THE MISTAKE

K.L. SLATER

bookouture

Published by Bookouture
An imprint of StoryFire Ltd.
23 Sussex Road, Ickenham, UB10 8PN
United Kingdom
www.bookouture.com

ISBN: 978-1-78681-244-5
eBook ISBN: 978-1-78681-243-8

For Francesca Kim x

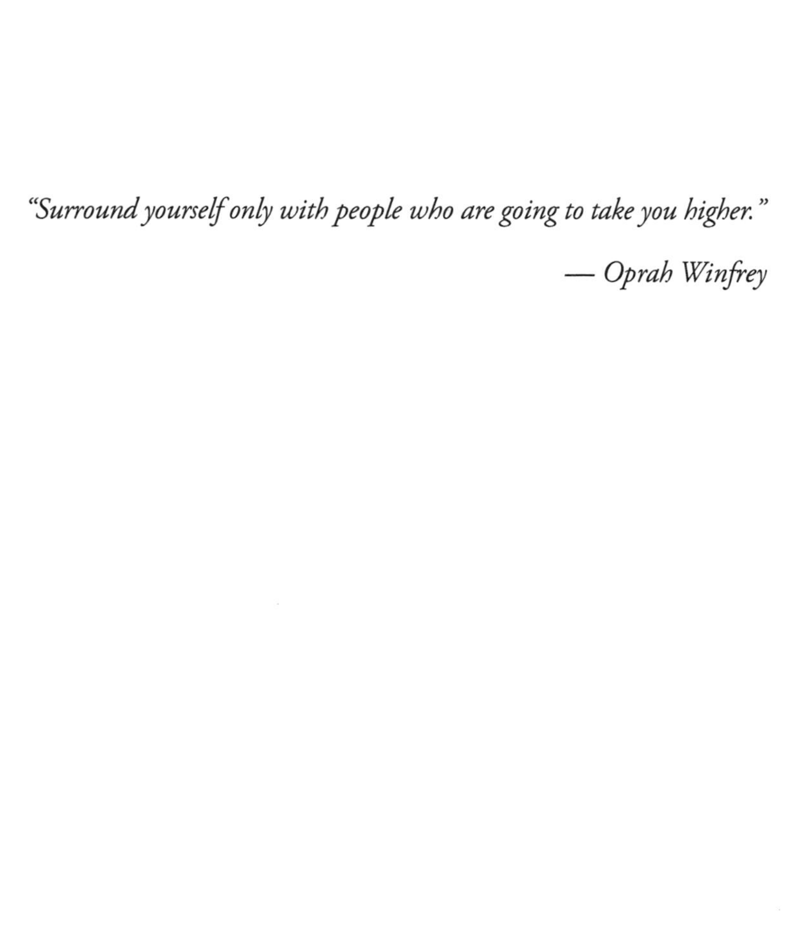

"Surround yourself only with people who are going to take you higher."

— Oprah Winfrey

BILLY

SIXTEEN YEARS EARLIER

The kite had dived-bombed around here; he knew it. Even though he couldn't see it yet, he felt confident he would find it.

It was a perfectly blustery day, the exact reason he and Rose had decided to take the kite for its maiden flight. Slate and silver clouds marbled the powder-blue sky, misting the weak sunlight but taking none of its warmth.

But here in the undergrowth, Billy could see none of that. His bare arms felt cool, his forearms prickling as he stumbled over ancient exposed roots that felt like gnarled bones beneath his unsteady feet.

Still, Billy bravely ventured further into the dense woodland, beating a pathway through with his trusty stick.

He had a good sense of direction. His class teacher had said so last summer when they went on the mini-beast hunt, here at Newstead Abbey. And so Billy forged ahead, his inner compass telling him that the kite was definitely around here somewhere.

He wanted to show his big sister how grown-up he was, by recovering the kite and bringing it back to her. If he behaved himself, Rose might take him out again.

They hardly ever did stuff together these days, didn't even play Monopoly or anything.

Billy heard a rustling sort of noise behind him. Ceasing the kite hunt for just a moment, he peered into the thick greenery but he could see nothing.

Perhaps it was a fox. Rose would be scared of that but Billy certainly wasn't. He was eight years old now and Dad had said big boys like him weren't scared of bears or wolves and certainly not foxes.

Billy inhaled the cool, damp scent of the earth, batting back the leaves and branches, eagle-eyed and waiting to spot the bright blue-and-white kite that Rose had bought him for his birthday just a few weeks ago.

A snapping branch and more rustling behind him. Billy spun around, brandishing his stick in case a fox was moving in to attack. His eyes caught a shadowy movement and then a figure stepped out of the foliage, towards him.

Billy breathed out and frowned. What was *he* doing here?

'I'm looking for my kite,' Billy said by way of explaining. 'I don't need any help.'

It would be just like him to take all the glory with Rose.

Billy looked up at him and thought how his face looked… different, sort of angry and he hadn't answered him yet or explained why he was there. And yet Billy knew he hadn't done anything wrong. His mouth felt dry and his chest burned.

'I've got to get back to Rose now,' he said, turning to run from the bushes, but before he could dodge past him, two strong arms shot out and held him fast.

Billy heard the chatter of voices close to them and he tried to call out but found he couldn't because there was a powerful hand clamped over his nose and mouth.

He kicked and struggled but quite soon he couldn't get his breath at all. He heard a crow cawing up ahead and he thought about his new kite, torn and lost in the undergrowth.

Billy strained to pull in breath to his straining lungs through fingers that were wrapped around his nose and mouth like an iron mask.

The voices he'd heard before sounded muffled and far away from him now.

Slowly, like a fading light switch turning, everything around him went very, very dark.

CHAPTER ONE

ROSE

PRESENT DAY

I sweep the book scanner across the two large-print Catherine Cookson novels Mrs Groves has spent the last thirty minutes selecting, and wait for the beep. Once I've checked they've successfully updated to the Library Management System, I push them back across the counter.

'Would you like to sign our petition, Mrs Groves?' I ask.

The old lady slides the books into her shopping bag and peers at the list of signatures I'm holding in front of her. 'What's it for, dear?'

'We're campaigning to save the library,' I explain. 'The local authority have issued a list of possible closures for next year and Newstead library is on there.'

'Really?' Mrs Groves frowns. 'But that's preposterous.'

'I know but it could happen if we don't actively do something about it,' I explain. 'It's happening all over the country. Libraries are closing on a monthly basis.'

Mrs Groves looks at me. 'You know it's wonderful, the work you do here in the village, Rose. You make the library such a friendly place to come…' Her face changes and I brace myself. 'All in spite of everything else you've had to cope with… the tragedy you went through…' Her eyes shine.

'Thank you.' I lower my eyes and smile *the smile* before moving on. 'But this is about standing up for what we believe in, isn't it? They've taken so much from our village as it is.' I push the petition a little closer to her.

Mrs Groves adjusts her spectacles and takes the paper and pen.

'Very true but I'll tell you now, they're not going to take our library, dear.' Her spidery scrawl fills the next available box on the petition grid and she looks up defiantly. 'We'll make sure of that.'

I smile, silently wishing it were that simple. Newstead has one of the smallest libraries in the county of Nottinghamshire. We open for a total of just three days a week; all day on a Wednesday and a mixture of mornings and afternoons on the other weekdays.

I like working here and I've never had ambitions to move to one of the bigger libraries. I started my career about eight years ago, when I finished university, as Assistant Librarian to Mr Barrow. And when Mr Barrow eventually retired and I'd had the requisite interview, they made me Librarian.

The library is housed in a flat-roofed building tucked neatly away off the main road and sits opposite the primary school at the entrance to the main village. On a fine day, from the main desk, I can see the woods beyond the busy Hucknall Road that skirts past us.

The sun, on the days it shines, bathes my workspace from mid-morning to mid-afternoon.

Inside, the library decor is tired and the whole interior is now rather grubby in places. The wiry, grey carpets are worn worst where the heaviest footfall lands and the fabric on the edges of the chair cushions in our comfortable reading area is torn and frayed.

In winter the cold air seeps in through the rotting wooden window frames and the antiquated warm-air ducted heating system probably malfunctions on more days than it works.

But people like coming here all the same.

Miss Carter, a lifelong resident of the village now in her mid-eighties and living on Abbey Road with her thirteen cats, reliably informs me she can sense the library has 'a subtle, sacred energy'. I suspect she might change her opinion if she heard Jim Greaves, the part-time caretaker, cursing loudly in his broad Geordie accent when the heating is on the blink again.

Still, I do know what she means. Even though it desperately needs upgrading, the place has a nice feeling about it. I put it down to all the wonderful books we have here. Shelf upon shelf of sparkling characters, addictive storylines and worlds that feel real enough to get lost in for a spare hour here and there, or for days on end.

I run a couple of fundraising events a year and from the proceeds, we've managed to buy some colourful bean bags to brighten up the children's fiction corner a little, and we also had enough left to equip a mother and baby room, located next to the main toilet.

The flat roof sprung yet another leak last week, prompting Jim to buy another brightly coloured bucket from petty cash, and the whole place is desperate for redecorating, but I like working here.

I feel comfortable and safe, despite everything that's happened.

My job allows me full contact with the villagers and even some of the new people who've moved here in recent years, without having to get fully involved in their lives. I've learned how to wear a convincing mask during my working hours. I say the right things, smile that smile and reassure everyone that despite the tragedy that happened here sixteen years ago, I'm OK and soldiering on.

I've realised that's all they really want: to show me that they haven't forgotten about Billy, and for me to say that *yes, I'm fine now*.

So that's exactly what I give them and watch with a weary resignation as the relief floods over their concerned faces.

Nobody ever mentions Gareth Farnham.

The full horror of what he did here is still too much for the village psyche to handle. But the legacy of him hovers, like an undulating cloud of flying insects, above the heads of all of those who remember.

Over the years, I've learned the correct response to every question, each sympathetic look and every well-meaning touch of the arm. I can keep it up no problem until I get home and close the door behind me.

Then it's a different story altogether.

Today is a half-day at work, so on the way home I plan on stopping off at the Co-op to pick up some bits for both myself and for Ronnie, my next-door neighbour.

As I sit re-jacketing a couple of our well-worn titles, I can't help worrying a bit about him.

A fiercely independent man now in his late seventies, Ronnie has been out of sorts for the last few days with a nasty stomach bug and on top of that, his legs have started playing up; stiffening up and aching terribly if he walks too far. Yet I have to virtually beg for him to let me help him.

'You've enough to do, Rose, without worrying about me,' he'd complained when I'd popped round yesterday and checked on the sparse contents of his cupboards and fridge.

I'd rolled my eyes at him.

'Ronnie, I'm just getting you some milk and bread on my way home from work tomorrow, OK?'

'OK.' He'd given me a little smile, suitably chastised.

Ronnie might be just a neighbour to some but, to me, he feels more like family. He's always been there. I was born in this house and I remember Mum telling me that, virtually as soon as I could walk, off I'd toddle next door to the Turners' house to get spoiled with sweets and Sheila's legendary home-made strawberry ice cream.

'Ronnie used to leave the little gate between our back gardens open so you could nip through and see Sheila whenever you liked,'

Mum remembered fondly one time. 'And when Ronnie and your dad went for a pint, you used to try and follow them down to the Station Hotel.'

From the first moments Billy went missing, Ronnie and Sheila Turner were there for us. Ronnie stayed up all night to co-ordinate a community search of the abbey grounds and the local woods early the next day, and Sheila made drinks and sandwiches for everyone while we all waited for news. The legion of police, drafted in from all over Nottinghamshire, said they'd never seen anything quite like it.

When they found Billy's body two days later, Ronnie and Sheila were there to catch us as we fell. We were feathers in a storm for days that bled into weeks then months and they held us down, stopping us from drifting into oblivion.

Sheila died just over five years ago and now, with Mum and Dad both gone too, there's just me and Ronnie left. And I owe him.

Picking up a few bits for him from the store is never going to be a problem.

CHAPTER TWO

ROSE

PRESENT DAY

From my desk, I keep an eye on the clock and watch the unstoppable tick of the hands towards one o'clock.

Most people can't wait to knock off work but it's never like that for me. I always dread finishing time.

Once the last customer has left the library, Jim locks the external doors and stands rattling his keys. When I tell him I have some things I need to finish off, his face drops and he disappears into the back office again.

I feel bad because I know he can't go home to Janice, his wheelchair-bound wife of forty years, until the building is empty.

But it's just one of those days and I don't feel strong enough to leave yet. I need to work up to going home.

I start by running an update to the LMS software while I tackle the big pile of today's checked-in books, returning them to the shelves.

Paula, my assistant, only comes in on Wednesdays when we stay open all day. On half-days, I'm on my own. I don't mind it, I like the variety and find that the simplest duties – like re-shelving the returns – bring back happy memories of when I first volunteered here and life was still safe and simple.

Books helped me get well back then and I feel happiest now when I'm around them. Sometimes I wish I could put up a camp bed in the back office, and then I'd never need to go home at all.

I load the returns on to a trolley and push it down to the bottom wall of shelves: the Crime section. It's probably the most popular genre in the library.

Our customers love a good mystery, a page-turner. They seem fascinated by terrifying tales or awful deeds that could quite feasibly happen to them in their own ordinary lives. But of course that's because they are *safely* afraid; they can close the book at any point and keep those emotions firmly in check.

When I was younger, I used to love reading crime novels for exactly this reason. My choice of late-night read before sleep beckoned was often a classic Agatha Christie or a chilling Ruth Rendell mystery.

But I haven't touched a book like that in sixteen years.

Reading about deceitful personalities, the hidden underbelly of society and unreliable characters who appear to be one thing but are soon found out to be something else entirely… all that stuff now fills me with a curdling discomfort that can last for days.

After I've re-shelved the returns and checked that the update is complete, I enter the new books that were delivered mid-morning onto the system inventory.

We've a copy of the new Jeffery Deaver novel and two copies each of the latest blockbusters from Martina Cole and Val McDermid. They are all reserved and have been for weeks. In fact, one of the Martina Coles has Jim's wife's name on it. Hopefully, that will be a small consolation for her when he rolls home late from work yet again, courtesy of *moi*.

We have lots of keen readers in the village who still struggle to make ends meet, even all this time after the pit closed. They've never fully recovered, and never will. Especially the older residents. They were once valued contributors to the UK's national coal supply and now, well, they're just about managing on their reduced pensions.

They almost certainly haven't got the funds to splash out on their favourite author's latest hardback.

Next job is sending out the emails, texts and in some cases, for our less technical, older customers, I ring, leaving a message to tell readers their long-awaited books are now available for collection.

Tomorrow, in they'll stride with purpose, their faces bright, their smiles of anticipation in place, and for a few hours, they'll forget about their problems.

And when they return their books, we'll have lengthy conversations about what they thought of the storyline, the setting, the characters. It's one of the highlights of my job and it's a massively important function of this library.

Jim's face lights up when I hand him the book.

'This will help my Jan with the pain far more than her medication ever could.' He looks genuinely touched and pats the cover of the novel. 'Cheer her up no end, this will. Thanks, pet.'

I smile and feel a sense of resolve inside. This is precisely why we can't afford to let them close the place down.

The moment I leave the building, all positive thoughts desert me and I catch myself in exactly the same tortuous place; relentlessly checking again.

Every single day, for goodness knows how many years, I've promised myself I'll try to stop doing it. But once I'm outside in the open air, even if there are plenty of people around, it's an automatic reaction.

It honestly feels like there's not a thing I can do about it.

Looking behind me every thirty seconds, monitoring the cars driving past to check the same one doesn't keep passing me. I never listen to music while I walk; I couldn't possibly. I need to be fully aware of any footsteps approaching behind. I cross the road if I pass by bushes or trees and I always give a wide berth to shadowy alleyways.

Years ago, Gaynor Jackson, my therapist, said, 'This compulsive behaviour will exhaust you, Rose. You have to stop.'

But even after all this time, it's still the only way I can feel remotely in control.

One of the reasons I stopped turning up for my therapy appointments was because I couldn't stand listening to the constant utopian ideology that Gaynor spewed on an endless loop.

She'd repeat the same clichéd phrases: 'You can learn to manage your fear' and 'you must strive to live in a state of relaxed awareness.' She believed in the stuff she told me, really believed it could work and it might have done. If only it were as easy as it sounded.

Gaynor meant well, I'm sure. But her advice all came from a textbook. It was clear from her sunny disposition and naïve expression, when I tried to articulate my terror, that she had never been in fear of her own life.

She'd never lain awake in the summer months, sweating buckets in a stifling bedroom because she was too scared to open even a small window in case someone climbed up the drainpipe and forced his way in.

She'd never had to run to the bathroom to be physically sick when she heard a noise out in the garden at dusk and felt too afraid to peer out of the curtains.

It wasn't Gaynor's fault, of course. I realised a long time ago that unless a person has experienced true terror, there is nothing you can do to make them understand how utterly debilitating it can be.

Or how your safe, ordinary life can disappear in the space of a heartbeat.

CHAPTER THREE

SIXTEEN YEARS EARLIER

At first, Rose hadn't even realised that someone was watching her.

Weighed down with an enormous black art portfolio case, a shoulder bag and a large wallet that was full of art supplies, she juggled her load, swapped hands, but still almost tumbled from the passenger platform.

The bus stop was situated on Hucknall Road, which traced the edge of Newstead village leading to the A611 towards Nottingham. The village sat on one side of the road and Newstead woods on the other, a curious merging of the sharp steely edges of a moribund industry and the soft green haze of nature.

Rose sighed as her feet touched the pavement. After a good day at college, the same familiar air of resignation had settled over her during the journey.

It happened every day. As the bus trundled closer to home, the heavier her heart felt, hanging there in her chest.

It hadn't always been that way. The atmosphere at home had grown steadily worse over the last few months. Mum and Dad screaming at each other, both saying awful things designed to inflict the maximum hurt.

But Rose had noticed a new, unwelcome development. When they tired of insulting each other, they seemed to have taken a liking to turning on *her*. Voicing everything that was wrong with her, everything she'd done wrong, every way she continuously disappointed them.

Every day, Rose asked herself how much longer she could stand it.

She would turn eighteen years old in June and that was just a couple of months away now. If she really wanted to, she could leave the village and make a new start somewhere a long way from here. Nobody could stop her.

It felt good and powerful to imagine it without considering how she'd begin to support herself. And Rose knew she could never leave Billy. So it wasn't a real option but still… it sometimes helped when she tried to block out the worsening situation at home.

Looking at the telltale small puddles here and there in the uneven pavement, Rose could tell it had rained here quite heavily earlier in the day. She hadn't noticed the weather at college, snug in a classroom, absorbed in her art.

But it had begun to rain again and, as Rose stood there, still trying to shuffle her various loads into a manageable position, she could smell the dank, old earth and fresh, young leaves; not for the first time, she thought how strange it was having a wood so close to the road.

She'd barely found her balance in her flat, sensible shoes, when the pneumatic doors whooshed closed behind her and the bus rumbled off down the road. She lost her grip and the bulky wallet slipped from her hands, spilling out her precious soft pastels on to the asphalt.

'Looks like you might need a bit of help,' a voice said behind her. 'Can I carry something?'

She turned to see a man with an amused expression standing watching her. The first thing she noticed was that he looked quite a bit older than her, she guessed probably in his late twenties. He stepped clear of the trees and she noticed his waxed green jacket shone with droplets of water and his hair was damp, stuck to his forehead and cheeks.

She looked up to the sky but it was still only spitting, certainly not enough to fully douse someone.

'I know, I'm wet through.' He grinned, displaying slightly crooked teeth in an attractive smile. 'I've been climbing up in the trees and brushing against the leaves. For the photos, you see.' He held up an expensive-looking camera.

Rose thought how quiet it was, now that the bus had gone. There was no one else around. The rainclouds had gathered moodily above them and she wondered how long it might be before the heavens truly opened.

She lay down the portfolio case and began to gather up the scattered pastels, praying none had reached a puddle. There was no way her parents would be able to afford more and it would be another thing for them to chastise her about.

He was staring at her. She felt her cheeks begin to heat up, despite the chilly air.

'So, what do you say?'

'I'm sorry?' She packed the last crayon back in the wallet, stood up and swapped the ungainly portfolio case over to her right hand.

'Can I help you carry anything?'

'Oh, yes.' Her cheeks heating up, she held out the large portfolio case. 'Thanks.'

Although she couldn't deny part of her was intrigued, Rose wished the stranger would just go on his way and leave her alone. She was only too aware she looked like an idiot. Bright red cheeks to match her pale-red hair. What a mess.

'Gareth Farnham,' he said. 'I'd shake your hand but you've got me laden like a donkey here.'

He had offered, she reasoned. Rose looked at him, wondering whether to defend herself, and then he grinned. She gave him a little smile back and looked at the pavement.

'Lead the way then and I'll follow,' he said cheerily.

They crossed the road and headed for the village. It felt strange, walking with a man. He was taller and broader than her and she found she quite liked how that made her feel. Would he walk all the way home with her, she wondered? He was just helping her out, after all. He couldn't possibly like her… could he?

Anyway, he was too old for her for there to be anything *like that* in it. Her mum would have a fit if she saw them together and she didn't want to begin to think what her dad might say. The mood he'd been in lately, he might well throttle her.

Nevertheless, Gareth was quite good-looking. And very grown-up compared to the lads at college, who still acted like twelve-year-olds.

He coughed and she realised he'd said something.

'Sorry, I—'

'I said my name's Gareth.' He stopped walking. 'You seem a bit distracted… are you worried about your homework or something? Maybe I could help you with it.'

He grinned and winked and a flush of heat began to slowly crawl up her neck.

'Sorry. I meant to say, I'm Rose,' she said and he stopped walking. She looked back at him and her feet stopped too.

He tilted his head to one side and frowned as if he was trying to recall something and then he began to recite words, loud and dramatically.

'Oh! Snatched away in beauty's bloom,
On thee shall press no ponderous tomb;
But on thy turf shall roses rear
Their leaves, the earliest of the year.'

He beamed at her and waited.

'A poem?' She felt the heat in her face increase tenfold.

'By Lord Byron, whose gaff, as you know, is just across the village.' He grinned. 'What's the place called again?'

'Newstead Abbey.'

'That's it, Newstead Abbey. I thought I'd impress you by reciting a poem with your name in it, you see. I've got a good memory like that, never had trouble with exams.'

'I *am* impressed.' She couldn't help smiling. She felt very self-conscious but perhaps she needed to make a bit more effort at making conversation. 'I – I haven't seen you around the village before.'

'You won't have, I just moved here a couple of days ago,' he said. 'I'm renting one of those new apartments on Lacey Grove; everything's still in boxes, I'm afraid. I'm going to be managing the new regeneration project. Have you heard about it?'

'I think so,' Rose replied, nodding. 'They're making a park and a fishing lake where the pit used to be?'

'That's the one.' Gareth seemed pleased she knew of the project. 'You've simplified it quite a bit but it's a very high-level programme.'

'Oh,' Rose said.

'Put it this way, I've had to speak to some pretty high-level people in government to get this thing up and running.' He paused and looked at her expectantly. When she didn't comment, he continued. 'It'll breathe new life into the village, just you wait and see.'

They crossed the road from the bus stop and headed into the village, leaving the dripping greenery behind them.

'The project sounds really good,' Rose remarked, although privately she thought fishing cruel. That said, it could only be a good thing that funding was finally trickling into the stricken village.

The government's regeneration in the area was a positive start but even Rose had to acknowledge that it would take more than a bit of grass seed and water to transform it back from the ghost town it had turned into when the pit closed in 1987.

CHAPTER FOUR

SIXTEEN YEARS EARLIER

The rain started to beat down a little faster now as they walked around the perimeter of the primary school's fence.

Rose shuddered at the brightly painted, polyurethane children that lined the road. They were essentially bollards, providing a visual warning that drivers were about to pass a school; unseeing eyes that watched Rose walking by, their tight little immoveable mouths barely concealing their disapproval.

The brick terraces came into view, dour against the grey sky. They had been built to last, originally for the mineworkers, and, although that purpose had now passed, they remained solid and fused together like links in an iron chain.

'I'll take that now, if you like.' Rose slowed her pace and reached out for the portfolio case with an arm that was already hooked with two bags. 'Thanks for helping me.'

Gareth drew the portfolio closer to his body.

'It's no trouble to see you home.' He smiled. 'I'll walk with you.'

Rose's heart began to thump. What would happen if her mum saw her with Gareth or, even worse, her dad saw? She'd hate to give them something else to moan at her about.

Her father had become so unpredictable in the years since the pit had closed, spending most of his time down at the Station

Hotel nursing the same pint of bitter all night because he couldn't face the screaming rows with her mum if he spent precious funds on more than one or two drinks.

Ray Tinsley had been 37 years old when the mine closed. He'd worked there all his life, since leaving school at fifteen. Ray had been a face worker – spending twelve-hour days and sometimes nights, in 38-degree heat, crawling through and toiling in a tunnel barely wider or higher than his own body.

Suffering the hardest work but paid the most money, Ray and his fellow face workers were afforded status in the local community. Overtime had been plentiful and, consequently, money had never been a problem in the Tinsley household.

The day the pit closed, Stella had told Rose some years later, Ray had opened an investment account and banked his redundancy payment, adamant he wouldn't end up on the 'scrap heap' as some predicted and therefore wouldn't be needing the money anytime soon.

'I'm not an old man, I've still a lot to offer,' he'd confidently said as he'd left his wife and five-year-old daughter, bright and early for the Job Centre, on his very first day without work.

He had steadfastly applied for numerous jobs around the area, even as far as the sprawling hosiery factories in Mansfield and Nottingham. But so had lots of the other redundant miners and some of them were younger than Ray.

Two months after losing his job, Stella had noticed her husband's applications tailing off. His step slowed, his head hung a little lower. Nobody seemed remotely interested in employing a man who possessed such specific mining skills and who wasn't far off knocking at the door of his fortieth birthday.

'So, what do you say, Rosie?'

'Sorry?' Rose jerked back to the present. She felt the art supplies wallet slipping in her clammy hand. He'd called her *Rosie*. Nobody had called her that since her grandad when she was small.

'You were deep in thought there,' Gareth said, smiling at her. 'I asked if you fancied going to the Odeon in Mansfield, say on Wednesday night?'

She watched him as he frowned up at the burgeoning rain clouds. 'You don't have to, of course, it's just, with being new to the area and all that… I don't really know anyone yet. Gets a bit lonely, just watching TV on my own every night, you know?'

Rose thought about when she'd first started at West Notts College, in Mansfield. Other people from school, who she knew by face, had also gone there. But there was no one she knew on her actual art course, so she spent her breaks and lunchtimes alone, watching other people laughing and discussing their lessons.

She'd hated it and had begun planning how she could back out of her art course and get a job somewhere. The fantasy included escaping everything, including her parents. And then Cassie had ditched her place doing hair and beauty at Clarendon College in Nottingham and had joined Rose's art course instead.

That was Cassie all over. Up and down, back to front.

'No pressure but what do you say?' Gareth continued. 'You can choose which film we see?'

He was too old for her but it would be rude to just say no outright. The thought of escaping the horrible atmosphere at home, even for just one evening, was tempting.

Nothing exciting and new ever happened here and now something had.

She'd be a fool to turn Gareth down. Besides, the look on Cassie's face when Rose told her she had a *date* would be priceless.

'Thanks,' she heard herself say. 'The cinema would be really nice.'

The closer they got to home, the jumpier Rose became. Gareth was still chattering on and she kept having to ask him to repeat himself.

If her dad was sitting in his chair with the net hooked back, looking out of the window like he so often did, he'd interrogate her for hours.

If she went straight up to her room, he'd complain she should be helping her mother with the tea. If she stayed downstairs too long, he'd question her commitment to the art course. Rose was heartily sick of his constant mantra: 'It costs us to support your education, you know.'

Gareth seemed to sense her discomfort. When she told him they'd reached her street, he handed her the rain-spotted portfolio case.

'So, what's your number?' he asked, pulling out a Nokia phone from his pocket.

'I – I haven't got a mobile,' Rose confessed.

'What? How come?'

She wasn't about to tell him there was no spare money in the house for mobile phones. She couldn't even get a Saturday job in the village; there was just nothing going at all. She'd just started volunteering at the library on Wednesday afternoons as she had no lectures then, but she didn't get paid a cent for that; she just liked being around the books.

She hated having to rely on her mum and dad for things. It made her feel like a little kid and she felt guilty that she made no contribution. Particularly when shortage of money was the main cause of antagonism between her parents these days.

'Never mind.' He winked at her. 'Give us your landline number, I'll call you on that to sort out the arrangements for Wednesday.'

Rose opened her mouth and closed it again. She couldn't give Gareth the number because she didn't want her parents to know she'd arranged to see him. Yet she'd look like a silly kid if she said as much.

Gareth stared at her for a moment and then his face broke into a broad grin.

'Oh, I get it. I've got to be your dirty little secret, right?'

'No!' she said, mortified. 'It's not that at all. It's just – well, my dad, he's…'

'Say no more.' Gareth's fingers hovered above the keys of his phone. 'Just give me the number and I'll call you tomorrow night; they won't know it's me. Does eight prompt suit?'

'But—'

'All you have to do is make sure you're right by the phone. They'll just think it's a friend.'

Rose was uncomfortable with the arrangement, but he seemed so enthusiastic, she didn't want to burst his bubble. She supposed she could give him one wrong digit but then how would he get in touch? He did seem really nice. And even though Rose fully intended to lay it on thick with Cassie about the fact she'd been asked out on a date, truthfully it was really only a film and a bit of company because Gareth didn't know anyone else who lived around here.

There was nothing sordid in it. If her dad wasn't so uptight at the moment, he'd have probably understood.

Meeting Gareth felt like a chance too good to miss. It was very early days, she knew that, but this could be the start of something positive in her dull village life… if she didn't muck it up by letting her own insecurities and family worries intrude.

'You forgotten your phone number now?' Gareth narrowed his dark-blue eyes, and for a brief moment she thought he was annoyed, but then he smiled and his eyes twinkled again.

Rose rattled off the number.

'Good,' he murmured as he tapped the digits into his phone. 'Eight o'clock it is, then. Tomorrow night.'

She nodded. He winked and smiled that sexy smile again and her heart did a double flip.

When she reached the gate and looked back, she saw he was still watching her. He raised a hand to wave and she smiled but her hands were full so she couldn't wave back.

CHAPTER FIVE

SIXTEEN YEARS EARLIER

Rose pushed the back door open with her foot and staggered awkwardly inside, trying to balance all her art supplies.

Her eight-year-old little brother, Billy, had obviously arrived home just before her. He sat on a stool in the kitchen, kicking off his scuffed trainers.

'I saw you standing with a bloke at the top of the street.' Billy smirked, stuffing a handful of cola bottles in his mouth and watching as Rose struggled inside. 'He was carrying your stuff for you. Is he your boyfriend?'

She glanced anxiously towards the door, wondering if her parents had heard but she could hear the TV in the front room so they were both probably in there, eating their tea on trays.

'Keep your voice down,' Rose hissed at her brother. 'He's not my boyfriend.'

'What's his name?'

'Gareth.'

'How do you know his name then, if he's not your boyfriend?' He laughed and dodged her hand as she dropped the portfolio case and swung for him.

'He's not my boyfriend, Billy.' Rose bit her lip. 'Do you want to get me into trouble with Mum and Dad?'

He pulled out more sweets from his pocket and shook his head solemnly. She wasn't the only one suffering her father's bad moods. Judging by the state of his unruly mop, Rose could hazard a guess that he hadn't brushed his hair at all that day. She dumped her bag and art materials on the drop-leaf table, and smoothed his ruffled locks. Billy jerked his head from side to side in an effort to avoid her fussy finger-combing.

'Stop saying it then, else they'll hear you. Let's have a drink.' She pulled two glasses from the cupboard, walked over to the fridge and searched for fresh orange juice but there was none. 'What did you do at school today?'

'Just boring stuff.' Billy pulled a face.

She'd had countless talks with Billy about trying harder at school.

She sighed. 'Are you serious about being a pilot when you grow up?'

He shrugged but didn't reply.

'What's the attitude for?' She made up two glasses of orange cordial instead.

'Carl Bennett in my class says it's just a stupid dream, Rose.' Billy looked at her over his glass with soulful brown eyes. 'He says people who come from round here never have exciting jobs, they just go to work down the pit because that's all there is.'

'Not any more,' Rose said. 'Pit's been closed for ages now and that's done local young lads like you a favour. You can do what you like, if you put your mind to it.' She took a long draft of juice. 'Remember how we talked about getting a good education?'

But Billy had already stopped listening; he began to lay out his football cards in precise lines on the other side of the table.

Rose was dying to call Cassie and tell her about meeting Gareth but the telephone was situated in the hallway and her parents would definitely be able to overhear. She'd just have to keep him to herself for now. It felt like a delicious secret that was only hers to tell.

Later, it took a long time for Rose to get to sleep.

The next day at college, Cassie met her off the bus and was instantly delirious when Rose told her.

'What, he's actually asked you out on a *date*?' Cassie exclaimed.

Rose grinned as she thought about how those big blue eyes looked in serious danger of popping out of their sockets.

'How old is he?'

'I don't know, exactly. But like I said, he looks quite a bit older than me.' The girls sauntered up Nottingham Road towards West Notts College, perched on top of the hill. 'I reckon he's maybe in his mid-twenties.'

Cassie's face shone. 'I bet you'll *do it* with him on Wednesday. He'll be your first one, you wait and see.'

'Cassie! We're only going to the cinema, for goodness sake.' Rose scowled but found she couldn't fully hide a grin.

'Yeah, you'll tell me anything. Look at you – you're gagging for it. Little virgin.'

She squealed and jumped back as Rose swung her shoulder bag at her. Cassie proceeded to dance around her, singing Madonna's 'Like A Virgin'.

'Cassie, pack it in,' Rose hissed, glancing round to see if any of the other students walking nearby had overheard.

'Seriously though, this is definitely progress, Rose.' Cassie fell back into step beside her. 'I was beginning to think you'd eventually take over from Miss Carter as the village's official old maid.'

'Very funny.'

Cassie was the same age as Rose but rather more experienced when it came to boys. She'd had three steady boyfriends and had slept with all of them. Her relationships to date had been with lads from college, all the same age as her, but Rose noticed that she seemed to find Gareth's age particularly attractive.

'I'd kill to shag an older man,' she said dreamily. 'All that experience.'

'Cassie!'

'It's true, I would!' She stuck her tongue out. 'If you're going all prim Miss Jean Brodie, you can introduce him to *me*. Maybe I could teach him a thing or two.'

'And, get this… ' Rose said, ignoring her crude comment, 'he recited me a poem by Byron.' She waited for her friend to pale in admiration.

'Now I know you're having a laugh,' Cassie snorted.

'It's true!' Rose giggled and nudged her. 'It even had my name in it, the poem. Something about a rose's leaves being the earliest of the year.'

Cassie's grin slipped from her face. 'Rose, you lucky cow, he sounds like a dream. For God's sake, don't mess it up.'

'Mess it up, how?'

'By being *naïve*. You need to show him you're not a kid just because you're a lot younger than he is.'

'How do I do that?'

Cassie gave a heavy sigh. 'We'll talk about it later. Come round to mine tonight and I'll give you a masterclass in how to snare a man.'

She stuck out her boobs and bumped into Rose on purpose, and they dissolved into laughter.

Rose felt all warm inside. Life felt good. Exciting.

CHAPTER SIX

ROSE

PRESENT DAY

I walk into the small, local Co-op store where I do my food shopping.

There are two major supermarkets within about four miles of the village and I'm fully aware that they offer a much broader choice and cheaper prices but I feel more comfortable staying local.

Here, I know all the checkout operators, the shelf-stackers and even the store manager. I can take my time and relax a little as I browse, as much as relaxing in public is ever going to be possible.

Food is important to me, always has been. It's my companion, my undemanding friend.

Every morning when I wake, I push away the heavy, unwelcome stuff that rushes into my head with thoughts of food. What I'm having for breakfast, what I'll take into work for lunch and, of course, the main event of the day: what I'm having for tea.

I start each day promising myself I'll do better, I tell myself I can stop the destructive eating pattern. But something inside of me is broken and I always let myself down… By nightfall, the early morning hope has turned full-circle, back to self-loathing.

The double wardrobe in my bedroom is crammed full of old clothes I won't wear any more. I can count on one hand those that I still look OK in: a pair of jeans, a pair of black work trousers, a blouse and two brightly coloured cardigans that help to disguise the multitude of glaring body faults I see the moment I look in the mirror.

I know I ought to sell the old stuff on eBay and use the money to buy one or two good quality new items that fit me properly. If I could just gain a few pounds in the right places, then I'd have dozens of outfits become wearable that are currently baggy on my bony shoulders or hang off my scrawny hips.

Plenty of people would swap bodies with me, I know. But that's because they don't know the full story. I'm not healthy, not attractively slim. I'm dry, malnourished and I'm hungry.

Most of the time I'm *so* bloody hungry.

Periodically, a voice inside me urges me to do something about the destructive cycle that on one level, I know I'm in. I've tried to come up with a plan many times but all those faddy diets in the women's magazines… they seem to feed the fear rather than allay it.

So last week I did a bit of online research on eating well and came up with my own solution.

Basically, it amounts to eating three sensible meals a day, cutting out sugary snacks and generally making healthier choices. Sounds simple enough when you commit it to paper.

Yet even as I noted down the meal ideas, I knew the fear of gaining weight would almost certainly outweigh the probability that I could ever eat normally.

You see, with me, it's always been *all* of the food. I just have to have it, to fill up the gaps of nothingness, the holes that run through me like in a slice of Swiss cheese. The only thing I feel in control of is what happens *after* I've eaten it all.

When I had my 'food problem' – Dad named it thus to avoid the stigma attached to the official medical term and it stuck – it was ages before my clothing started feeling looser. Once the weight loss did start, though, it just didn't seem to stop.

I reach into my handbag and pull out the scrawled list I compiled. I'd been moved to do it yesterday when I sat down at my desk with my sandwich lunch. My eyes flashed over the chicken salad wrap, the packet of cheese and onion crisps and the small banana I'd packed at home that morning and felt what can only be described as a raw panic.

If I kept eating like this, I'd swell, grow fat again.

Those words, the ones that had leaked from his cruel, stretched lips as he grabbed my hair and pulled my head back; disgusting… vile… obese… sickening…

They'd bounced around my head yesterday like a ping-pong ball and I felt seized by an urgency to have another go at taking myself in hand.

Attending the council-run gym in nearby Hucknall and mixing with strangers was out of the question, as would be taking long walks alone in the fields that surrounded the village. Far too many hiding places there to conceal anyone wishing me harm. But I also knew that if I didn't do something, I'd just carry on, trapped in this negative and dangerous cycle.

Now I glance at the list of my optimistic ideas for nutritious, filling meals, and after grabbing a wire basket, I head off up the first aisle.

Before I've even reached the salad section I've exchanged pleasantries with a fellow villager and two members of staff. No deep, searching questions, thankfully, just observations about the weather and the agenda for the upcoming village committee meeting. This, I can handle.

I put a Romaine lettuce, two tomatoes and half a cucumber in my basket. I add a carton of eggs and a piece of cooked salmon with a chilli ginger glaze from the chill cabinet and, instead of my usual two litres of fizzy pop, I grab a two-litre bottle of water.

As I turn the corner on to the next aisle, I look down into the basket at what I have so far and I don't see fresh and healthy at all. I see only bland and tasteless with nothing to look forward to.

I'd desperately like food to cease playing such a major role in my life and control *it,* instead of the other way around, but the thought of cutting back on the sort of dishes I love makes my heart sink.

How on earth am I going to fill the long evenings, eating just a few leaves and a scrap of fish? I'm used to what I call my 'never-ending meals'. These consist of maybe a ready-made lasagne or spaghetti bolognese with a slice or two of garlic bread, followed by a nice fresh cream cake.

All this I usually wash down with a bottle of nice chilled Sauvignon Blanc, the first glass of which I consume immediately upon getting home from work, after locking and bolting the doors. Then, as I prefer to think of it, I 'pop upstairs'.

When I come back down again, I'll have a coffee and a few chocolate digestives or perhaps some cheese and biscuits.

Finally, I might down a couple of iced Baileys and, after taking a trip upstairs again, I usually fall asleep watching a box set on Netflix.

I'm aware it might not sound like much of an evening but it's my life. I've become accustomed to evenings spent alone by building this sort of sanctuary around myself, based largely on food, drink and television.

It's the way I forget about everything; what's happened in the past and the future I can never look forward to. Sometimes, it even works for a short time.

'Hello, Rose.'

Miss Carter stands in front of me in aisle two, holding a basket weighed down with cat litter and numerous tins of flaked tuna.

'Hello.' I smile.

'That's all looking very… healthy.' She peers into my basket and then looks at me, narrowing her eyes. 'How are you feeling these days, Rose?'

I dampen down the flare of irritation that rises in my chest. Those five words might sound innocent but what she really means is, *I see you have lettuce in your basket… are you heading back to the food problem again?*

'I'm very well, thanks, Miss Carter,' I say, purposely keeping my voice bright. 'I feel absolutely fine.'

Her eyes flicker over me, hovering just a second or two over the waistband of my trousers. 'That's good to hear,' she says, clearly unconvinced. 'Don't go too mad with the salad though. You've still room to put a few pounds on, dear.'

One disadvantage of living in a small village with the same small-minded people all your life is that they never quite grasp you're no longer the clueless teenager they once knew… that now you're a functioning adult who doesn't need their rude and often thoughtless suggestions.

People around here have very long memories. Ask any ex-miner and they'll happily point out the 'scabs': the derogatory name reserved for the men who refused to strike back in 1984.

The villagers all knew about the bulimia, how could they not? It was impossible to hide at the time. After Billy's death, I lost around a pound in weight every few days for weeks and looked like death warmed up, due to my digestive system all but breaking down.

It was a very public disappearing act I tried unsuccessfully to pull off.

I mumble some excuse to Miss Carter and move on to the next aisle. The plastic tubing on the basket handle slips in my clammy hand and I feel a trickle of moisture gather in the small hollow at the bottom of my back.

I stand for a moment, staring at the shelves, and when my vision finally clears, I see row upon row packed with cakes and biscuits.

I breathe out, feel my shoulders relax. Comfort at last.

CHAPTER SEVEN

ROSE

PRESENT DAY

I exit the supermarket and, loaded down with over-full plastic bags, I walk across the village whilst still running my observation checks.

There's just a few minutes to walk now until I reach my house but it feels like it's taking a lifetime to get there.

As my heartbeat races faster still, and despite being fairly sure there is nobody to fear anywhere near me, I keep my gaze on the pavement in front of me and begin to count my steps. I begin to feel a little easier as my narrow, brick-fronted terrace comes into view. Familiarity is good. I crave it. Need it.

Seeing Miss Carter, and having her mention my food choices, opened up a can of worms I was totally unprepared for.

Sometimes I can build up my defences if I know the past is going to be mentioned in some way. It might just be someone who's using the library facilities referencing what happened long ago and asking if I'm OK. I take it in my stride.

But when I'm unprepared, like today in the supermarket, a couple of ill-considered comments can knock me off my feet and it can take days for me to restabilise.

I glance down at the bulging bags, the handles of which are cutting into the soft flesh of my palms.

I'd rushed away from Miss Carter and by the time I'd reached the checkout, my proposed healthy eating plan had been shelved indefinitely and I'd ended up clutching *two* wire baskets filled with comfort foods that would serve to act as a powerful balm for the painful memories she'd inadvertently disturbed.

My pace picks up as I hasten towards number thirteen, my house. But before I can go home and close the door behind me, I need to look in on Ronnie and drop off his shopping.

I push open the small, wooden gate to number eleven. Glancing behind me to make sure I'm alone, I walk briskly down the little cut through between the houses, round to the back of his property.

Damp patches begin to chafe the sensitive skin under my arms. I catch my breath and hurry round the back of the houses.

The concrete paving slabs feel cracked and uneven beneath my worn, flat soles.

I peer down at the chickweed borders that spill over onto the path. The green, leafy bunches are dotted so prettily betwixt tiny innocent-looking star-shaped flowers that will surreptitiously strangle any other sign of life.

Ronnie keeps his back door unlocked when he's at home, so I just tap on the kitchen window and step quickly inside.

I've tried to warn him about opportunist thieves and rogue callers but he won't have it. He still thinks it's the eighties when he and the other residents of the terraces lived and worked in the midst of a mutual community trust they took for granted.

There are as many new people in the village as original residents now. Strangers. Bumping into faces that nobody recognises at every corner.

It's a danger I know only too well.

Usually, when I pop next door, Ronnie will be in the kitchen, pottering around in that hesitant, forgetful way he has these days.

Sometimes he likes to sit at the tiny table in the single chair, poring over the cryptic crossword he can never seem to finish any more.

But today he isn't in here.

I put the carrier bag that contains his shopping on the worktop and dump the others and my handbag by the door for when I leave.

'Hello?' I call as I walk across the room. He doesn't usually like to settle down in the living room until the evening programmes begin, so maybe he's upstairs in the bathroom.

I hesitate at the bottom of the stairs. I've been coming round here all my life to see Ronnie and Sheila and yet I still find it strange to stand quietly in the mirror image of my own home, feeling it so utterly different.

I crane my neck around the door leading to the living room.

The furnishings in here are all very dated but of a quality that's lasted well through the years. A blue-and-brown patterned Axminster carpet runs through the hallway into the living room, where a walnut sideboard and television cabinet crowd the space. The burnished oxblood Chesterfield three-seater and matching high-backed winged chair sit rather grandly in the cramped room and heavy velvet drapes in a similar shade frame the single net-curtained window.

It's dark and drab, but Ronnie and Sheila were never fans of the light, minimal look. They came from a generation that preferred clutter; the more elaborate, the better. All these quality furnishings were selected with love and purchased with a good living earned from the pit, where Ronnie was known as the Overman, a sort of underground foreman.

When Dad – the then-young Raymond Tinsley – first started at Newstead Colliery after leaving school, Ronnie was already well established and respected in the mining hierarchy there, and, as he knew the family well, he took Dad under his wing. That's the way things worked around here for years when everyone looked after each other.

Ronnie isn't here in the living room either.

I begin to climb the stairs, a sense of foreboding laying heavy on my chest.

'Ronnie?' I call.

I hear a scrape, and, as I near the top and the landing, a soft groan. When I reach the top, I tap tentatively on the bathroom door, my heart thumping.

As I push open the door, Ronnie's socked feet and skinny white ankles immediately come into view and when I step into the tiny room, there he is, lying prostate on the floor, his face pinched with pain.

I walk forward and clasp my hand across my mouth and nose at the stench of vomit and worse. He looks at me with rolling, wide eyes and murmurs, and I step back out of the room to take a breath.

'Don't worry, Ronnie, I'll get an ambulance.'

And then I run downstairs for my phone.

CHAPTER EIGHT

ROSE

PRESENT DAY

I grab my phone from my handbag and call emergency services immediately, praying that the ambulance doesn't take too long to arrive.

Back upstairs I place a folded towel under Ronnie's head, flush the gruesome contents of the lavatory and step over his legs and the cracked, worn Linoleum, to open the small, frosted window next to the bath.

'The ambulance is on its way, Ronnie,' I tell him. 'Did you slip and fall?'

He doesn't answer but his eyes widen further and he swallows hard, his mouth crooked. I wonder briefly if he's had a mild stroke and pray I'm wrong.

'You're probably just weak from the bug you've had the last couple of days, Ronnie,' I say, trying to comfort him. 'Did you black out?'

His whispered reply is so faint I nearly miss it. 'No.'

His mouth is moving, like he's trying to say something else but he can't seem to manage it. I make sure he's as comfortable as I can make him and head back downstairs to look out for the ambulance. Within minutes, I'm showing the two paramedics upstairs.

'What's the patient's name?' the taller one asks me as we all troop up.

'His name's Ronnie.'

'And is Ronnie conscious?'

'Yes, but he's not moving and he can't seem to speak very well,' I explain.

'How did it happen?'

'I don't know. I just found him up there on the floor when I popped round to bring his shopping. He's been a bit unwell with a stomach upset the last couple of days.'

'Any idea how long he was up there before you found him?'

'I don't know, sorry.' I feel hopeless, as if I somehow ought to know more helpful details.

One of the paramedics stands on the landing as the bathroom is too small for them both to attend to Ronnie. I hover at the top of the stairs for a minute or two but I'm just getting in the way, so I come back down.

Ronnie does well, at his age, to keep the house tidy but sitting here in the kitchen, instead of my usual dash in and back out, I can see the tell-tale signs of neglect. The floor is desperate for a sweep and the worktops are covered in dull smears and stale crumbs. It's obvious that a thorough clean is long overdue.

I feel bad. I should have thought to offer Ronnie my help before now, to help him keep on top of things.

The Turners couldn't do enough to help my family when Billy was taken and yet I'm ashamed to say it had never occurred to me to offer to pop round once or twice a week to help Ronnie with his chores.

I'd seen recently in the *Nottingham Post* that there were a couple of retirement villages in construction closer to the city. They seemed to be springing up everywhere; smart, purpose-built accommodation with integrated facilities to make life easier for the ageing-but-still-able population.

I could see Ronnie settled somewhere like that but I probably won't suggest it. The elderly villagers tend to stay here until the end of their days; it's as if they've got the pit dust running in their very blood. Even though all the new housing at Jasmine Gardens has brought new people here, there's an underlying sense that they're not the 'proper' villagers. Not like Ronnie and, I suppose, me.

'Could we have a glass of water up here please, love?' one of the paramedics calls down.

I open a number of cupboards looking for glasses and I have to use my hand to push stuff back in, some of them are so bunged up with clutter. Finally, I take a glass of water upstairs.

I hand it over. 'How is he?'

'He's in a bit of a bad way, poor chap. Dehydrated. Does he live alone? Is there any family close by?'

'His wife died about five years ago so he's on his own now. He has a son, Eric, but it must be ten months or even longer since he's visited Ronnie. He lives with his own family in Cornwall.' I shrug away my disapproval. 'But I live next door and we're close neighbours. I see him every day, even just if it's to pop my head round to make sure he's OK. You know, see if he needs anything.'

'I wish more folks were like you.' He looks regretful. 'Doesn't take much to check in on elderly neighbours, does it?'

The other paramedic's head appears from around the bathroom door.

'Good job you checked up on him today,' he says in a low voice, and looks at his colleague. 'It's a very nasty virus. We're going to have to take him in but he's far too weak to walk.'

I wait downstairs while they bring poor old Ronnie down on a stretcher. His face is deathly pale and he seems to have aged ten years since yesterday.

'Don't worry, Ronnie—' I squeeze his hand gently, feel his cool, papery skin pressing into my palm '—I'll lock up and feed Tina. I'll make sure everything's OK with the house.'

He opens his mouth as if he's going to say something but his breath catches in his throat and he starts to cough.

'Steady on, Ronnie,' one of the paramedics says. 'Just breathe, nice and easy. Don't try to speak.'

They wait until he stops coughing before moving again. But still Ronnie continues to murmur.

'D – don't – I—'

'What's that, Ronnie?' I bend my head closer to him. 'What're you trying to say?'

'Don't go—' He coughs, his voice raspy and almost incoherent.

'I think he wants me to stay with him,' I say. 'Is that it, Ronnie? You don't want me to go?'

He tries again and then, finally, I catch his words. I realise what it is he's been trying to say.

'Don't... go... upstairs,' he whispers.

CHAPTER NINE

SIXTEEN YEARS EARLIER

Rose wolfed down the plate of home-made Shepherd's pie her mum put in front of her and made her excuses to get out of the house as quickly as possible.

Her mum and dad were arguing about money again. Even Billy had made some excuse about going to play footie on the field and dived out of the house before her.

Cassie and her family lived on Byron Street, which was located over on the other side of the village, a steady ten-minute walk from Rose's own house.

It was a pleasant afternoon so she decided to walk the long way round to Cassie's house. As she walked, Rose thought about her classes that day. She'd chosen to draw classical figures with charcoal on paper but Cassie had used the brightest pastels and her modern explosions of colour were the polar opposite of her friend's conservative efforts.

Cassie loved Picasso and Banksy; Rose preferred Van Gogh and Turner. But that saying about opposites attracting… well, that kind of applied to her and Cassie.

Rose had known they were a great match right from their first day at primary school, when they'd swapped coat pegs and painting tabards; Cassie had wanted red and she'd wanted the pale pink.

Now, Cassie lived with her mum, Carolyn, and her older brother, Jed. Her dad, known to the locals as Bomber but whose real name was Brian, had been good friends with Rose's dad, Ray. When the girls were younger, the two men would regularly go for a pint down the welfare together after work and were members of the same snooker hall in Hucknall.

Bomber died on the coalface. Ray Tinsley had been working the same shift that day but quite a bit further down the line. The roof had collapsed at the end of the tunnel where Bomber had been working. For weeks afterwards, the village had rung with the story of how all the other men, including Ray, had dug at the earth with their bare hands, trying to reach him before the pit rescue team arrived.

They did get to him, but by that time Bomber had already gone.

When he'd come home, Ray had been broken. It was only one of two times Rose had seen him openly cry. Ray had said he'd never seen anything like it; Bomber's head had been crushed flat as a pancake. Rose had never told Cassie about that.

Her dad had nightmares for months afterwards. The National Coal Board denied any wrongdoing and the court ruled that the roof collapse was an 'Act of God' and could not be ascribed to any safety failings by the company.

The NCB voluntarily opted to give Carolyn a small sum, which the local press called a 'payment of goodwill'.

Rose raised her hand to knock at the door when Cassie's brother opened it.

'Hello, Jed,' she said.

He grunted and swept by her, heading off down the road.

'There's a man in a rush,' she said as Cassie appeared at the door.

'Ignore him.' Cassie rolled her eyes. 'He's a bloody sponger, living off Mam. She's just given him a tenner to pour down his throat at the Station Hotel. We've all just had a big row about it. Anyway—' she stood back '—let's get you upstairs and in front of the mirror. I'll have you looking like Christina Aguilera in no time at all.'

Rose grinned and pulled a face. 'You got a magic wand up there, have you?'

'No, just my amazing artistry skills. Step this way, madam.'

Upstairs in her cramped bedroom, Cassie had set out her full make-up kit on the dressing table. Rose sat down on the stool, touched her friend had gone to such an effort to help her. Cassie had been asking to make Rose up for ages and she'd agreed she could. But there always seemed something better to do when it came down to it.

'I have to be back for seven-thirty in case Gareth rings early,' Rose said.

'Yeah, you said… for the third flipping time!' She sighed. 'Chill out a bit, will you?'

Cassie pressed a button on her CD player and the room filled with Britney Spears singing, *I'm a Slave 4 U.*

Cassie grabbed a pair of mangled, worn tan tights from the floor and draped them round her shoulders. Then she started gyrating and twisting the tights so they resembled a snake.

'You look just like Britney at the VMA's, Cass… *not*!' Rose burst out laughing as Cassie whipped the tights off and flung them at her.

'Ugh.' Rose pushed them off her and on to the floor. 'Get on with it then or it'll soon be time for me to go home.'

Cassie turned the music down a bit.

'You're really pretty, you know, Rose,' she said, picking up a tendril of long, pale red hair and twisting it into a thick rope which she then pinned to the back of Rose's head. 'You just have to learn how to make the best of yourself.'

She instructed Rose to turn the stool around so she was facing away from the mirror.

'Just so it's a surprise when I've finished, like the makeovers you see on the telly,' she explained.

Rose's eyes flicked over the room. She noticed the single bed was unmade and the sheets looked dingy and in need of a good wash. The bedside table was covered in used mugs and plates and empty crisp bags and there was a pile of dirty washing in the corner of the room. No wonder there was a fusty smell in here.

'Soz, I know it's a mess.' Cassie shrugged, without embarrassment.

Rose forced her eyes away from the mess and fixed them on her friend's face instead.

Cassie was still obsessed by the pop group No Doubt even though they'd been around a while now. She'd modelled her look on the lead singer, Gwen Stefani. Hair bleached to within an inch of its life, heavy make-up and mostly skimpy clothes. It was a startling effect.

Sadly, Rose knew that even if you dressed up like a pop star, walking around a tiny village like Newstead didn't have quite the same effect as being the real singer, on stage. Rather than drawing admiration for her lookalike image to a famous singer, Cassie had quickly earned herself the reputation of being quite a tarty-looking wild child. It wasn't an entirely unfair description, thought Rose; she always had to go over the top.

'I'd rather face the mirror so I can see what you're doing,' Rose complained. 'I thought I was supposed to be learning how to apply all this stuff.'

'And I'll teach you,' Cassie said shortly, pouring a little make-up base on the back of her hand and dipping a rather grubby-looking sponge into it. 'But first I want you to see how good you *can* look. Just relax.'

But Rose couldn't relax. She didn't like Cassie being so close up to her face; close enough to see she had one eyebrow higher than the other, three chicken pox scars on her left cheek and a big angry red zit on her forehead. The only good thing being that she didn't have to look at herself in the mirror. Rose hated her Titian hair and pale skin. She hated these features with a passion.

On the one hand, it seemed as if she'd sat there for hours but, as she was keeping a close eye on the time, she realised it had actually only been around twenty minutes.

'Ta-dah!' She unpinned Rose's hair. It cascaded down and Cassie mussed it around her shoulders. 'You can turn around now.'

CHAPTER TEN

SIXTEEN YEARS EARLIER

Rose squeezed her eyes shut until she faced the mirror again and then opened them.

'Wow,' she breathed.

'Wow is right,' Cassie agreed. 'You look like a proper model. Like you're in your twenties, instead of about twelve.'

Rose pulled a face at her friend in the mirror but her eyes were soon dragged back to her own features. She couldn't stop looking at her reflection.

The model thing was pushing it but she definitely did look a lot older, far more worldly-wise and sophisticated.

She saw with approval that Cassie had framed her green eyes with subtle, smoky shades in chocolate brown and gold and that she'd used a fine black liner, which had redefined her round, deep-set eyes. Now, Rose thought, she looked less like a pig and more like a slinky cat.

Her pale, blotchy skin had been smoothed into a flawless porcelain canvas, and for the first time ever, her lips appeared plump and pouted seductively in a deep-plum shade.

'You look flipping knockout,' Cassie said, grinning. 'What do you think?'

'I can't believe it. I love it!' Rose turned, still seated, and hugged her friend close.

'Watch you don't smudge it all.' Cassie laughed, pushing her back a little. 'I don't want my amazing talent going to waste.'

'Thanks so much, Cass.'

'*De nada.*' She waved her thanks away. 'Now. Let's talk about what you need to be doing in the cinema with Gareth. Any ideas?'

Rose frowned. 'Watch the film and then talk about it afterwards?'

'No, no, no!' She shook her head in desperation in time with her words. 'When you leave the Odeon, you shouldn't have a clue what the film was about, silly.'

'How come?'

'Because you'll be *far too busy* to watch the film, if you get my drift…' Cassie sat on the edge of the bed and patted the space next to her. Rose dutifully sat down. 'So. Let's imagine we're at the cinema right now, yeah? The film's started and you're comfy and relaxed. About ten or fifteen minutes in, you could slide your hand onto his leg like this.'

She pressed her hand onto Rose's thigh and began stroking it seductively.

'Gerroff!' she squealed and sprang away, laughing.

'Rose! This isn't a game. Gareth isn't a kid, he's going to be used to dating *real women.* Confident women who know what they're doing. Get my drift?'

Rose shuffled back next to her.

'If you think that's a bit forward to start with then just lay your head on his shoulder or shift your leg a bit so your knees are touching, like this.'

Cassie's knee pressed lightly against her own.

'OK,' Rose replied doubtfully.

For the next half an hour, Cassie took her through the full spectrum of possibilities; from merely touching knees to nigh on having full intercourse in the cinema seat. Rose had no intention of doing any of it, of course, but she stayed quiet and appeared to pay full attention.

Rose had learned way back in primary school that once Cassie set her mind on an idea, there was no stopping her. It was easier to just let her have her say.

Cassie's mum popped her head around the door. 'I'm just off for a couple of drinkies down the Station Hotel with Barbara. Blimey, is that you under there, Rose? You look stunning.'

'Thanks, Carolyn.' She smiled shyly. It did make a nice change to feel positive about her appearance for once.

When Carolyn had gone, the girls went downstairs into the living room. Cassie turned her Britney CD up twice as loud as her mother usually allowed and Rose fetched the two Bacardi Breezers that Cassie had hidden for them earlier at the back of the fridge.

The girls gyrated seductively, bumped hips and bottoms in time with the beat and swigged from their bottles. Later they fell onto the settee, exhausted and unable to speak for laughing.

When Rose left it was already dark. She walked along the street at a steady pace, enjoying the cool air and the relative silence after the music blaring in her ears. She could hear a steady stream of traffic passing the village on the main road but there were no vehicles around on the smaller back roads.

It had been such fun tonight at Cassie's. When she'd first caught sight of herself in the mirror after her makeover, Rose had felt just like a butterfly emerging from a chrysalis. She really hadn't known she could look so… *attractive.*

Was that really a word that she could ever get used to using about herself?

Now, walking home, she felt like she'd been plucked out of a life of college-kid drudgery and transplanted onto a path to womanhood. A date with a real man and a hot new image in the space of a few hours… it was almost too much to get her head around.

But she would, she told herself silently, she *would* get used to it because it was a hell of a lot more exciting than what she'd had in her life so far.

As she walked under a lamppost, Rose glanced at her watch. It wasn't even seven-fifteen yet. There was no rush to get home, where she'd have to come down to earth with a bump and revert back into boring Rose. Although she was looking forward to speaking to Gareth, if not a little nervous in case her dad realised she was speaking to a boy.

She decided to walk the long way home and then cut through the park to bring her out near the end of her street.

As she walked she conjured up Gareth again in her mind: his neat dark hair, and soulful brown eyes. He was neither muscle-bound nor skinny; just the perfect build for his height, which Rose estimated to be around 5'10", maybe five inches taller than herself.

His voice was deep, masterful. He'd sounded so experienced and wise when they chatted... he was just perfect!

She shuddered with the anticipation of what it might feel like to kiss Gareth as she entered the small, grassed park area that, last year, the council had dotted with climbing frames and play equipment for the local kids.

On impulse, she sat on a swing and, keeping her feet on the floor, rocked herself gently. She closed her eyes and smiled, leaning her head against the freezing cold chain and imagining her cheek pressing into Gareth's chest.

A noise over to the left caused her eyelids to snap open involuntarily. She stood up and peered into the gloom of the bushes where the sound, like a snapping twig, came from.

'Hello?' She walked a little closer and then stopped again to listen.

Nothing. It was probably just a cat. She shrugged and chuckled to herself when she thought about her man-dreaming on the swing. That's what drinking alcopops and dancing wildly did for you.

Still, she couldn't remember feeling so excited and nervous in equal measure.

Rose sighed, thinking that she'd better get home so she wasn't late for Gareth's call.

She walked to the park exit and crossed the road to where her own house stood, lights blazing in the front room.

She didn't look back. She didn't see the figure step out of the bushes and watch her as she used her key to open the front door.

CHAPTER ELEVEN

SIXTEEN YEARS EARLIER

Back in her bed later that night, Rose found it difficult to get to sleep. When she finally dozed off, she snapped awake at two a.m. in a state of exhausted excitement.

It was the thoughts, the possibilities. Mostly, it was the replaying of Gareth's deep, seductive voice in her head that kept her from resting.

He'd called her last night, just as he'd promised he would. Eight o'clock on the dot.

It had been a stressful wait because her mum's friend Kath rang the landline unexpectedly at seven-thirty. The two women had been known to chat for England, so Rose breathed a sigh of relief when Stella ended the call after twenty minutes, so she could watch *Masterchef*.

'Why are you sitting on your own out here, Rose?' Billy enquired loudly when he passed her on the bottom step, next to the telephone table.

'It's my new reading spot,' she said with a tight smile.

'So, where's your book then?' That kid was just too smart for his own good at times. But she knew how to get rid of him.

'Tell me about school today, Billy. What lessons did you do?'

He frowned and mumbled something incoherent, shuffling off into the kitchen. She heard the back door open and close. It was just before eight; too late for Billy to be going out. Why wasn't her mum calling him back? It was too close to Gareth calling for Rose to get involved now.

The last five minutes of waiting was torture. Her dad got up from his chair and walked past her on the step without speaking. She wasn't even sure he'd noticed her sitting there; he seemed to be in a world of his own these days.

Rose heard him pottering around in the kitchen. A minute or two later he walked by again with a sandwich and a can of lager.

Rose wondered if she'd be able to speak if the phone rang. Her lips were dry and her skin was still stinging from where Cassie had scrubbed off the make-up in a huff.

'I've gone to all that trouble and now you want it taking off.' She'd scowled, pummelling at Rose's face with a pungent face wipe. 'You should have just said if you hate it.'

'Cass, of course I don't hate it. But what do you think my dad's going to say if I go home looking like this?'

'Like what?'

'All glammed up. I think you've done an amazing job but I don't want them asking questions when I go out with Gareth tomorrow night, do I?'

'Suppose not,' Cassie had conceded moodily.

The truth was, Cassie might have done a really super job with her make-up but the more Rose looked at her reflection, the more she felt decidedly uncomfortable. It didn't look like *her* in the mirror, for one thing. Not as she liked her ordinary appearance but she thought it might be a slightly better idea to start with make-up that was a bit more natural looking; a look that didn't transform her into someone else entirely.

She wasn't about to tell Cassie that. It was more than her life was worth.

The shrill ring of the phone made her jump.

'I'll get it, it'll probably just be Beth from college,' Rose called through to her mum and dad just before she snatched up the phone. They didn't respond.

'Hello?'

'Hello, Rose. It's Gareth here.'

The hairs on her forearms prickled. 'Oh, hello.'

She tried desperately to act as casual and relaxed as she would with a college friend but she thought she probably sounded more like a nervous teen. She hoped that Gareth would soon gather Rose was having a double-sided conversation, just in case her parents were tuning in next door.

'Are you OK to talk, Rose?' he asked.

'Yes, that's fine.'

'So, what have you been up to today then?'

She could hardly talk about her day at college, seeing as it was supposed to be Beth Teague on the phone, who was on the same art course and whom her parents had met a couple of times.

'I popped round to Cassie's house earlier.'

'Oh, I get it.' Gareth laughed. 'I'm a college girl now, right? I'll have to start wearing a dress and high heels and gossip about the fittest boys.'

Rose giggled.

'Cassie's your friend, I'm guessing?'

'Yes. She lives on Byron Road.'

'Right. And what were you doing there?'

Rose hesitated. She couldn't very well say Cassie had shown her how to apply make-up and lectured her on how to fondle him on their cinema date.

'Sorry. Was that an awkward question to answer when your parents are listening?'

'No, no. We just hung out in her bedroom. You know, playing music and talking. Just the usual stuff.'

'Teenage girls, talking about which boys they fancy, eh?' He gave a low, throaty chuckle.

Rose felt her cheeks begin to heat up and she couldn't think of what to say.

She and Cassie might still be college students but legally they were adults now as both had turned eighteen. They weren't still silly little girls, which is how he'd made it sound… did Gareth think she was younger than she actually was? Maybe Cassie was right and she did need to slap on the make-up a bit.

They arranged to meet the following night.

'If you walk to the top of your street, I'll wait for you in the slip road just by the school,' Gareth said. 'I have a silver Ford Escort.'

He had a car! For some reason this excited Rose even further.

'And have you thought about which film you'd like to see?'

She had. She'd browsed the film lists in the local newspaper earlier that day.

'I thought maybe… *Shrek*?'

'*Shrek*?'

She was embarrassed at his surprised tone. It was the sort of film she'd usually see with Cassie; they'd go halves on a bucket of popcorn and relive the Disney films of their childhood. 'I just thought it was… I don't know, nice and light. Funny.'

'OK. Well, I said you could choose, so *Shrek* it is.'

'No, honestly,' she said quickly. 'If there's a better film on then—'

'Well… how about *The Mummy Returns*?'

'I don't mind, if you'd rather see that.'

'That's sorted, then. You'll have to cuddle up to me if you get scared.' She heard the tease in his voice. 'But if you really want to see *Shrek*, then just say so.'

'No, honestly. *The Mummy Returns* sounds great. Perfect.'

'Excellent. See you tomorrow at seven, then. We'll go for a drink first.'

Rose said goodbye to 'Beth' and ended the call.

She remained sitting on the bottom step for a few minutes, basking in the secretive gloom of the hallway. What had she done to deserve someone as classy as Gareth asking her out? She might be eighteen but to all intents and purposes she was just a college kid who lived in a boring little village where nothing ever happened.

She didn't even know how to apply eyeshadow properly, for goodness sake.

She felt a bit sick now. Would he take her for a drink at some sophisticated cocktail bar?

Gareth had told her he'd only just arrived in Newstead to begin working on the regeneration project. Rose felt sure when he saw the other village girls – Cassie herself with her rock chick looks – or perhaps Stephanie Barrett, who was a curvy brunette who came third last year in the local Miss Mansfield beauty pageant, he'd realise he was wasting his time on pale, uninteresting Rose Tinsley.

To Rose's eternal shame, and Cassie's amusement, she'd never so much as kissed a boy and now a good-looking *man* with a job and a car had asked her out.

Despite feeling like the plainest girl in the village and worrying about whether Gareth was too old for her, Rose couldn't ignore the continuous fizz of excitement that threaded through her veins.

CHAPTER TWELVE

ROSE

PRESENT DAY

The day after Ronnie's collapse, I get to work a little earlier than I need to.

The library's staff entrance door is open but I'm pleased there's no sign of Jim. I'm very fond of him and he's such a gregarious soul but sometimes he doesn't know when to stop rattling on and leave me to get on with my work in peace.

His loud booming laugh and sharp Geordie wit is enough to make any librarian cringe; we're well known for our love of quiet whispers, after all.

The library isn't due to open to the public for another fifty minutes so I make myself a coffee and sit in the easy chairs over in the reading corner to scan through a thick wad of documentation. I've been putting off looking at what amounts to a pile of official spin from the local authority, detailing why they are intending to close up to fifteen libraries across the county of Nottinghamshire.

It starts with a covering letter explaining their officers will be visiting each library to view the facilities and meet librarians personally. I enter the date for Newstead's visit in my diary and skip ahead.

A chill crawls the length of my spine when I think about what will happen if I lose my job. I feel so safe here; I know the area. I feel I'm amongst my own and I know nearly all of the people who regularly use the library.

I'd be forced to get another job.

I have some savings but barely more than a couple of months' salary. The very thought of starting anew somewhere… maybe even being forced to move to a different area… makes my lungs feel as if they are about to burst.

I can't afford to dwell on it. I'm still not strong enough to contemplate how I'd even begin to get through such a massive life change when I'm still wrestling to get through each day.

'Morning, Rose,' Jim says over my shoulder, making me jump. 'Sorry to startle you. How's Ronnie?'

Word had already got around the village about Ronnie's ill health. Just a few minutes after the ambulance took him to hospital, a small, concerned group of our closest neighbours gathered, eager to offer any help Ronnie might need.

'Morning, Jim.' I take a breath to calm myself again and turn in my chair to face him. 'I rang the hospital first thing and they said he'd had a bit of a restless night but he's now comfortable. I'm popping in to see him later this afternoon.'

'Give him mine and Janice's best regards, will you, pet? And give me a shout if his garden needs tidying or anything of that nature. They don't make them like Ronnie any more, that's for sure.' Jim's smile dissolves into a sad expression. 'Did everything he could for our Joe, I'll never forget it. Tried to resuscitate him right there at the pit gates in front of that baying crowd. Ronnie Turner, he's got the heart of a lion.'

We all knew the story. Jim's twin brother, Joe, was one of a small number of miners who decided not to go on strike in 1984. Consistently referred to by the striking miners as 'scabs', the men were vilified and the subject of much intimidation locally.

One morning, when the National Coal Board bus carrying the working miners edged past the furious crowd of those men who were on strike and penniless, the restraining police line failed. As the men got off the bus, the crowd surged forward and objects were thrown.

Half a flying brick hit Joe Greaves on the back of the head. Joe never gained consciousness and the culprit was never found.

There were lots of similar incidents that documented the troubled years, as they'd come to be locally known, although none had been quite as tragic as that one. But the lack of justice following Joe's death had bred a suspicious discontent that still simmered under the surface of the community to this day.

'I'll tell Ronnie you were asking after him, Joe,' I said, standing up. 'You can open the main doors now, if you like. There'll probably be a stampede, all those lovely new books waiting to be collected.'

'Aye, you should've seen my Jan's face when I took that book home last night, her nose was straight in it.' His expression grew mock-stern. 'I had to make my own tea, mind.'

I grin and move over to the main desk as Jim opens the doors. Predictably, there are a handful of people already waiting, most of whom I'd left a message for yesterday.

But the first questions were not about their long-awaited books.

'How's poor old Ronnie?' Mrs Brewster heaved her considerable bulk over towards me and leaned on the desk to catch her breath. 'I've been thinking about him ever since I heard.'

Miss Carter followed her over and I told the two of them what the nurse had said when I called the hospital this morning.

'I thought about starting a little collection for Mr Turner,' Miss Carter said, shyly. A whip-thin elderly woman with a grey bun, she peered at me through school-ma'am spectacles. 'If you don't think it too presumptuous of me.'

'I think that's a lovely idea.' I smiled at her, hoping she'd have no more questions about my eating habits. 'Ronnie will be very touched, I'm sure.'

CHAPTER THIRTEEN

ROSE

PRESENT DAY

After work, I drive straight to Kings Mill Hospital to see Ronnie.

I know the ward number already, so I bypass the main reception and follow the signs directing visitors to the upper floors.

Visiting time has already begun so I don't have to wait around behind everyone else. I buzz the intercom at the secure-ward entrance door and lean forward, speaking back to the disembodied voice. 'I'm here to visit Ronnie Turner. I'm a friend, his neighbour.'

There is no further reply but an audible click and I push open the heavy swing door.

The smell of antiseptic hits me as I walk into the ward, the quiet emptiness of the corridor outside replaced by the hustle and bustle of a busy staff and patients' visitors milling around. I approach a nurse at the reception desk.

I explain who I am again. 'I'm a bit more than Ronnie's neighbour really,' I say. 'I'm a good friend. I'm the one who called the ambulance.'

'I see. Well, I'm afraid Ronnie is resting at the moment,' she says. 'He had a bit of a setback this morning.'

'A setback?' I swallow, worried what she's about to say.

'He's been having breathing difficulties, so the doctors have put him on oxygen and they've lightly sedated him.'

'Can I see him, just for a few minutes?' I ask but she shakes her head.

'He's completely out of it at the moment; he won't even know you're there. You should come back tomorrow but I'd suggest ringing the ward first, to check he's up to receiving visitors.'

'OK,' I say, and sigh. 'Can you tell him I came?'

She nods, already distracted by another visitor.

Driving home I think about what the nurse said and begin my usual trick: telling myself the story of how things could get worse. I feel awful leaving without seeing Ronnie. I worry he'll wake up and be the only patient without someone at the side of his bed.

I know it's times like this that older people can feel neglected and alone, feel like there's no one left who cares about them anymore.

I wrack my brains. I can't see him in person right now but surely there's something I can do for him that will show I'm there for him… show I've been thinking about him?

And that's when it occurs to me.

Ronnie's house is in a bit of a state. The least I can do is make sure it's clean and tidy and pleasant for him to come back to.

I think that's something that would make a difference.

When I get home, I make a cheese and tomato sandwich and a cup of tea. I don't fancy anything else, even though the cupboards and fridge are still full of treats from my impulsive bulk-buying session at the Co-op.

My mum was always a big fan of baking and loved making hearty meals from scratch. Practically everything I cook is shop-made and I sometimes feel I ought to make more effort to make nutritious home-cooked meals for myself.

I think it's generational; women today have it drummed into them that there are more important things to do in life than cook, as though somehow it's demeaning to enjoy doing a domestic activity. There always seems to be somebody out there that knows what women ought to be doing better than we know ourselves.

By the time I've finished my tea I feel quite tired. I'm a low-energy person anyway, always have been. I'd really like to run a bath and soak for half an hour and then go to bed early with a tub of Ben & Jerry's and my latest novel: one of the Man Booker Prize shortlisted titles.

As a librarian, I often feel a bit of a pressure to set an example and read some heavyweight, literary fiction; the sort I sometimes quietly have to keep going back to and reading the last half a page again before it makes any sense.

Tonight is definitely one of those times that a nice bit of light women's fiction would be preferable.

Still, taking a bath and going to bed early to read isn't going to help Ronnie. So instead I choose a few cleaning products from the cupboard, grab a couple of cloths and head next door.

I leave the lights on and lock my back door, slipping my keys into the pocket of my fleece. It's dark outside now and the air feels cool on my face and hands.

My heart starts up, beating its irregular rhythm on my chest wall. I talk myself calmer, just like the therapist taught me all those years ago.

I'm fine. I'm safe. I am breathing myself calm.

I open the small gate, the same one I've slipped through hundreds of times as a young girl when I'd pop round to see Ronnie and Sheila.

My mind flits back and for a few seconds I hesitate at the gate and allow myself to slip back in time. I imagine Mum and Dad are in the living room. Billy is building one of his Lego masterpieces on the kitchen table and here I am, just popping next door to take Sheila this week's *Woman's Own* magazine that Mum has finished reading.

A dog barks in a nearby garden and the vision dissolves. I press my hand to the gate, feeling the damp, splintered wood beneath my fingers.

The moment I'm imagining existed once and yet I barely noticed it back then. My family were just there. Nothing to feel grateful for; in fact, quite the contrary. Lots to be irritated by: Mum and Dad bickering about money; Billy constantly asking questions about this and that or badgering me to play another never-ending game of Monopoly.

Annoying me. That's all they all ever seemed to do back then.

I wish they were still here to annoy me. I wish I'd taken the time to talk to Dad about how he felt, being stripped of his job and his standing in the community within a single day. I wish I'd suggested to Mum we go for a walk together in the abbey grounds, just to get her out of the house and talk about something other than the lack of money and Dad's drinking.

And Billy. How I wish I had another chance to spend some time with Billy.

I should have played a thousand more games of Monopoly with my brother and talked to him about keeping safe. I should have stressed that it was OK just to turn your back and walk away from any situation that made you feel uncomfortable.

Even if it meant being rude to someone you knew.

Someone like Gareth Farnham.

I hear car doors slamming on the street and shake myself out of the fog of the past. It serves nobody, this kind of indulgent reminiscing. Least of all me.

Regrets don't solve anything. Regrets won't bring my family back, that's for sure.

I reach into my pocket and fish out Ronnie's spare key. It's lived in the kitchen drawer for years but I've never had occasion to use it over the years.

Ronnie has never taken ill like this before. He doesn't go on holiday – not even for a weekend break – and aside from popping to the local shops or very occasionally down to the Station Hotel for a pint he's literally never out of the house.

I know one thing though: in the future, I don't want to wish there were things I'd done for Ronnie in his time of need. I want to support him the best I can right now and repay a little of the kindness he's shown over the years to me and my family.

He's always done his best to help anyone he can and now it's time for me to show my own personal gratitude. I think about Miss Carter and her planned 'get well' collection and Jim offering to tidy up Ronnie's garden while he's in hospital.

There's a lot of love for him in this community.

I open the door and step into Ronnie's kitchen, snapping on the light. There's a bit of a fusty smell in here. I've never noticed it before but it can't have just appeared in the space of a day.

I realise, to my shame, that there's a lot I haven't noticed about Ronnie. He's just been a comforting figure in the background up until now; he's always there. Like my own family were, I suppose.

I set down the bag of cleaning products on the kitchen worktop. It sounds like Ronnie's hospital stay might extend a little longer beyond that which I first thought but that's OK.

By the time I go back home tonight, the downstairs rooms of this house will be fresh and pristine, ready for Ronnie coming home.

And tomorrow, despite Ronnie's odd instruction as he left for the hospital, I fully intend to tackle the upstairs.

CHAPTER FOURTEEN

SIXTEEN YEARS EARLIER

After what felt like a lifetime of waiting for her first ever date, at last Rose was ready to leave the house.

She'd left plenty of time to walk up the street and meet Gareth just after the bend at the top where he said he'd be waiting in his car on the slip road.

'Where did you say you were going again?' Ray Tinsley took another swig from his can of lager and belched, throwing Rose a disapproving look as she said goodbye from the safety of the hallway.

'You look lovely, Rose,' Billy whispered from behind her and she reached behind her and squeezed his hand.

Despite Cassie issuing detailed instructions, Rose had decided to dress down in the end. She really had no choice if she wanted to keep her date a secret.

She had on a pair of black, tailored trousers, sensible low-heeled court shoes and a white silky blouse her mum had bought her last year from Marks and Spencer. Basically, it was the outfit she'd worn for her art course interview at college last year.

In Rose's view, it qualified as 'dressed up' compared to the jeans, T-shirt and flat shoes or trainers she usually wore day in, day out. But it was an outfit Cassie simply wouldn't be seen dead in. Hot date or no date.

'It's nice to see you making an effort to dress up, love. You look really nice.'

'Thanks, Mum.' Rose looked at her father to address his question. 'A few of us from college are going for a drink and then to the cinema, Dad. I won't be back late.'

'I should hope not,' he grumbled. 'It hasn't taken you long to start going out drinking, since you started at that place.'

'Now, Ray, that's not fair.' Stella lay her hand on her daughter's arm. 'Our Rose is a good girl and she hardly ever goes out. Have you got enough money, love?'

Rose nodded. 'I'll be off then.'

'How are you getting there?' her father barked.

'Bus,' she said curtly, as though it should be obvious. Thankfully, Ray didn't reply.

Rose stepped back into the hallway. 'Oops, forgot my jacket. I'll just grab it from upstairs and then I'll be off.'

'Have a lovely time,' her mother called, settling back down in front of the television with a bag of potato chips.

Rose ran back upstairs and quickly brushed on some blusher and a smear of pale-pink lipstick. She'd already used a lick of mascara but that was as much as she could risk in case her parents got suspicious.

If Cassie could see her so dressed down after all the effort she'd put in the other night, she'd be livid.

She rushed back downstairs and straight out of the back door. Billy stood outside in the small yard. 'I'll walk up to the bus stop with you, Rose,' he said.

'No!' Her heart was already banging. 'Not tonight, Billy.'

'But I'm fed up. I've nothing to do.'

Rose glanced at him and thought he really did look miserable. Since she'd started college the previous September, she'd not spent much time with her brother.

There was a ten-year age gap between them but she adored Billy. They used to play board games together: Cluedo; Scrabble; and Billy's favourite, the seemingly never-ending Monopoly.

But now, with her art course studies and the new volunteering commitment at the local library, she seemed to have a lot less spare time on her hands.

As she looked at him, he turned slightly and she caught sight of a shadow on his jaw.

'Is that a bruise?' She reached out a hand towards him.

'The ball hit me,' he said glumly, stepping back from her. 'Last night, when we were playing footie on the field.'

'Look, tomorrow night, we'll do something together.' She walked towards the alleyway at the side of the house and turned back to look at his forlorn face. 'I promise.'

'What'll we do though?'

'I dunno, Billy. Whatever. Think of something you fancy and then tell me in the morning.' She didn't look back at him again; she needed to get going.

Rose reached the agreed meeting place on the slip road a good five minutes early and was surprised to see there was already a silver Ford Escort parked there.

She felt the blood rush to her face and it took all her resolve not to run back home again.

As she approached the car, she heard loud music and realised Gareth had his window wound down. 'All Rise' by boy band, Blue, boomed out, drawing a look of disapproval from a dog walker over the road who, fortunately, Rose didn't recognise.

Ducking her head and peering through the passenger-side window, she checked that it was definitely Gareth in the car. He winked at her and so she dragged in a lungful of air and opened the door.

'Hello, Rose.' Gareth smiled and turned the music down. 'You look nice.'

'Thanks.' She climbed into the car. He turned in his seat and stared at her. The heat in her face and neck increased. 'What's wrong?' she asked.

'Nothing's *wrong.*' He smiled, touching her cheek. 'I'm just looking at your loveliness. That's all right, isn't it?'

'Yes,' she squeaked, silently wishing the ground under her seat would suddenly open up and swallow her whole.

And anyway, it wasn't alright, not really. Even without a mirror, she knew she looked one big awful mess; red hair, red face. She was clearly out of her depth and should never have come here.

Gareth twisted back to face the steering wheel and turned the key. The ignition coughed but didn't catch. He turned it a couple more times.

'I love your colouring,' he said, watching as she pushed her hair back from her face. 'Your red hair and smooth skin.'

Rose didn't want him to say things like that just to try and put her at ease. She hated the way she looked.

'You're lovely.' He smiled at her, still watching as she became engrossed in picking at a nail. 'Not used to compliments, are you?'

She shrugged, wishing he'd just get off the subject.

'Well, you'd better get used to it because I think you're beautiful.'

The car kicked into life at last and Gareth pulled out onto Hucknall Road. Rose silently released a long breath.

'You got out of Colditz OK, then?'

'Sorry?'

'Past your dad, I mean? I thought your old man was the reason I had to pretend to be a college girl on the phone last night?'

He grinned at her and Rose found herself laughing at his comment and, in turn, she felt her shoulders relax a little.

'It was fine,' she said. 'Dad questioned me a bit about where I'm going and how I'm getting there. Then my little brother, Billy, offered to walk me up to the bus stop, which I could've done without.'

'Little brother, eh? Sounds like a little nuisance, more like.'

'He's no trouble, really.' Rose smiled impishly. 'In small doses.'

CHAPTER FIFTEEN

SIXTEEN YEARS EARLIER

Initially, Rose had felt a little vexed that the journey to the cinema would drag on painfully, hampered by her lack of confidence. But they chatted on quite easily about this and that.

'Where did you live before you came here?' Rose asked.

Gareth fiddled with the music, turning it high and then low again.

'Before you came to Newstead, I mean,' she went on. 'I can't quite place your accent. It doesn't sound like Nottinghamshire but—'

'I wouldn't know where to start,' he cut in. 'I've lived all over the place. All over the country, the world even.'

'Wow,' Rose said, genuinely impressed. 'Like where?'

'Is this a formal interrogation? Do I need my lawyer?' He laughed and she joined in.

'I'm just envious,' she said. 'I've never even been abroad yet.'

'Really?' He looked at her, his face shining. 'That's so sweet.'

'It's not sweet, it's sad.' Rose pulled a face. 'Furthest I've travelled from the village is to Newquay, in Cornwall.'

'A proper little girl next door, aren't you, Rosie? Pure and unspoilt.'

She clamped her lips together and looked out of the window.

'My dad was in the army,' he said. 'He was based in Germany but we've been all over the place.' He hesitated before carrying on speaking. 'To be honest with you, my family broke up when I was younger. Silly, really, but I still find it painful to talk about.'

'Oh! I'm sorry,' she said quickly, berating herself for not behaving more sensitively. 'I totally understand and I didn't mean to pry.'

A few moments of awkward silence and then they began chatting again.

Gareth seemed far more enthusiastic discussing the upcoming regeneration programme he was involved with.

'We've a whole roster of stuff planned that will eventually provide jobs for the local people.'

'It sounds brilliant, just what the village needs.' She beamed. 'If things improve around here we'll all be very grateful to you, Gareth.'

He laughed. 'It's all in a day's work for me; I've never been one for a lot of fuss. Soon we'll have a whole team of people working on the project, including local volunteers. You know, if you wanted… oh, it doesn't matter.'

Rose looked at him. 'What were you going to say?'

'Just that if you were interested, we could probably use your help as a volunteer but I know you already do some of that at the library.'

Rose thought about her dreary afternoons with Mr Barrow, who unwrapped his ham salad sandwich each day at precisely noon and measured the book spines with a ruler so the labelling remained exactly level.

She loved working amongst so many wonderful books but time spent there was staid and predictable rather than exciting, as she felt sure it would be working with Gareth and his team.

'I only do Wednesday afternoons at the library,' she said quickly. 'I'm sure I could find a bit more spare time to help out with the project.'

'That would be brilliant, Rose.' Gareth's eyes stayed on her longer than they ought to, seeing as he was supposed to be watching the road. She held her breath until he turned his attention back there. 'This project is going to get the whole village back on its feet and it would be so great to have you be a part of that.'

'I really hope you're right,' Rose said, suddenly feeling a little downcast. 'My dad is a shadow of the man he used to be. The day they closed the pit, he started to fade.'

'He hasn't found another job yet?'

Rose shook her head. 'It's not through lack of years of trying but there's just nothing going around here.'

Gareth took a sharp right turn and Rose saw they were suddenly in a car park. In the end, the journey to Mansfield had seemed to take no time at all. They'd chatted easily and now she felt much more relaxed. Even her face felt a normal colour again.

Gareth turned off the engine.

'I *am* right about the village improvements. Hopefully, you'll learn to trust my judgement.' He winked and she felt the heat begin to crawl into her neck again. 'Stick with me and your life will get better. Do you think you can you do that? Can you trust me, Rose?'

'Well – yes, I think so.' She faltered under his intense stare, wondering if this meant he was already planning to invite her on another date.

Later, when she replayed their conversation in her mind, she would think it was a rather strange thing for him to ask, seeing as they had only just met.

CHAPTER SIXTEEN

ROSE

PRESENT DAY

On Fridays, the library is only open in the afternoon, from two until six o'clock, so I decide I'll put the morning to good use and continue my surprise sprucing up of Ronnie's house.

Last night, despite feeling quite tired, I'd enjoyed making a difference and had worked until fairly late next door before coming home.

Often my empty evenings stretch on a bit, which is why I tend to go to bed early most nights if I'm not watching something on television. It's surprising how slowly the hands of the clock can turn when you've nobody to discuss your day with or put the world to rights with over a glass of wine.

I suppose I ought to be used to it by now. Still, it made a change for the hours to fly by like they did last night.

I fed Tina, Ronnie's cat, and then started in the kitchen, wiping down all the worktops and cupboard doors. I thought about emptying the cupboards and wiping out the shelves but I worried that might be overstepping the mark a bit. I didn't want Ronnie to feel like I'd been intrusive while he wasn't home.

Besides, I could see, after a cursory glance, that some of the cupboards were stuffed to the brim with all sorts of bizarre items – balls of wool, unopened packets of brand-new clothing pegs and sewing materials – they must've been stuck there, frozen in time since Sheila's death five years ago.

After I'd cleaned and wiped everything down, I mopped the kitchen floor and then closed the door behind me, leaving it to dry.

In the small hallway, I pulled out the compact cylinder vacuum cleaner from the understairs cupboard and moved into the living room.

After dusting, plumping cushions and finally vacuuming the patched, threadbare carpet, I resolved that, the next day, I'd pull back the heavy velvet drapes and throw open the windows. It would feel good to get some fresh air circulating in the place.

And now, this morning, it's time to finish the job.

I step out into my small garden and inhale the early morning dank, earthy air. It's not altogether unpleasant; I've happy memories of playing here when I was younger.

I remember various family birthday gatherings out here with beef burgers and warm soda pop, the adults sitting on uncomfortable striped, metal-framed deckchairs that Dad had crammed on to our small, marshy lawn.

Those were the days when he was still working at the pit and overtime was regular and plentiful. Even when the pit closed, there was a sense that things would turn around somehow.

Like generations before him, Dad assumed his whole future was mapped out, working for the National Coal Board, the NCB, as it was called back then, and then retiring on a nice comfortable pension. Every penny of it honestly earned by tens of thousands of hours spent filthy and overheating, slogging more than three thousand feet underground, on the coalface.

Mum liked being in the garden. She kept the borders full of burgeoning colour from springtime onwards and she'd mow the lawn with her little orange Flymo. She was a creative soul, happiest planting in the garden or baking in the kitchen.

I just about manage to keep the yard tidy these days but I haven't got Mum's green fingers, or her creativity.

I step through the gate into Ronnie's garden where it's a different story altogether. His back yard is entirely concreted over. I remember him doing it himself some years back.

'Grass is just too much trouble,' he'd grumbled to Dad over the low fence. 'Better to be living life than breaking your back in the garden, eh, Ray?'

They'd laughed and Dad had agreed but he'd wrinkled his nose at Mum when Ronnie had gone back inside.

'Lazy bugger,' Dad had complained. 'Doesn't take much to keep a postage stamp of grass tidy, does it?'

'Doesn't take *you* very long but it takes a good bit of my time,' Mum had pointed out.

Now the concrete in Ronnie's yard is dirty and deep cracks radiate out from the centre like disused roads on an expired map.

I let myself in next door and feel gratified that, after yesterday's cleaning spree, the kitchen looks as fresh and clean as I've seen it in years.

After opening the small window located next to the oven, I take the stripy rug I'd set going in the washing machine last night and peg it out on the clothes line just outside the back door. The air is crisp and breezy today, so I know it won't take long to dry.

In the living room, I pull open the curtains as far as they'll go and open the top two windows.

It occurs to me that maybe I ought to have a word with Ronnie about exchanging these heavy velvet drapes for some short, neat curtains made from a lighter fabric.

I'd be happy to go shopping with him to buy some new soft furnishings but I have a sneaky feeling he won't want to change… too many memories of Sheila lie preserved in the dust and folds.

I stand at the bottom of the stairs looking up, clutching my bag of cleaning products, and I spot that a thorough vacuum is also long overdue up here.

I've never thought about how Ronnie copes keeping this house shipshape. Like most couples of Ronnie and Sheila's age, their roles in the home remained traditional for most of their married life, and Sheila was a formidable housewife, taking much pride in keeping her home pristine and in good order.

He must have felt completely out of his comfort zone when she died, and he let things slide while he grappled with his grief.

I begin to climb up to the first floor, deciding I'll vacuum the stairs later. It's only half way up that my feet stop moving and Ronnie's words echo in my head.

'Don't go upstairs' were the last words he'd whispered before they carried him off on a stretcher.

I think I know why he said that. More than likely, it's because it's in a bit of a state up here and he feels embarrassed that I might see it. Trust Ronnie to be worrying what people think of him when he should only be concerned with getting himself well again.

Of course, I wouldn't want to glaringly defy Ronnie's explicit instructions but I really do need to freshen up the bathroom for his return. The dreadful smell yesterday had been testament to the fact that Ronnie had obviously been ill in here, prior to me finding him. As much as the thought of it turns my stomach, I need to bleach the loo and mop the floor at the very least.

Fortunately, the tiny bathroom window has been left wedged open overnight so the air isn't as bad as I expected in here.

I whisk a good dose of bleach around the toilet bowl and leave it to do its work, and then I clean both the sink and the bath.

My heart squeezes in on itself when I spot a cluster of dated, feminine toiletries crowded into one corner of the bathtub.

It's another legacy of Sheila from which it seems poor Ronnie just can't bear to move on.

CHAPTER SEVENTEEN

ROSE

PRESENT DAY

I leave the bathroom, intending to pop downstairs to the kitchen to fetch the mop and bucket to give the lino a good dousing, when I notice that Ronnie's bedroom door is ajar.

Just like my own house, the main bedroom overlooks the road while the smaller second bedroom is tucked away at the back.

Curiosity gets the better of me and I decide to take a little peek in Ronnie's bedroom. I know he'd be embarrassed if he were here now but I so want the whole house to be nice for his return. Changing the bed and airing the room will make a difference, especially if he needs to rest up for a while after he's discharged.

I push open the door slightly and peer around. Good old Ronnie, he's made his bed and it's quite tidy, considering. I can vacuum in here when I do the rest of the upstairs but for now I just crack open a window to get the air circulating.

Back on the landing, I see that the second bedroom door is firmly closed.

If Ronnie is anything like me, his spare room is probably a bit of a dumping ground, used for storing stuff. More clutter that should have been thrown away years ago, I suppose.

I might as well take a quick look and then I'll have seen the whole house and know exactly what needs to be done.

I head across the landing, open the door a little and stick my head in.

I can't help smiling. I was right; Ronnie is definitely using his spare room as a bit of a dumping ground. In fact, I think it might even be in a worse state than mine, which is saying something.

Boxes upon boxes of stuff. It all looks undisturbed and I wonder when the last time was that Ronnie looked in here or actually needed anything.

I jump slightly as I hear a shuffle and a thump behind me.

'Oh! It's just you, Tina,' I say to the cat and she stares back at me accusingly. 'Yes, I know. Ronnie told me not to come upstairs and here I am. Well, this is just between us, OK? Come on, let's go downstairs and get you some food.'

I reach for the door handle to pull the door closed again and Tina bolts past me, swiftly disappearing amongst the stacked boxes.

I huff and head downstairs, leaving the door open. I reckon she'll come out when she's ready.

Thirty minutes later, I've vacuumed the stairs and the landing and Tina is *still* ensconced in there. I wind up the cable of the vacuum and stand in the doorway, hands on my hips.

'Time to come out now, Tina,' I say to her, beyond the boxes.

A shuffle, a scratch and then silence. I begin to wonder if she's got a mouse back there. There's a bit of a funny smell but that could just be the fact the room remains closed up most of the time.

The window is over on the far side, a barrier of boxes and stuffed bin bags blocking its access. If Ronnie hardly comes in here, then it's hardly worth breaking my neck to let some air in.

'Tina?'

Silence.

I imagine her crouching there, taking a perverse enjoyment from my impatience, in the way that cats so often do. Such mutiny calls for desperate measures. I head downstairs and return with a cat treat from a bag I spotted on the kitchen worktop.

I whistle and click my tongue, waft the treat in the air a bit to tempt Tina but she's staying put.

'OK, have it your way.' I sigh, turning to leave.

I can leave the spare room door open and let her come out when she's ready. But then it occurs to me that I don't actually know what's in all those boxes. Perhaps Ronnie leaves this particular door closed for a reason.

I don't want him unexpectedly arriving home when I'm at work and finding Tina has ruined fabrics or scratched his sentimental keepsakes.

But if I leave the door open, Ronnie will know I've been in here snooping – which I haven't been really, but it could easily look that way.

I step inside and pull out a few boxes to carve a channel further into the room towards the centre, where I heard Tina scuffling. If I can only spot the little pest, I can grab her and whisk her out of here. Then Ronnie won't be any the wiser.

Most of the boxes are the sort you pick up free from under the supermarket counter. They're not proper packing boxes with interlocking upper flaps, so I'm able to see the contents of most of them as I pull them out.

Yellowing newspapers, no doubt containing articles that were once of interest to Ronnie or Sheila, lots of old, fusty-smelling clothes and boxes full of photographs in yellow and red Kodak envelopes and a couple of boxes full of old cables that now look positively antiquated.

It's fairly safe to assume, I think, that Ronnie hasn't thrown anything out for the past decade at least.

I see a flash of tawny fur as Tina burrows deeper into the room, behind yet another stacked box. I pull it out and swipe down quickly, grasping Tina as gently as I can, while she emits an indignant yowl.

'You didn't really think you'd get the better of me, did you, madam?'

I try my best to dodge her extended claws and hold her in front of me as I turn to wade back out of the room but I'm not quite quick enough and she catches my forearm with a hooked talon, leaving a nasty red welt.

'Oww!' As I stumble, I kick against a small box that has actually got closed cardboard flaps. It tips and the contents scatter on to the floor.

Keeping a grip on Tina, I step over the mess, resolving to come back in here and tidy up once I've got her downstairs again.

A small triangle of red fabric catches my eye.

There's something about the texture of it… the colour…

The world stands still for a second and my heartbeat relocates in my head.

My brain makes an instant match. It looks just like—

'*Billy's blankie*,' I whisper so faintly I wonder if I said the words out loud.

I'm vaguely aware of Tina hissing and jumping from my arms and I realise I've been holding her too tightly.

I bend down and touch the exposed edge of the fabric with my fingertip. Brushed fleece. So soft.

I sway slightly. As my centre of gravity deserts me, I sink to my knees next to the box.

Taking hold of the edge of the small triangle with my finger and thumb, I gently tug at the fabric. The body of the small, red blanket rises up from underneath the other stuff in there and then I'm holding it in my hands.

I stare at it. There are pale patches where the colour has faded.

I lift it to my face and inhale.

There are a lot of red blankets out there, says the voice in my head. *This could be another blanket that just looks like Billy's.*

It's possible, I think, as I tighten my grip.

And then I see it, right there in the corner. The little gold 'B' embroidered by Mum. Purposely designed to be discreet enough not to embarrass him but to aid identification of the blanket, if ever it were lost.

Mum's efforts did the job she intended. There is no doubt about it; *this* is my brother's blanket.

The one he took out with him for our little picnic at the abbey.

The one the police never found.

The one Billy had with him the day he died.

CHAPTER EIGHTEEN

ROSE

PRESENT DAY

Concealed for years below the packets of tissues and folded pillowcases, my brother's blanket lies now in my lap.

I don't know exactly how long I've been sitting here on the floor, in Ronnie's spare room. The light looks a bit different and it feels harder to breathe in the thickened air.

I haven't got my watch on but it must've been hours. Work briefly enters my mind and drifts back out again.

I'm trapped in a parallel universe where nothing makes any sense. Where, if I don't shake myself out of it, day might merge into night, as real life is suspended.

I am in a space where the impossible happens.

I look down at Billy's blanket.

We searched for weeks. The villagers, the police and people from surrounding areas. Even after they found Billy's body, we were told it was vital to the investigation to find his blanket.

And that's when I think maybe I shouldn't have touched it. This is no longer my brother's comfort piece; it is evidence. Crucial evidence that may contain traces of a killer.

Ronnie's face flashes into my mind.

I think back just a few months ago when he accompanied me to Billy's grave, as he's done every single year since Mum and Dad passed on.

It used to be me, Sheila and Ronnie but when she died, Ronnie and I continued to visit Billy every year at the cemetery.

Sometimes it's not on the day he was found, it might be on the day we had his funeral. It doesn't matter, so long as we remember.

Years ago, when we first lost him, I had to force myself to cut down the number of visits. The therapist said it was for the best, that I was in danger of seriously delaying my recovery. But it had been Ronnie's own words that really struck home.

'You can't live life constantly visiting the dead, Rose,' he'd said gently when he came round to visit me in the darkened room I barely left for over a year after my parents died. 'Billy was full of life. He would never have wanted this.'

And through the smog of grief that had suffocated me for so long, the truth in Ronnie's words broke through like a shining beacon of light and I instinctively knew he was right.

Ronnie Turner didn't destroy life; on the contrary, he saved it.

He had helped me *to live.* He'd helped us all through, as we struggled to survive after Billy… there's no way he could have had anything to do with my brother's death.

I must refuse to even consider it.

All of the wonderful things that Ronnie has done for me whirl round in my head like scraps of torn paper in a gale-force wind. I want to stop and to sweep everything into a neat box so I can feel in control enough to start the thinking process from scratch again.

There has got to be a logical reason as to how Billy's blanket could have been concealed here, in this tiny room, for so many years.

I try and think it through again but the whole concept just feels too big. What I've discovered this morning is simply too obtuse to even begin to deal with.

I bury my face in Billy's blanket, and breathe in the fusty smell of Ronnie's spare room again. It's all that's there now, all there is left to smell. But it doesn't matter.

It's enough to know that my brother loved this scrap of cloth. Took it to bed with him each night and stuffed it in his rucksack to take out with him when he could get away with it. He was a bit of a lonely soul, hadn't really got any mates to rag him about having it.

After he'd gone missing, Mum had to scour his room and tell the police if everything was in place, if there was anything out of place. She saw immediately that his rucksack and blanket weren't there.

'I've found it now, Mum,' I whisper to the blank, white walls.

CHAPTER NINETEEN

SIXTEEN YEARS EARLIER

Rose considered their first few dates to be a great success.

Gareth turned out to be a big film fan so they'd visited the cinema on nearly all their outings.

Cassie had been right on one detail; on each occasion, Rose had barely watched the film. But that was due more to her burying her face in her hands at the gory, stomach-churning scenes in Gareth's favoured horror films than because he had his tongue down her throat.

Quite the contrary, Gareth was a perfect gentleman.

He often took her for drinks at an inconspicuous little bar near the cinema. Gareth had a pint and Rose had a small white-wine spritzer.

She needn't have worried, as she had in the beginning, about it being a sophisticated cocktail bar affair. The place was unobtrusive and quiet, and Rose felt perfectly comfortable there.

To his credit, Gareth wouldn't hear of her paying a penny towards the drinks or film tickets.

'I'm working, earning a damn good salary as it happens, and you're just a student. Let me look after you, Rose,' he said firmly, the first time she'd tried paying for the popcorn.

So she did. She let him help her into her seat, hold doors open to let her through first and she didn't even mind when he insisted on choosing which flavour of ice-cream she'd have, after asserting that the chocolate and raisin would be far superior to the boring vanilla she'd initially chosen. And he was right; it was much nicer this way.

It was a lovely feeling, letting him take charge and fuss round her like that, Rose thought. It felt as if he really cared about her, although she knew that couldn't possibly be the case, so soon.

It made such a change to her mood, getting away from what felt like the constant criticism she got from her parents at home. Rose neatly explained each time they met that she was seeing friends from college. It had been surprisingly easy to slip out undetected and enjoy time out of the oppressive atmosphere.

She'd noticed Billy had stopped pleading to come with her and, although he'd been a bit quiet and withdrawn lately, he'd found a way of coping without her around.

Gareth had said it would do him good and she believed him to be right.

After the film, Gavin drove her home each time, dropping her off at the same slip road where they met, well before the eleven o'clock curfew her dad had set for her a year earlier and which he'd never changed.

As Rose rarely went out, it hadn't seemed to be a problem before now.

'Don't want to get you into trouble with your old fella, do we?' Gareth grinned as Rose breathed a sigh of relief at arriving back on time.

This time, he kissed her chastely on the cheek as usual and asked if he could see her again on Friday evening.

'The weather is supposed to be fine. Any ideas for a nice walk around here, for a change to the cinema?'

'Yes, we could take a picnic up to Annesley Church,' she suggested. 'There's lovely woodland there.'

'Oh. I thought we might have a look around the abbey and then take a walk in the gardens. And then you could come back to mine for a drink, if you fancy it,' he said. 'How does that sound?'

'Lovely,' Rose replied, nodding, excited that he'd invited her back to his place but already wondering what excuse she'd make to her father.

Gareth tipped his head to one side, seeming to recognise her dilemma.

'Are you going be able to escape Colditz, do you think, Rosie?'

She shrugged, biting her bottom lip. 'I'll think of something.'

She didn't have to worry about her parents right now. She just wanted to enjoy the last few minutes she had with Gareth.

He insisted on walking with her to the top of Tilford Road and, after scanning the street, he placed a single, gentle kiss on Rose's trembling lips.

She felt like skipping home but she walked steadily away, feeling the burn of his eyes on her back. He watched her all the way down the street and they both waved when she slid her key in the front door.

This, their fourth date, simply couldn't have gone any better. Rose had left the house feeling like a silly college kid and returned feeling like a real woman.

Gareth would be a catch for any girl round here but he'd chosen *her* to date and to invite round to his home. He really did seem keen.

Cassie was going to be *so* jealous.

Rose had glided dreamily through college the next day. Returning home on the bus in the afternoon, she smiled as she replayed Cassie's reaction when she'd told her all about their evening.

'Seriously, do you think this could actually be love, Rose?' Cassie had asked, her eyes wide.

'How can I *love* him, you silly moo?' Rose had snorted. 'We've only just met.'

But Cassie had always been in love with the idea of being in love.

'Gareth sounds so intense and besotted. I think he might be in love with *you*, even if you don't feel the same way yet.' Cassie had squeezed her arm. 'I'm mad with jealousy!'

Rose hadn't denied Cassie's suggestion about Gareth's possible feelings. In fact, she'd found she quite liked the idea.

Cassie had wanted to know every last detail of Rose's chosen outfit and make-up for the last date. She had been predictably annoyed when Rose had come clean and told her the truth.

'Seriously? You basically wore your bloody college jeans and tee?' Cassie had grimaced, aghast. 'You need your head testing. What an absolute geek you are, Tinsley.'

'Gareth said I looked lovely,' Rose had pointed out.

'Well, of course he did, it's early days!' Cassie's voice had dropped lower. 'Did you… you know, have a bit of a fumble in the cinema at last?'

'No.'

'What about in the car when you got back?'

'No!'

Cassie had shaken her head slowly and stared at her, as if there was no hope for Rose.

'Well, my advice is to definitely ramp it up next time. You've been out with him a few times now, and, well… you don't want him getting bored, do you?'

Rose had been forced to admit she didn't want that to happen.

'When are you seeing him again?'

'Friday night. We're going for a walk in Newstead Abbey and he's asked me back to his, if I can think of a suitable excuse to tell my parents.'

Cassie's face had dropped. 'But I told you last week, Mum's at Auntie Noreen's for the night, so it's drinks round ours on Friday, remember?'

'Gosh, I'm sorry, Cassie. I forgot all about it.'

'Great.' Cassie had folded her arms in a huff.

'Don't worry, I'll rearrange with Gareth.'

'Really?' Cassie had given her a sheepish smile. 'That's sweet of you, Rose, thanks. It wouldn't be the same without you. In fact—' her face lit up '—why don't you bring Gareth along with you?'

'Oh!' Rose had swallowed. 'I don't know, I mean—'

'What?'

'Well, he's quite a bit older than everyone else who'll be there, and he might feel a bit uncomfortable.'

'Oh, I see. Aren't we good enough for you now?'

'Don't be daft.' Rose had shoved her playfully. 'I'll ask him, OK?'

'You do that.' Cassie had grinned. 'We could do with some eye candy amongst all those spotty little college boys and our Jed's no-hoper mates.'

Gareth had arranged to call her again that evening at eight o'clock and Rose had giggled when he'd said they'd keep the same arrangement when she answered the phone.

'I'll put my frilly dress on again and be your little college friend.'

'Beth,' Rose had clarified.

'Yes,' he'd said. 'I'll be Beth.'

As she hopped from the bus now, she thought about how to broach the subject of changing her date with Gareth.

Truthfully, she wasn't in the least bit fussed about going to Cassie's house on Friday evening. She'd thrown these so-called 'drinks parties' before and they were boring as hell unless you got wasted, which Rose never did.

Still, she felt guilty pulling out at such short notice because she'd already made a commitment to her friend.

She felt sure Gareth would understand.

CHAPTER TWENTY

SIXTEEN YEARS EARLIER

Gareth rang at the agreed time and Rose told him about the mix-up in plans right at the beginning of the call.

'What do you mean, you want to rearrange?'

'It's not that I *want* to,' she faltered. Her parents were both next door in the living room so she had to be mindful of her words but luckily the television was blaring. 'I'd forgotten I'd promised to go round to Cassie's house as her mum is away for the night.'

'I see,' Gareth remarked dryly. 'And I suppose you've been worrying about what you're going to tell your dad about our date, too.'

'Well… yes.' Rose felt quite relieved he'd managed to work out excuses were difficult for her. 'That's true. Even so, Cassie will be annoyed if I let her down.'

'I can understand you preferring to see your friend than come out with me,' he said tightly. 'I suppose there's nothing I can do about that but just be careful is my advice, Rosie.'

'Careful?'

'I know you and Cassie are good friends but think about it; a good friend wouldn't stand in the way of someone they cared about like this.' He sighed. 'If you ask me, she's just jealous that you've met someone who actually cares about you. Just be careful she doesn't try to ruin things between us, that's all.'

He sounded really fed up and Rose felt terrible. 'I don't think she'd do that, she's pleased for me, but I'm really sorry I've disappointed you, I—'

'I just wish I hadn't turned down the chance of a weekend in London.'

'London?'

'Yes, some friends of mine are leaving Friday lunchtime for a jaunt to London. Usually I'd be the first in line but I didn't hesitate in turning this trip down. Seeing you was easily my first choice. Never mind.'

'Oh!'

'You mustn't feel bad, Rose, I understand,' he said kindly. 'I suppose we'll still see each other around the village sometime this week and I hope you'll still help out with the project soon.'

Rose thought about what a lovely time they'd had on their dates together and how, up until meeting Gareth, she'd just hung out at Cassie's house every weekend to get out of the house. Bored to death and watching reruns of the Simpsons on television. Was she mad, even considering cancelling their plans?

It was starting to sound as if this upset might change things between them.

'Please, just forget I said anything,' Rose said, feeling suddenly resolved.

'It's fine. I don't want to force you to spend the evening with me, if you'd prefer to be in Cassie's company,' he said firmly. 'I understand you want to see your friend.'

'But I don't prefer her!' Rose bit her lip and lowered her voice to little more than a whisper. 'I've realised that now. I'd much rather see you.'

'And what about your old man?'

'Don't worry about him,' she said. 'I'll think of something.'

*

On Thursday, Rose smiled to herself as she got off her bus and began the walk home.

It was hard to believe that, in the space of just two days, her life had turned completely on its head in a good way. Previously boring days and nights were now full of expectation and excitement for what the future might hold with Gareth.

It had been a bit tricky for her today at college, telling Cassie she couldn't make it after all on Friday evening.

'Huh! Nice to know you're ditching me already.' Cassie pressed too hard while shading and snapped the pastel crayon she held.

'Cassie, that's not it at all,' Rose told her. 'I just made a mistake double booking, that's all, and now Gareth has cancelled a weekend in London because he's supposed to be seeing me.'

'Bully for Gareth,' Cassie mumbled.

Rose looked at the top of her head as she bent closer to her drawing pad. She was pretending to be absorbed in her artwork but Rose could tell it was a smokescreen so she didn't have to look at her.

Maybe Gareth was right after all and Cassie really was jealous of them being together.

'Boo!'

Rose squealed as someone jumped out from nowhere when she neared the house.

'Billy!' Her hand flew over her heart. 'I've told you time and time again not to do that. You'll give me a flipping heart attack.'

'Fancy a game of cards?' he asked as they walked around the back of the house.

'I've only just this minute got home, Billy,' Rose said, sighing. 'And I've got to—'

'But you said we could do stuff together tonight,' Billy whined.

'And we can,' Rose said, cleverly covering up the fact she'd completely forgotten about her earlier promise to her brother. 'Have you thought about what you'd like to do yet?'

'Well, we can't play Monopoly because Dad's busy in the living room,' Billy frowned.

'Busy with what?'

'Dunno. He's talking to someone in there.' Billy shrugged. 'Mum said I can't go in.'

'Well, we could set the game up on the kitchen table,' Rose suggested. 'After tea though, or we'll get in Mum's way. I've got a bit of college work I need to do first, anyhow.'

Stella was in the kitchen rolling out pastry when Rose walked in the back door.

'Hello, love,' she said, wiping her brow with the back of a floury hand. 'Good day?'

'Yes, thanks, Mum.' She nodded towards the closed living room door. 'What's Dad up to in there?'

Stella smiled. 'He said to send you through when you get back.'

'Can I go in too?' Billy piped up.

'No, Billy,' Stella said firmly. 'Just Rose.'

The boy scowled and sat down heavily on a rickety stool in the corner.

'Who's Dad talking to?' Rose asked again.

'I'm not sure exactly, love. Just get yourself in there.'

Rose slipped off her trainers and left her canvas college bag at the bottom of the stairs. She stood listening for a moment, trying to identify the muted voices to no avail.

When she pushed open the door, Billy slipped into the room behind her but she barely noticed.

Rose caught her breath when her eyes settled on her father's visitor.

CHAPTER TWENTY-ONE

SIXTEEN YEARS EARLIER

'There you are!' Ray announced and both men stood up. 'Gareth, this is my daughter, Rose.'

Gareth stepped forward and held out his hand.

'Hi Rose, Gareth Farnham. Nice to meet you.' His eyes drilled into hers, dancing with mischief. 'Your dad's been telling me what a brilliant artist you are.'

Her dad had actually said something nice about her?

Rose's face flamed. Her whole body felt as if it was overheating. How could it be that Gareth was *here*? He knew where she lived – of course he did because he'd walked her home enough times – but…

'Where are your manners, Rose?' her father asked sharply. 'Cat got your tongue?'

'Sorry,' Rose said softly, reaching for Gareth's hand. His fingers closed firmly around hers and he gave her hand a tight, meaningful squeeze and a surreptitious wink.

Billy stepped forward and pointed at Gareth. 'Hey, Rose. Isn't that the—'

'Billy!' Rose said sharply, realising in an instant that Billy had clearly remembered he'd spotted the two of them together at the top of the street just a couple of days ago. 'You're not supposed to be in here. Go and help Mum set the table for tea.'

Billy slunk out of the room. Rose was relieved to see her father hadn't seemed to notice the implication behind Billy's words.

'Gareth's involved in the new regeneration scheme, Rose. The one in the paper last week,' her father said brightly. 'They're looking for experienced villagers to help them out and apparently my name has been mentioned.'

Rose looked at her father's flushed, hopeful expression and something pulled tight inside her chest.

'Good news, eh, Rose? I can hardly believe it.'

'That's really great news, Dad,' she replied, without looking at Gareth.

'I've explained to your dad, it'll be on a volunteer basis at first,' Gareth said smoothly. 'But we'll be expanding quickly once we get going and there'll definitely be some paid positions we'll need to fill in the future.'

'I can't believe it,' Ray said again. 'All these years on the scrap heap and now I could end up with a plum job right on our doorstep. To tell you the truth, I thought I was washed up good and proper, Gareth.'

Whilst Ray stared out of the small paned window onto the road, Rose stole a glance at Gareth but she couldn't bring herself to smile at him.

'Far from washed up, Mr Tinsley. We need people like you on board, folks that know the village and the community. I'm really interested to hear your ideas for the future.'

'It's Ray. Please, Gareth, call me Ray.'

'Ray it is then. Now, Rose, I was just telling your dad I'm new to the area and trying to find my way around. He was saying you're a bit of an authority on Newstead Abbey. It's one of the places I'm really keen to see.'

'Not really, I mean I don't know that much about it—' Gareth shot her a meaningful look '—but… I'd be glad to tell you what I do know.'

'Great. I was thinking of popping over there tomorrow actually, after work.' He turned back to her father. 'Is there a shortcut through the village at all, Ray?'

'Why don't you go with him, Rose?' Ray seemed inspired by his own suggestion. 'You could tell him all about the Abbey's history then, while you're there.'

Both Gareth and her father watched her closely. Rose swallowed but her throat felt parched. Her head pounded, trying to reconcile the fact that Gareth was here, in her house, talking to her father.

And now Ray himself was encouraging her to meet up with him. It all felt so underhand.

Perhaps she ought to feel glad but, the truth was, she didn't want to see her dad being made a fool of. He'd suffered enough, scouring the area for years in search of a job and now… well, he looked so optimistic. She hadn't seen him this buoyant for a long, long time.

But why hadn't Gareth warned her he was going to call at the house?

Ray coughed. 'So what do you say then, Rose? Are you going to show Gareth round the abbey on Friday, or not?'

'Yes,' Rose said with a small smile. 'That's a good idea, Dad. I'd be glad to.'

CHAPTER TWENTY-TWO

SIXTEEN YEARS EARLIER

On Friday, Gareth picked her up outside the house.

Anyone would think it was her dad who'd got the date, Rose thought, the way he was stalking up and down and peering through the window every few minutes.

'He's here, Rose!' Ray called excitedly, holding back the net curtain.

When she saw Gareth's car, her neck and shoulders began to cramp.

Ray raised his hand and looked pleased when Gareth waved back. 'Have a nice time, love,' he said as she left. She couldn't help thinking how different it was to their first date and his barrage of awkward questions.

'Looking gorgeous again.' Gareth beamed as she slipped into the passenger seat. He started the car. 'I suppose we'd best get straight off. We can't sit here with your dad watching us. I might not be able to keep my hands off you.'

This time Rose knew he must be joking because she'd left the make-up off altogether, pulled her hair back into a severe pony tail and wore her usual boring jeans and T-shirt. Her dad had taken a real interest in her leaving the house so everything had to appear normal.

'Don't forget, Rose. If you get the chance, tell Gareth all about my managerial experience at the pit,' Ray had instructed her. 'I don't want him thinking I was just a cart horse down there.'

Managerial was stretching it a bit but Rose had smiled and assured him she would. After all, her father had barely said a bad word to her since Gareth's visit.

At the top of the street, Gareth indicated and pulled into the slip road by the school where he'd first picked her up.

He leaned over and planted a kiss on her cheek.

'Hey, why the long face?' He cupped his fingers under her chin and turned her face to look at him.

'I just feel a bit stressed out,' Rose said lightly.

'Aww, drawing with your pretty crayons at college is classed as stressful now, is it?'

She searched his face, trying to decide if he was being serious when his mouth relaxed into a wide smile. 'I'm just kidding, Rose; you're so tense. What's wrong, gorgeous?'

Rose squirmed at what she considered to be a ridiculous compliment. 'You just turning up at the house like that… it – well, it was a surprise.'

'Did the trick though, didn't it? Here you are and with your old fella's blessing, too. Just call me a genius!'

'I just wish you'd told me what you were planning,' she said in a small voice. 'Then it wouldn't have been such a shock.'

'It was a spur of the moment thing.' He shrugged. 'I didn't realise it would be a problem for you, me meeting your family.'

'It's not that,' she said quickly, watching as his face dropped. 'It's just… I'd have liked to have known and – and—'

'Go on.'

'It's just that I don't want Dad to get his hopes up if—'

'If what?'

'If you just said all that about him working on the project to get on his good side, I mean.'

'What do you take me for, Rose?' He looked down at his hands. 'I can't believe you think I'd pull a stunt like that just for the fun of it.'

'I'm sorry, I didn't want to upset you. It's just that Dad's been like a different man since you've been round to the house.' Gareth seemed to have taken great offence at her ill-chosen words. She stammered on, trying to rescue the situation. 'Y—you see, the pit closing took everything away from him; he's been sort of hollowed-out inside for years. Yet in the short time you spoke to him yesterday, you've really given him something to hope for.'

Gareth's face darkened as she watched him. 'So why are you throwing accusations my way, if he's happy about it?'

'I'm not accusing you of anything, Gareth. I just wondered if it was real. Saying Dad could work on the project, I mean.'

'Yes, it's real. Satisfied?' Gareth said shortly. 'I'm sorry you have such a low opinion of me, Rose. I truthfully explained to your dad it would be a voluntary position at first. I can't be any clearer than that, can I?'

'No. And I'm sorry,' she apologised yet again.

'It's an awful shame you have such a low opinion of me and of your father, too. You seem to have made your mind up that he's a bit of a no-hoper.'

'That's not true,' Rose said, wounded. 'It's not Dad's fault that there are no opportunities round here and it's not his fault that the pit closed in the first place.'

Gareth frowned at his watch.

'If you really think I've no scruples then maybe we shouldn't bother with the abbey visit,' he said curtly. 'And maybe it's a bad idea after all to get your dad involved with the project, if you consider that I'm just leading him on.'

A flood of images filled Rose's mind. Her father's crumpling optimism, Cassie's incredulous face and her own boring, featureless life making a swift and unwelcome comeback.

'No!' she heard herself say. 'Just ignore me, I'm sorry. I honestly didn't mean to insult you, I—'

He placed his forefinger over her lips and she fell silent.

'I forgive you,' he said softly. 'Let's start over again, yes?'

'Yes.' She sighed with relief. 'I really am sorry, Gareth.'

'Let's just forget about it now,' he said, his expression intense. 'You can make it up to me later.'

Rose felt a small jolt of panic and then she saw him grinning and realised he was having her on again. She smiled back at him. He was such a joker.

'I hope you don't mind, Rosie, but I got you this.' He opened the glove compartment and took out a small, silver mobile phone and charger. 'It's charged and ready to go. I know it's awkward for you, speaking on the landline. Now we can talk from the privacy of your bedroom.'

'Oh! Are you sure? This must've been expensive.'

'Of course I'm sure. Nothing's too much for my girl.'

Rose took it from him, her eyes bright. 'Thanks!'

'I'll feel better knowing you can always get in touch with me.' He leaned over and kissed her on the cheek. 'If you need to, that is.'

A warm feeling flooded her solar plexus. Cassie was going to be green with envy.

She blushed. 'That's really nice of you.'

'There's more.' He reached into the back of the car. 'Before we get off again, I want to give you this. Sorry it's not wrapped.'

He handed her a rather tatty olive green, cloth-covered book with faded gold lettering on the cover. She peered closer, in an effort to read the words.

'It's a book of Byron's poetry,' he told her.

'Oh, thank you,' Rose breathed, opening the yellowed pages and inhaling the pleasant fustiness of a genuinely old book. 'It's lovely.'

'It's got our elegy in it, look.' He took the book from her hands and leafed through, holding both pages open.

'Here it is.'

Rose saw that Gareth had made a couple of pencilled amendments so that the line read, *My Rose is here.*

'My Rose,' his voice echoed as she silently read the words. 'I'll never let anyone snatch you away.'

CHAPTER TWENTY-THREE

ROSE

PRESENT DAY

Sometimes, misery is a comfort to the soul… like a bitter poultice.

For so many years, grief has wrapped itself around me like a heavy cloak the second I walk through the door, as I walk through the rooms full of memories and family belongings.

Sixteen years after it happened, I still don't feel ready to walk away from it.

I don't want to escape my family and the past. My discovery has bound me to revisiting the raw pain of it all.

I sit in my kitchen now and I can almost hear the sound of Billy's feet hammering up and down the stairs, Mum shouting for him to quieten down and Dad roaring with frustration in the front room as Forest let in another goal.

Other times, the silence serves to remind me of just how alone I am.

And a backdrop to it all is the ticking 1930s' Westminster chime mantel clock Mum was so proud of. She was fond of telling us how it had been in her family for years and that it was a valuable antique, worth thousands of pounds.

After she died, I looked up similar versions on eBay and found it was worth around fifty pounds at the most.

I'm glad Mum never got to know that. There are small things in all our lives that have no importance to anyone else but that keep us breathing, keep us believing.

There's other stuff around the house too. Dad's record player, Mum's sewing box and Billy's torn felt slippers. I keep these things in the living room so I have them close to me at night as I watch television or read.

I sometimes like to look across and believe that nothing changed that day, sixteen years ago.

It might sound pathetic to some people, you know the sort. The 'it's time to make a fresh start' brigade.

I must have heard that phrase a thousand times and it's always uttered by the sort of people who mean well but who've never had to make a fresh start in their life.

Never had to construct a new existence from the ashes of a tragedy.

New things can't ever erase what happened or make it right again.

But the discovery I've made this morning pours petrol on the glowing embers of my grief and I know now that everything I thought I knew for sure has already changed.

CHAPTER TWENTY-FOUR

ROSE

PRESENT DAY

The thought of what I might find if I continue to poke around Ronnie's house fills me with a crawling dread but I instinctively know this is no time for dithering.

He's still in hospital, thank God. This might be my only chance.

I swallow down a sickly taste and pick up the phone and dial the hospital, tapping in the direct extension for the ward.

'I – I'm just checking on Ronnie Turner's progress,' I falter when they pick up. 'And I wanted to ask when he's likely to be discharged? I'm looking after his house, you see.'

The nurse covers the telephone receiver for a moment and I hear her speaking to someone else nearby. All the sounds, the voices, are muffled. I imagine Ronnie lying in his hospital bed. Will he be worrying about what I might find while he's away?

'Hello?' she says impatiently and I realise she's already said it once.

'Sorry,' I say. 'I'm here.'

'He's comfortable, still no exact date for discharge but shouldn't be long now.'

I thank her and end the call.

Frankly, I'm not worried about how Ronnie is feeling any more. I'm relieved he's out of the way so I can investigate a bit more.

I need to gather as much evidence as possible before I go to the police.

Fifteen minutes later I'm back next door.

I climb the stairs, my clammy hand gripping the rail because I don't trust my sense of balance.

The air around me feels thick with my own trepidation and yet I know nothing has changed here. What I discovered in Ronnie's spare room this morning has *always* been here.

All those times I've sat in the Turners' kitchen chatting to Sheila.

All the times Mum and Dad have called round to thank them for their support.

Every time Ronnie has been with me to the cemetery.

Billy's blanket has been buried up here, just like my brother is, in the cold, hard ground.

My heartbeat is in my throat. I swear, in the echoing silence, I can hear it thrumming relentlessly. I can't be sure if it is warning me off or urging me to continue but I know I have no choice but to do this.

I owe it to Mum and Dad.

I owe it to my poor, dead brother.

Systematically I unpack each box right down to the bottom and then replace its contents, moving to the next one.

I don't know what I'm looking for but I keep on going.

I have three hours before I'm due in at work but because the hospital didn't seem to think Ronnie would be out anytime soon, I've no intention of ringing in sick. There should be plenty of time to get this done over the next couple of days.

I plough through about a third of the boxes before I stand up, groaning and pushing the heels of my hands into the bottom of my back. My clothes may hang off me but I'm so unfit and inflexible. My back is now aching with a vengeance.

I arch and brace back and forth a bit before making my way into Ronnie's bedroom.

Everything I see here is offering another unwelcome suggestion: a pair of shabby, heavy boots, sat next to the oak freestanding wardrobe; a walking stick with a carved brass wolf for a handle; a solid glass paperweight on the bedside table.

All perfectly ordinary items unless you attribute them to a monster. A murderer.

Is that what Ronnie Turner is?

I ignore the tight feeling in my chest and press on. I search through drawers, rummage in wardrobes, check under the bed. I open a dusty old wooden ottoman at the bottom of the bed to find it full of candy-striped brushed-cotton sheets, the sort I remember my gran had when I was small.

I'm careful to take out and replace everything as I find it.

But that's just it.

I don't find anything else at all.

CHAPTER TWENTY-FIVE

SIXTEEN YEARS EARLIER

'I'm sorry I said we'd go, Gareth. It'll just be a really quick visit, I promise.' Rose lay on her bed and whispered into the mobile phone. 'It's just that Cassie is dying to meet you. *Everyone* wants to meet you.'

'We'll only be staying half an hour at the most,' Gareth replied.

'I know. I've told her that.'

'When you say *everyone* wants to meet me, who do you mean, exactly?'

'Just my friends. Beth, Carla, Clare.' Rose wracked her brains. 'Andy, Pete and Jed, Cassie's brother and a few of his mates, probably.'

A beat of silence. 'You've got male friends, too? You never mentioned that.'

'They're just boys from college.' Rose shrugged, staring at the same spot of flaking plaster on the ceiling. 'We all hang around together at lunch sometimes.'

'*You* might think they're just friends but I can guarantee the boys have got other ideas. They'll be after getting in your knickers.'

'Gareth! That's so gross.'

'Gross is right. What do you think people say behind your back about girls who spend their lunchtimes hanging out with boys?'

'We just talk, that's all. We're all on the same course.' It kept happening. She opened her mouth without thinking and managed to upset Gareth without fail. 'I'm sorry,' she said softly.

The silence at the end of the line lasted so long that Rose looked at the handset to see if the call had cut off. 'Hello?'

'Give me Cassie's address. I'll meet you there at eight.'

'I'm sorry if I've upset you,' she said again, after reeling off the address. 'There's nothing in it, honestly. We just hang out together sometimes.'

'I don't like the thought of it, Rose,' he mumbled. 'I didn't have you down as the type to be flirting around boys at college.'

She snapped back a retort without thinking. 'You're trying to suggest it's something seedy and it really isn't. We're just mates, is all. Why can't you get that?'

She expected him to snap back at her, but after a short pause his voice was soft and conciliatory.

'Why do you always think the worst of me, despite everything I do for you and your family? I'm just trying to look out for my girlfriend. I'm sorry if that annoys you, Rose.' He sounded genuinely troubled.

'I'm sorry,' she said, chastised. He'd said she was his girlfriend. He'd actually said that and he was right about the other stuff, too. He'd done so much to restore her father's hope and confidence. Why couldn't she just be happy about it?

'I don't like Cassie's influence, Rose. I trust you implicitly but your friend's morals are sadly lacking.'

Rose felt a twinge of loyalty towards Cassie but she didn't say anything. She really didn't want to make a bad situation any worse.

She swallowed down the grizzle that started up in her throat whenever Gareth got annoyed. She'd read an article in a magazine only last week, warning girls about the signs of being in a controlling relationship; constantly walking on eggshells, afraid of saying the wrong thing. It was worrying.

'Promise me you'll stop. No more hanging out at lunchtimes with boys.' Gareth paused and sighed. 'I'm like this because I care about you, Rosie. I care so much about you, it physically hurts me at times.'

She could hardly believe the wonderful words that were now tipping from his lips like rose petals.

'I promise I'll stop,' she said, instantly forgiving his earlier suspicions.

He wasn't trying to control her, she realised. Gareth *cared* about her.

Maybe she'd got so used to being snapped at by her parents and living with the backdrop of their continuous arguments, she'd forgotten what it felt like to have someone looking out for her. Someone who cared deeply.

Rose supposed that sometimes meant saying things she didn't necessarily want to hear.

Gareth ended the call pretty quickly after that, saying he had some important paperwork to do.

Rose could sense he was annoyed about the plans she'd made for him to meet her friends the next day but Cassie was chewing her ears off, desperate to meet him.

Anyway, she shouldn't feel guilty, she resolved. It was natural for him to meet her friends, wasn't it? Hopefully, it would settle his doubts; he would see that her male friends were perfectly harmless.

They'd been dating a while now, still managing to keep it secret from her overbearing father who, miraculously, was now Gareth's greatest fan.

It felt like their relationship was going from strength to strength. She could feel it.

CHAPTER TWENTY-SIX

SIXTEEN YEARS EARLIER

Rose had agreed to go to Cassie's house straight from college so she could help her prepare for the party.

They walked straight upstairs, past Jed and a group of his wolf-whistling mates who were gaming in the living room. Rose pushed thoughts of Gareth's fury, if he heard them, out of her mind.

'They'll be gone soon,' Cassie told Rose when they got up to her bedroom. 'Gives us time to get ready, anyhow. Tonight is the night you show Gareth how grown-up and glamorous you can look.'

Rose began to object but quickly realised it was hopeless. She might as well let Cassie just get on with it.

Twenty minutes later, Cassie put the last lick of mascara on with a flourish, and said, 'Ta dah!'

Rose turned around and stared at herself in the mirror.

Cassie had layered make-up on her eyes, far heavier than last time. With the deep-plum lipstick and shimmery pink cheeks, Rose thought she rather resembled a painted doll and not in a good way.

Cassie frowned. 'Well, don't get too excited.'

'Sorry. It's great, you've done brilliantly, Cass.' Rose pressed her lips together. 'I just don't know if it's the right look for me, that's all.'

'Don't talk wet! *Of course* it's the right look. You look completely different.'

'I know and that's the problem, really. I'm not sure Gareth will want me looking—'

'Sod Gareth! It's what *you* think that matters and you want to look glam, don't you?' Cassie backcombed and mussed at her hair until Rose felt like a wild banshee. 'He'll love it, trust me. And anyway, he's your boyfriend, remember? Not your bloody keeper.'

Rose sighed and sat on the bed while she watched her friend layer on her own rainbow eyeshadow.

'I've got two pairs of these.' Cassie held up miniscule hot pants – one black pair and one pink. 'And I've got two tight white tops to go with them.'

Rose refused to be bullied into wearing the shorts but, on Cassie's insistence, she slipped on the top and found to her surprise that it fit perfectly in all the right places.

She turned this way and that in front of the mirror, admiring her own slim curves and imagining how Gareth might think she looked womanly.

When they heard Jed and his mates go off to the pub, the two girls went downstairs and began their lengthy preparations.

While Cassie tidied round and organised the music CDs, Rose emptied packets of crisps and nuts into dishes and dotted them around the poky living room.

Then they trotted back and forth up and down the garden, lugging in the big brown bottles of beer and the packs of alcopops that Cassie had hidden behind the dilapidated garden shed to foil Jed and his thirsty friends.

When Rose looked at her watch she was surprised to see it was already seven-thirty. Cassie was still upstairs in the bathroom when there was a knock at the front door. Rose called up to her but there was no answer so she tentatively opened the door, stepping back in surprise.

'Gareth, you're early!' She smiled and took a step towards him, holding her face up to his for a kiss. 'There's nobody here for the party yet but come in, you can meet Cassie.'

Gareth didn't move.

'What's wrong?' she asked, stepping back, wide-eyed.

'What have you done to yourself?' His voice sounded low and strange.

'You mean this?' She grinned and wiggled her fingers around her face and hair. 'Cassie made me up, for the party. I – I wanted to look nice for you tonight.'

Rose grinned but she could feel the heat building in her cheeks under the thick, cloying make-up.

He didn't speak, so she placed her hands on his shoulders.

'I'm glad you're here.' She smiled.

'Rose,' he said slowly. 'It doesn't look like you. At all.'

'That was sort of the idea.' She giggled, rather pleased at his shocked expression. If he'd thought her a college kid, it looked like this new image had vastly changed his mind. 'I wanted to look glamorous for a change.'

'But it makes you look cheap, Rosie.'

His eyes flickered over the tight T-shirt that clung to her body and she folded her arms across her chest.

'You don't need all that stuff smeared all over your pretty face.' He stepped inside the kitchen and gripped her upper arms. 'You don't need to show off your body to everyone. That's not who you are, Rose.'

She felt hot and itchy and the contents of her stomach curdled, as if she might throw up at any second. She'd let Cassie convince her to try something different and it had backfired horribly.

Gareth pulled her to him and wrapped his arms around her. 'You're beautiful as you are, Rose, a *natural* beauty. You don't need all this crap.' He licked his finger, pressed it to her mouth and dragged it slowly across her cheek.

Tears prickled as she felt her lipstick smear across her face. Shame felt like a red heat and it spread everywhere. Under her skin and swimming in her eyes.

'I just wanted to show you I could look sophisticated,' she sobbed, tears now in free-fall. She wished she could just drop dead.

Gareth wiped his sticky fingers on the front of her T-shirt and hugged her closer to him. His chest felt sturdy and dependable. She felt sorry she'd made him so angry and yet, at the same time, she couldn't understand why it had.

'Sophisticated is the last thing I want to see you looking, Rose. I like you fresh and natural.' Gareth kissed the top of her head and bent down to whisper in her ear. 'I like you looking young.'

Her forearms prickled with goosebumps and she pulled away from him.

'What do you mean, you like me looking *young*?'

It sounded so… so utterly gross. Like Gareth was some kind of pervert.

He laughed and pulled her close to him again.

'I don't mean *like that*, silly. I mean I want you to look like *you*; young and unaffected. Not like some painted…' He hesitated. 'Not like Cassie.'

Why had he said that? He hadn't even seen Cassie before!

But should she feel upset that he wanted her for who she was, not for how sexy or glamorous she could look? Most girls would probably think that was wonderful.

'I only want the best for you, Rosie, believe that.' He held her tightly in his arms and she breathed a sigh of relief.

That's all it was. He was only thinking about her.

He was always thinking about her.

CHAPTER TWENTY-SEVEN

SIXTEEN YEARS EARLIER

Rose heard Cassie's footsteps bouncing across the ceiling above their heads.

She pulled away from Gareth's embrace and hastily wiped her wet eyes with the back of her hand. Black and purple smears appeared there and she could only imagine the extent of the awfulness of her messed up make-up and how she now looked.

She looked down at her chest, at the livid purple stain Gareth had wiped over her crisp, white T-shirt.

Cassie appeared at the bottom of the stairs.

'Cassie, this is Gareth,' Rose said hurriedly, swallowing down her panic.

'What the hell has happened to your make-up?'

'I – I think I'm going to take it off, Cass.'

Cassie frowned and looked at Gareth, her eyes narrowing as she joined up the dots. 'Did you make her cry?'

At first, Gareth didn't answer. His eyes travelled down past her tight T-shirt and even tighter pink shorts, over legs that were glowing orange with developing false tan, to her strappy high heels. Then they travelled back up again to her heavily made-up face.

Rose shuffled on alternate feet.

'Have you upset Rose?' Cassie demanded, jutting out her chin.

Gareth's mouth twisted up as if he could taste something nasty. 'What if I did upset Rose? How is that any of *your* business?'

Rose looked in horror at the two of them. Her best friend and her new boyfriend were already at loggerheads. *This* was never the plan.

'It's my business because she's my best friend and she looked lovely before *you* got here.'

'You look lovely too, Cassie,' Rose said meekly.

Gareth looked over at Cassie, threw his head back and laughed. 'Lovely is an interesting adjective to use, Rose.'

'Are you going to let him speak to me like that?' Cassie glared at Rose, her eyes sparking with indignation.

Rose stood silently looking at Gareth. Her arms hung down by her sides, fingers twisting against themselves.

'Go upstairs and wash your face, Rose,' Gareth said calmly, holding Cassie's defiant stare. 'And then we'll get going.'

'But the party—' Rose began.

'It's time to make a choice, Rose,' Cassie said without breaking the glare between herself and Gareth. 'You either tell this… this *bloke* you just met to fuck off and stop trying to control you, or you ditch your best mate of thirteen years and go with him. Your call.'

'Can't you two just say sorry and start over?' Rose blurted out, looking wildly at both in turn. 'This is horrible, it wasn't meant to be like this.'

Gareth reached out and took her hand. His fingers felt soft and cool. He gave her a gentle, encouraging squeeze.

'Pop upstairs and wash all that crap off your face, Rosie, there's a good girl,' he said, smiling that smile that always made her knees feel weak. 'I'm taking you for something to eat, somewhere nice and romantic. Just the two of us.'

Rose looked at him and then looked at Cassie. Both were looking at each other in a strange way that made her want to throw up again.

The back door was slightly ajar and she could hear birds singing in Cassie's small, neglected garden. The air was warm but too early in the year for the heat to be oppressive. As Rose's heart sank further down inside her, a cool breeze drifted through, kissing her clammy skin.

Tonight should have been perfect. Instead, everything was now ruined.

To be fair, Cassie had immediately attacked Gareth as soon as she came downstairs. Rose knew she was only being protective of her, but still…

She let go of Gareth's hand and headed towards the stairs.

'Sorry, Cassie,' she said. 'I can't stay now.'

'If that's your choice, then fine.' Cassie turned to look out of the window. 'At least I know where I stand now.'

Gareth winked at her as she walked past him.

Upstairs, as she lathered her face with soap, Rose wondered if they were still standing staring at each other in the kitchen.

Both stubborn and refusing to be the one to walk away from their silent battle.

A whole week passed and still Cassie wouldn't take Rose's phone calls or answer the door to her.

She had steadfastly ignored her at college every day and made Rose look foolish by teaming up with a group of other girls that they wouldn't ordinarily consider hanging around with. They would all giggle whenever Rose walked by and she coped with it by keeping out of their way as much as possible.

But just before she left on Thursday afternoon, Cassie cornered her in the common room. Rose's heart gave a little hopeful leap.

'Don't think for a moment I want to be friends again, Rose.' Cassie grabbed her arm. 'You made your choice and that's up to you. But for all the good times we've had together, I need to say something to you.'

Rose took a breath and waited. She had the distinct feeling this interaction wasn't going to end at all well.

'Be careful of Gareth Farnham. How long have you known him, really?' Cassie didn't wait for Rose to answer. 'Three or four weeks at the most. He's a total control freak, Rose; surely you can see that?'

Rose shook out of Cassie's pincer grip and stared unseeingly out of the window. It was natural for Cassie to jump to conclusions about Gareth's motives but she didn't see the other side of him – the gentle way he treated her, as if she were made of glass.

But now wasn't the time to start explaining how protective Gareth was, how wonderfully he treated her when they were alone. Cassie would only scoff and make fun of her. Probably delight in telling the other girls at college.

But neither did Rose intend to listen to Cassie's poisoned, bitter litany. Gareth had warned her this very thing might happen. He'd said he was certain that Cassie had instigated the argument at her house last week because she was jealous of his and Rose's relationship.

'It might be hard to hear but he *is* controlling you, Rose. He controls how you look, who you hang around with… he's even controlling your own dad now he's got him volunteering with the village regeneration project.'

Rose sighed but she didn't bother replying.

Cassie didn't really have anyone who really cared about her. Carolyn, Cassie's mum, let her and Jed do as they pleased. Carolyn spent too much time out of the house drinking with Cassie's Aunt Noreen, who lived in Mansfield Woodhouse.

Rose had been the closest person Cassie had in her life and now she was bitter, angry. She'd honestly hoped that Cassie and

Gareth could be friends but now Cassie had turned against them both, big time.

'Rose, you're doing everything Gareth tells you to do and it's not right. You even admitted he chooses the flavour of the fucking ice cream you eat. He's swallowing up your personality, can't you see that?'

Rose now deeply regretted telling Cassie about their dates in such detail.

'I'm sorry it's come to this, Cassie,' Rose said calmly. 'But Gareth loves me. He only wants the best for me and if you want to call that "controlling", then I suppose that's your prerogative.'

'Please yourself, I'm only trying to make you see what's happening,' Cassie snapped, pushing her face closer to Rose's. 'If he's so wonderful, then why is he sneaking around with you behind your dad's back? Maybe somebody ought to tell your parents exactly what's going on. That would put an end to slimy Gareth Farnham.'

Rose gasped, but before she could think of a retort, Cassie had stormed off.

CHAPTER TWENTY-EIGHT

SIXTEEN YEARS EARLIER

Rose's work had been selected for a special display in the college gallery. It was to be screened that very Friday but she stayed home, telling her mother she felt unwell.

Her parents were both out. Ray was working on the regeneration site. He'd proudly told Rose last night that Gareth had put him in charge of organising the other volunteer labourers.

'He recognises I have a lot of unused skills from my days at the pit,' Ray boasted. Rose smiled to herself as he puffed out his chest like one of the abbey's resident peacocks. It was great to see him so motivated. The knock-on effect was that he seemed to be less argumentative all round, which had improved the atmosphere at home no end. 'Plus I know everyone who's helping out, I know who'll be good at what, you see.'

Stella was providing a bit of a drinks/snacks service up at the site to keep everyone going. She'd baked some flapjacks and muffins last night, humming happily to herself in the kitchen. Rose had never seen her parents so engaged in something they chose to do together.

Love him or hate him, Gareth had transformed all their monotonous lives.

At twelve-thirty, Rose walked round to Gareth's small flat as they'd planned when she texted him earlier to say she needed to talk. But her phone had just pinged with a message to say he'd had to delay his lunch slightly and would be ten minutes late.

She stood round the side of the house, away from prying neighbours' eyes. Gareth's flat was on the ground floor of a new property that looked rather like a town house from the front but was actually four small flats.

She jumped as a hunched figure appeared, clutching two large bin bags. Rose had seen the man before around the village and had the feeling he was the grandad of a girl at college but she couldn't be sure. Although she knew most villagers by sight, she didn't know all their names.

'Who are you?' The crotchety old man stared at her with watery blue eyes.

'I'm just waiting for my friend,' she said quickly, praying Gareth wouldn't appear. This guy might be old but if he was anything like the other senior citizens around here, he could probably still gossip quite well.

'Well, I hope there won't be any more racket tonight. The bloke in the flat above me seems to like a party lifestyle.' The man scowled and shuffled past her to the bins. She heard the clang of the metal bin lid and he came back past her without speaking again.

Rose looked around nervously, wondering how long Gareth might be.

He hadn't offered her a spare key yet. Perhaps he wouldn't until they'd been seeing each other a bit longer.

Gareth had first invited Rose back just over a week ago, before he and Cassie had their fall out.

'This is it,' Cassie had gasped when Rose told her she would be going round to the flat that evening. 'Say goodbye to your virginity Rose.'

Rose had tutted and shook her head but Cassie had frowned. 'You're not dealing with an immature college boy now, you know.

Gareth is a hot-blooded man. You'll look like a silly kid if you put up too much of a fight.'

'I'm not going to be railroaded into doing something I'm not comfortable with,' Rose had said firmly.

'There really is no hope for you,' Cassie had sighed. 'Answer me this: do you fancy him, yes or no?'

'Yes!'

'And do you want your relationship to continue?'

'Of course I do.'

'Then what's the problem?' Cassie had shaken her head in frustration. 'It's natural you'll start having sex soon, I'm surprised he's been patient for so long.'

'Natural for you, maybe,' Rose had replied, scowling. 'But I don't feel ready yet, and anyway, he's invited me over to his flat for dinner and a film, not a full-blown orgy.'

Cassie sniggered. 'You're *so* gonna end up like Miss Carter and her cats.'

Rose had pushed half a Pringle in her mouth and stared at the muted TV. Another episode of *The Simpsons* had been just about to start.

'We could run through what to do, if you like. You know, a bit of *foreplay*.' Cassie had cackled.

'No thanks,' Rose had said curtly. 'Can you turn the sound up on the telly, please?'

Later, at Gareth's house, Rose had wished she'd taken Cassie up on her uncomfortable offer of a 'what to do' conversation. She felt sick with an incompatible mix of excitement and dread.

The evening hadn't quite turned out to be the romantic, candlelit affair she'd envisaged. It transpired that Gareth's offer of dinner was actually a frozen pizza, supplemented by a lukewarm beer each. Rose had had the distinct feeling that he'd wanted the food out of the way as soon as possible. When she'd cleared away the plates, they'd moved over to the faux leather settee.

Gareth had kissed her on the lips. His lips had lingered there and she'd responded before gently pulling away.

'Hey.' He'd touched her cheek. 'Are you OK, baby?'

'Yes, fine,' she'd said, trying and failing to sound relaxed. 'Shall we watch the film now?'

'Relax, princess.' He'd given a throaty chuckle. 'It's nice to spend some time together, isn't it? Just you and me, without your brattish brother interrupting us.'

He'd nudged her to show he was only teasing but she didn't like it when he made remarks like that about Billy. She'd let it go, keen for the evening to be a success.

'Yes,' she'd said. 'It's lovely, being together like this.'

He'd kissed her again and this time she'd felt the gentle but insistent push of his tongue into her mouth. His right hand had slid from the top of her arm onto her breast in one smooth movement.

Rose had pulled away. His hand had been on top of her clothing but she'd still felt a bit panicky and rushed.

'What's wrong?' His hand had dropped away and he'd looked at her.

'Nothing!' She'd felt a bit out of breath. 'I'm just, I don't know, a bit nervous, I suppose.'

Gareth had laughed softly. 'There's nothing to be nervous about, Rose.'

'I know, but—'

'But what?'

'I'm not very good at this sort of thing. I've never—' Her entire face, neck and chest had burned. She'd felt so foolish. 'What I mean is—'

She'd pressed her lips together; it was all proving too painful.

Gareth had sucked in air. 'Are you trying to tell me you're a virgin, Rose?'

She'd given a single nod and looked at her hands. Her heart and head had both pounded in awful unison.

'Don't be embarrassed.' Gareth's hand had encased her fingers. 'I knew you were and I think it's wonderful.'

She'd looked at him.

'You *knew*?'

'Yes. The moment I saw you, I thought to myself, I've found a genuine beauty here. An unspoilt, innocent beauty in a sea of tarty wannabes.'

'Gareth!'

'It's true, Rose. You're a breath of fresh air. You're beautiful inside and out, and I love you.'

She'd looked away.

'I love you,' he'd repeated. 'And that's why I want to be close to you. As close as I can possibly be.'

The skin on her hands had tingled. She'd wanted to hold him and run far away, all at the same time.

'I can't help but touch you,' he'd whispered in her ear. 'I want to be part of you… inside you.'

His hand had crept over her forearm and up her body, massaging her breast over her clothes. Rose's breath had caught in her throat. She'd swallowed back the silent protest inside.

Relax, Rose, she'd told herself. *Just relax.*

CHAPTER TWENTY-NINE

SIXTEEN YEARS EARLIER

She wanted him, she really did. But then she felt so sick when she thought about the fact she was so completely out of her depth.

All manner of things might go wrong if they had sex too soon. Not least it would expose her as the inexperienced, stupid young girl she was. Surely it was better to wait until it felt a bit more special than this, and she felt more confident.

Gareth's hand dropped away and she felt herself breathe freely and then his fingers touched the skin of her stomach and quick as a flash, his hand was under her top and slipping under the wire of her bra. She sat up straight and his hand fell away.

'For God's sake—' He took a breath and the edge fell from his tone. 'Rose, what's wrong? Don't you care about me?'

'Yes! I do, I just—'

'Then *please*, let's make love. I've waited until now because I totally respect you, you know that, right?'

'Yes,' she whispered, still struggling to push the feeling it was happening too soon out of her head.

'Well then. I love you, you love me. Let's cement that, so we belong to each other properly.'

Rose bit her lip and Gareth looked at his hands.

'I don't like mentioning it but since I moved here I've had girls throwing themselves at me, do you know that?'

She looked at him. She *hadn't* known that.

'I barely notice it, Rose, because I only have eyes for you. I only want *you*.'

Cassie's words came back to her; the bit where she said Gareth would think she was just a big kid unless she shaped up. He was a man, not a spotty college boy. *Of course* the local girls were going to be throwing themselves at him, it made perfect sense. Girls like Cassie, who gave it up to anyone without a second thought.

They'd been dating a few weeks now and Gareth had always been a perfect gentleman. Hadn't pushed her at all. If only she could make him understand how she felt.

'I just don't want to rush things,' she tried again, hating how pathetically young she sounded.

'Of course you don't and I don't want that either,' Gareth said softly. 'But we're not rushing because we've been together a while now. This is a natural progression in our relationship. Do you trust me, Rose?'

'Course.' She nodded, thinking it was still only a few weeks, no matter how he dressed it up.

'Then show me.' His leg pressed next to hers. She could feel his hot breath on her cheek and she gasped as his hand slid out from under her top, delving between her legs. 'It's time, Rose. I want you to belong to me.'

'I just…' Rose squirmed beneath his grasping hand. 'I don't know, Gareth.'

Rose gulped as all of a sudden he reared up over her and then his weight was upon her, pressing her down.

'Do you want to be mine, Rose?' His tongue wriggled into her mouth again before she could answer.

She lay frozen beneath him, her body a buzzing mass. She felt confused whether she was aroused or scared but she thought she wanted it to stop.

'Do you love me?' he asked urgently, pressing his groin into hers, his hand lowering from her breast to the zip of her jeans.

'Yes,' she gasped. 'But—'

'Then relax,' he urged, unbuttoning her jeans. 'I need to know you're mine, Rose. I only want you, you know that, but I need us to be closer. Do you understand?'

Rose knew there must be lots of local girls who fancied him like mad. And she supposed it had to happen sometime; she couldn't stay a virgin forever.

At least Gareth was kind and loved her and she loved him too. She did. And she wasn't going to bloody well turn into Miss Carter, like Cassie constantly teased her.

'Yes,' Rose whispered as he lowered her zip and began to pull down her jeans. 'I understand.'

After that, she'd been to Gareth's flat most days. They hardly went out together at all any more. As soon as she got there, he just wanted to take her to bed.

And now, here she was again, waiting to see him on his lunch break.

She heard scuffling around the corner on the path and suddenly he appeared.

'Sorry, Princess.' He rolled his eyes. 'Those idiot volunteers, they haven't a brain cell between them. They should've shut them all down there on the coalface to perish when they closed the pit.'

He caught her expression and laughed. 'I don't mean your dad, Rosie, just some of the others.'

She followed him into the flat.

He glanced at his watch and turned to her. 'Fancy going to bed for half an hour?'

She had a sudden thought. 'Do you know who lives below you?'

'Some old bloke.' Gareth shrugged. 'Why?'

'While I was waiting outside, this old guy said that the man above him had a party last night.'

'Well, it certainly wasn't me.' Gareth laughed dismissively. 'Maybe one of the other tenants. Now, what's wrong, lovely? You look troubled.'

'I – I just wanted to talk to you,' she said, feeling a prickle in her eyes.

'Hey, don't get upset, Rosie.' He led her through into the small living room/kitchenette area.

'I don't know what I'd do without you,' she said to him when he laid a warm hand on her shoulder. 'You're the only person who wants anything to do with me these days.'

'I'm always here for you, Rose, you know that,' he whispered, tangling his fingers in her hair as she knew he liked to do. Sometimes he pulled a bit tight and it made her grimace. 'I'm yours and you belong to me. Every inch of you is mine from your glorious red hair to your cute little toes.'

She nodded, feeling relieved and thankful, burrowing deeper into his shoulder. She knew she could count on Gareth.

That's why she'd agreed to have sex with him. He'd been gentle and considerate and he'd even said her embarrassment and lack of experience only made him love her more.

CHAPTER THIRTY

SIXTEEN YEARS EARLIER

After years of acting like the proverbial couch potato, her father now always seemed to be out of the house these days, working in his volunteer role within the village regeneration project.

'He's a new man,' Stella had told her daughter on more than one occasion. 'We have a lot to thank Gareth Farnham for. You should be a bit friendlier to him when he comes round, Rose.'

But Gareth had told her it was important to keep their relationship a secret for now and so when he did pop round to the house to speak to her father about project business, she purposely made herself scarce.

'*We* know that a ten-year age gap is nothing but your parents are hopelessly old-fashioned,' he told her. 'I'll set the seeds but let them think it's their idea to get you more involved in the project and then we'll have an excuse to spend lots of time together with their full knowledge.'

'Why friendlier?' Rose prodded her mother, wondering how she might feel when she and Gareth finally announced they were a couple. 'I thought you'd think he's too old for me.'

Stella rolled her eyes. 'I don't mean friendly like *that*. He's told your dad he thinks of you in the way you might a younger sister. He's done such a lot for this family and he's going to be your dad's boss once there's a job going. You should make an effort to be a bit more sociable, is what I'm saying. Help out a bit more on the project.'

Rose had turned away and smiled to herself. Younger sister indeed! But it looked like Gareth's plan was working.

It was amazing the way he seemed to understand what made her parents tick. He was so sensible and wise. He always knew the right thing to do and that's why she found herself defaulting to his suggestions more and more. She trusted him completely.

But now, after her week-long ordeal at college with Cassie, she collapsed into Gareth's arms.

'What's wrong, Rose?'

'I just feel a bit low, that's all,' she said. 'I just needed to see you, talk to you.'

'Rosie. I think you need to think about leaving college.'

'What?' Her eyes grew wide. 'B—but I've another eighteen months until I complete my course.'

He led her to the sofa.

'But you haven't got that long if you pull out early. I can give you a job on the regeneration project and then we'll be together all the time.'

She felt a bolt of excitement at the prospect of working with Gareth, swiftly followed by the sickly worry of what her parents would have to say about it. Then she remembered Cassie's threat.

He lifted her chin with a finger. 'What's wrong?' he asked again, his eyes burning into hers. 'I can always tell when there's something bothering you. I know you inside out and back to front; you should have realised that by now, silly girl.'

So she told him what Cassie had said, her opinion that Gareth was controlling her.

Initially she'd thought to keep their conversation to herself because she couldn't imagine he would take it well. But of course, he'd been able to see right through her attempts to hold it all in.

'It's all rubbish,' Rose concluded, after she'd repeated Cassie's insults about him virtually word for word. 'I know what she's saying about you is wrong. She's deluded.'

She smiled up at him, relieved to unburden herself but Gareth didn't smile back.

'It's more than wrong. It's slander. Spiteful lies.' He bit down on his back teeth, setting his jaw. 'That little bitch, she's determined to split us up.'

'I honestly think she means well,' Rose said, eager to prevent one of Gareth's long, low moods that he now seemed to suffer on an increasingly frequent basis. 'She thinks she's talking some sense into me.'

'Don't make excuses for her,' Gareth growled. 'She's just jealous, pure and simple. Jealous of *us*.'

This made sense to Rose and she nodded. 'She did admit she'd love an older boyfriend. She couldn't wait to meet you, so I don't know why she's being so weird about things now.'

'Like I said, it's pure jealousy. I've never been anything other than polite to that girl,' he said.

Rose remembered how Gareth had dragged his eyes in such a derogatory way over Cassie at her house the week before but she decided it wouldn't be helpful to bring that up when he was already so peeved.

'There's… something else.' Rose hesitated but decided he had to know, just in case. 'I don't think she means it but—'

He raised an eyebrow, and waited.

'She threatened to tell Dad about us,' Rose blurted out. 'I don't think she would for a minute but it has worried me a bit.'

Gareth stayed quiet for a moment or two but Rose saw that his hands were balling into tight fists.

'She'd better not. If she ruins things for us, she'll wish she'd never been born.' His mouth bunched into a cruel sneer that made Rose's blood run cold. 'I'll make sure of that.'

CHAPTER THIRTY-ONE

ROSE

PRESENT DAY

The ambulance pulls up outside Ronnie's house and I take a deep breath, exhaling slowly, like they tell you to do for pain relief.

Breathe, Rose, breathe, I tell myself silently.

The thought of facing him, of talking to him…

I watch from behind the nets as the paramedics carefully wheel Ronnie through the narrow wooden gate. I move to the front door, open it wide.

I can do this. I have to.

'Come through,' I tell the paramedics and they lift Ronnie out of the wheelchair and help him down into his armchair.

He looks smaller and thinner, his skin crinkled like discarded wrapping paper. He's looking down at his hands but when I say his name, he looks up and gives me a thin smile, as if he's only just realised I'm there.

'Rose,' he says in a thin, hoarse voice, as if to remind himself who I am. He seems reassured by the familiarity, as if he's pleased to be home.

'Hello, Ronnie,' I say. The words wedge like a lump of gristle in my throat. I cough. 'How are you feeling?'

'Can't complain,' he replies. 'Glad to be home.'

His mouth stretches wide into a gapped grin. His thin lips are a dark pink and spotted purple in places. His chin looks sore and patchy with grey stubble. I feel my stomach turn.

'Excuse me,' I mutter and rush into the kitchen. I splash a little water on my face and hang over the sink for a moment or two.

'Are you OK?' The female paramedic stands watching me in the doorway.

'Yes, I'm fine.' I stand up straighter and wipe my mouth with the back of my hand. 'Sorry, I just felt a bit queasy.'

She looks at me curiously. 'Are you a relative of Ronnie, or—'

'His neighbour. We've lived next to each other for years.'

'Are you going to be OK looking in on him now and then, supervising his medication? He seems quite confused and he's still shaky on his feet.'

I don't like the way she still seems to be considering me, with her head tipped to one side. It's as if she can see through the thin façade I'm trying so hard to maintain.

Looking at Ronnie back there, I felt a rush of revulsion but now I almost feel guilty for that. Ronnie might not have done anything wrong. In fact, I have real trouble even mulling over the possibility that he could have even remotely been involved with Billy's death.

Surely, I'd know. Back then, *someone* would've known it.

Sheila's face appears in my mind's eye. I blink slowly and firmly. It's essential I get a grip here.

I realise I need to get rid of the paramedics and get Ronnie settled so I can speak to him privately.

'We'll be fine,' I say as confidently as I can manage. 'I'll ring the hospital right away if there's a problem.'

'Perfect.' She turns to walk back in the living room. 'If you want to come through we can talk you through his medication. There's rather a lot of it, I'm afraid.'

I follow her down the short hallway again and sit in the armchair. I angle my body away from Ronnie so I don't have to look at him for now.

'It looks tidier in here,' Ronnie says from my left. 'You've been cleaning up, Rose.' I turn to look at him then and he smiles at the male paramedic. 'She's ever so good to me, you know.'

My heartbeat grows louder in my ears as I grip the sides of the armchair.

'That's good because you're going to need all the help you can get, Ronnie,' I hear the paramedic says. His voice sounds soft round the edges like he's moving away from me. 'You've had a very nasty virus and you'll feel weak for a while yet. You've got to take it easy and give your body time to recover.'

'I cleaned the kitchen and the bathroom. I cleaned everywhere, Ronnie,' I hear myself say, my voice high and strained. 'Upstairs and down.'

Our eyes meet and I'm certain I see him falter, as if someone has prodded him sharply on the back of his head.

'Are you OK, Ronnie?' The female paramedic rushes to his side.

'Not really,' he croaks, looking away. 'I feel hot… I think I might be sick.'

But he isn't sick and after a few more minutes of fussing over him, finally, they leave.

I see the paramedics out and then I sit opposite Ronnie and look at him.

The room is gloomy; I can hear the ticking of the clock and each click feels like an arrow in my heart. I can't do this; I can't stay quiet any longer.

'Ronnie,' I say softly. 'Can I ask you something?'

'I don't know.' His breathing sounds laboured. 'I feel weak and I still feel I could be sick.' He grips the kidney-shaped cardboard dish as if his life depends on it.

I wonder if it's my imagination that Ronnie seemed to stop feeling sick when the subject of cleaning the house was changed.

'It's just the one question I have,' I say. 'A very important question.'

Ronnie shifts in his wheelchair. He closes his eyes and breathes in and out through his nose.

'Remember when they took you downstairs from the bathroom, just after I found you collapsed up there?'

He opens his eyes.

'You said something to me on the way out of the house, can you remember what that was?' He doesn't reply. 'You said, "don't go upstairs". That's the last thing you said, Ronnie, before they took you into hospital. What did you mean? Why didn't you want me to go up there?'

The silence falls again and the clock ticks.

I can almost feel the spare room weighing down upon us from upstairs, like it is ready to unburden its secrets at last.

'Ronnie?'

'I can't remember saying that.' His words sound strangled.

'You don't have to remember it, Ronnie, I promise you they're the exact words you said to me. I need to know, what did you mean by it?'

'I didn't know what I was saying, Rose. I felt so ill.' He pauses and pulls in a breath. 'They said if you hadn't found me so quickly I… I could have died up there.'

'I know you were feeling really ill, Ronnie, and I know you still don't feel one hundred per cent but have a little think. This is important.'

He's mumbling to himself.

'Ronnie?'

'I can't think straight,' he says, his fingers digging into the plastic covered arms of his wheelchair. 'Sorry. I just can't.'

I stand up and walk across to him, lay my hands on his wasted arms. Arms that I can clearly recall used to be strong and muscular.

The man he was, so many years ago… that person is still in there somewhere.

Truth never disappears or deserts us; it's there forever, shining strong. It can be covered and disguised but it's still there. You just have to know where to find it.

'Ronnie,' I say gently. 'You've been here through everything. You were here before and after Billy. We're like family, you and I. So, I have to ask you, why did you specifically tell me not to go upstairs?'

Ronnie's wrinkled hand reaches for mine and he squeezes my fingers.

'I'm so sorry,' he whispers, 'but I honestly can't remember a thing, Rose.'

CHAPTER THIRTY-TWO

ROSE

PRESENT DAY

I haven't slept. I have literally been awake the entire night.

People come into the library all the time and say casually, 'I barely slept a wink last night' or 'I was wide awake from two a.m.'… they're just phrases people use to indicate broken or disturbed sleep but I really mean it. I didn't sleep *at all* last night.

I can't go on like this. Not unless I want to undo all the years of therapy, of working so hard to keep myself functional.

I'm the first to admit that, compared to some, I've not got much of a life. But it's a life of sorts, bolstered by a routine I've made for myself in order to get by. And I'd like to keep it that way.

So, during the long hours of last night, as I stared up at the ceiling, walked around the house, sat in the kitchen with my third cup of coffee… I was thinking about the exact same thing.

Not what happened sixteen years ago, not finding Billy's blanket but this: What am I going to do about it?

I don't know what I expected Ronnie to say when I spoke to him.

I think I was hoping he'd immediately confess but come up with a totally plausible excuse as why the blanket was in his house. Something that made absolute sense to me.

I'd imagined myself smiling sadly and realising I'd let my imagination run away with me. I thought I'd feel relief that everything had been explained and I'd now be able to get my life back to normal.

Ronnie had looked so frail, just out of hospital, I couldn't bring myself to blurt out what I'd actually found in the spare room. He might have fainted, collapsed, anything… I'd felt I had no choice but to bide my time, to wait for the right moment so he was strong enough to explain himself.

I waver constantly between the certainty of Ronnie's innocence and his obvious guilt. A jury sits in my head and I present, very convincingly, both sides of an argument I can't possibly win.

I know Billy had his blanket when he was at the abbey that day. I saw it poking out of his rucksack.

When they found his body and the rucksack, the blanket was nowhere to be seen. And the police never found it despite a fingertip search of the area.

Now, after all this time, I have found that very blanket in Ronnie's spare room.

How can he possibly explain *that* away?

My head pounds and I feel sick. I've not eaten since teatime yesterday and I certainly can't face anything this early in the day.

I've managed to get myself ready for work on autopilot, and I've discovered that not sleeping is a bit like not eating. You get to a stage where you sort of get past it and just carry on as normal.

I know this is merely a little pocket of recovery, and sleep deprivation will return with a vengeance later, but for now I can just about see straight.

I look down at the pen and paper on the kitchen table. I think it was about three o'clock this morning when I wrote down my options as I saw them:

1) *Do nothing*
2) *Go to the police*
3) *Speak to Ronnie again*

Now, in the cold light of day, I can completely discount option one.

There is no way I can *unfind* the blanket now even though, during the past eight hours, there have been times when the voice in my head said, You know it was Gareth Farnham. You know it. He's serving a life sentence, being punished for what he did. The police at the time said it was a good result. So just leave it.

But if I ever want a decent night's sleep again, then I know I have to face up to the significance of what I found next door. I just have to.

Option two: speak to the police.

DCI Mike North was the one person who'd lived and breathed Billy's death almost like we as a family had done. To him, losing Billy wasn't just part of his job.

I didn't have that much to do with him during the actual investigation, of course. Quite rightly, he'd disappear into the front room with Mum and Dad and I'd get any developments second hand from them.

But I can remember Mum saying in conversation, only a few months after Billy died, that Mike North had retired due to ill health.

I doubted anyone senior on the original investigation would still be working for Nottinghamshire Police. As I recall, Mike North and his senior officers were all in their late forties/fifties.

Going to the police would mean explaining everything again to someone who hasn't a clue what happened here. And anyway, I'd say *what*, exactly? That I wanted Ronnie taken in for questioning because he says he can't remember what Billy's blanket is doing in his spare room?

The more I think about involving the police, the more ridiculous it sounds. The other villagers will bay for my blood, upsetting Ronnie when he has just been discharged from hospital.

But then… maybe there is a compromise to be had.

I might not be able to go to the police and make an accusation against Ronnie directly but it's possible, if I could only speak with Mike North, that I could discuss the case again with him. Find out if it was truly as watertight as it appeared at the time.

I don't know anyone I could speak to informally at Nottinghamshire Police about contacting ex-DCI Mike North but I know Sarah and Tom well enough, our local PCSOs. I don't want to put them in an awkward position, asking for protected data information, but it's a good place to start.

Option three: I can also speak to Ronnie again. Hopefully in a day or so, he'll be feeling physically stronger and not as confused. I know that, underneath, I'm still hoping Ronnie can clear it up, say something that negates all my doubt.

It's a long shot but it's all I have. I'll speak to him again later, hopefully when he is feeling a little better. The hospital has arranged a nurse and a carer to pop in and see him during the day and I've agreed to keep an eye on him at night and look in on him each morning.

In spite of all my logical reasoning, the awful thoughts still keep surfacing.

Did Ronnie have anything to do with Billy's death?

Is he lying about losing his memory?

If the answer to either of these questions is *yes*, then how can I possibly help him? How can I ever speak to him again?

For now, I have to push such terrible musings away.

One way or another I have to get some answers so everything can be packed back safely into the correct boxes in my head, as it was before.

I have to carry through my decisions now, or I risk slowly falling back into the bottomless pit of madness I've visited once before and hope I will never have to revisit.

I just don't think I'm strong enough to get through it all again.

CHAPTER THIRTY-THREE

SIXTEEN YEARS EARLIER

When the sirens first began their high-pitched screaming, they merged into Rose's dream and became part of it.

Then, as they travelled closer still, she finally roused from her slumber. She heard voices in the street. Doors were banging downstairs.

The red digits of her alarm clock declared it was one-thirty a.m.

Rose quickly got out of bed and pulled on her fleecy dressing gown. She crept across the small landing bare-footed and stood listening at the top of the stairs.

Strange, urgent whispers floated up and then she heard her father's voice.

'And you're sure… it's definitely Cassie?'

Rose flew downstairs.

'What's wrong?' She pushed past her father to find a small group of neighbours clustered at the door, their faces all struck with horror. It was then she realised that they were surrounding Jed, keeping him standing upright on useless, buckling legs.

'Come on, lad, let's get you inside,' Ray said, stepping back.

'Jed, what's wrong? What's happened?' Rose thought him drunk and incoherent at first and then she realised he was sobbing.

'Cassie. It's our Cassie—' And then, as if he could not bear the thoughts and feelings that presented themselves, he burst into a flurry of sobs and pushed his way clumsily from the crowd, stumbling up the street.

As people leapt after Jed, Stella took Rose gently by the arm and led her back inside. Ray picked up his boots, sat down and began loosening the laces, his face dark and menacing. The hairs on the back of Rose's neck prickled.

She pulled away from her mother, her skin suddenly burning.

'Mum, Dad? Tell me what's happening!'

'It's Cassie, love,' Stella said gently. 'She's been… attacked.'

Rose's hand flew up to her mouth.

'She's been raped, Rose,' Ray said grimly, pushing his feet into the boots. 'Some bastard's raped her.'

'Ray, don't—'

'She's not twelve any more, Stella,' her father's voice thundered. 'Rose needs to know… needs to know the danger out there. She'll find out anyway. Half the village is out there looking for him.'

'But – how…' Rose struggled to put the words in line. 'Where did it happen?'

'At home,' Stella said. 'Carolyn and Jed were both out. Cassie was home alone for the evening.'

'Do they know who it is, who did this?' Rose heard herself speaking, yet her voice drifted far away. She and Cassie had always spent Friday nights together, usually watching television with snacks round at Cassie's house. At least that was until she met Gareth.

Stella shook her head. 'They don't know who did it. Apparently, he didn't speak and wore a balaclava.'

'Was it someone she knew? I mean—' Rose's mouth hung open, the words refusing to come.

'Don't you worry, love.' Ray looked at her. 'We'll find out who did this and, when we do, we'll string the bastard up. That's all you need to know right now.'

When Rose got back to her bedroom she lay on her bed and stared at the ceiling.

Gareth's face floated into her mind. She would call him in a moment. He made her feel safe and he knew how to calm her down.

His last angry words about Cassie danced in her ears but she pushed them away. Gareth would be shocked about what had happened. Everyone was so shocked.

Things like this just didn't happen around here. The local police wandered around the village from time to time, talking mainly to Mr Sandhu, the owner of the convenience store. Also, they made a point of chatting to the teenage kids who hung outside the Miners' Welfare at night and at weekends because they had nothing else to do.

Probably the most shocking thing to happen in Newstead during the past year was when someone put a rock through the window of the chippy. But that only turned out to be Daft Davey, a big soft lad in his thirties who lived up Mosley Road with his elderly parents.

Apparently, he'd take offence when they wouldn't sell him all eight potato fritters on the hot shelf at the expense of the rest of the queue. Everyone knew that Daft Davey lived for his potato fritters.

But now this nightmare had happened. And it had happened *to Cassie.*

Newstead had always been a friendly place to live, Rose reflected. What had happened to Cassie though… it felt so shocking it had happened here, right in the heart of the village. It felt like a much-loved family dog that you trusted, turning on you without warning.

Stuff like this just didn't happen in such a safe, dependable place where generations lived together in relative harmony and everyone knew everyone. Did it?

Rose reached under her pillow for the mobile phone that Gareth insisted she kept turned on, even through the night, in case he needed to reach her. He was forever fretting about her keeping in touch, keeping safe.

She called him on speed dial. There was only one number programmed into the device and that was Gareth's own.

Rose listened, her heart beginning to pump harder as she waited for the shrill ringing to fill her ear. The call went to answerphone. She would have liked to have heard the reassurance of Gareth's voice, strong and sensible, but there was just the standard recorded message.

She rang back four times in the next half hour but got the same response each time.

Where could he be? He'd said he had a meeting after work that would doubtless go on until late and that he was having an early night ready for a one-day weekend conference in Birmingham the next morning.

Granted, it was nearly two a.m. but she'd assumed he also kept his phone on all night, seeing as he was always so insistent she did it. He must have turned it off. Perhaps the meeting had gone on much longer than he'd expected, she pondered.

Silent tears of misery and regret slid down Rose's flushed cheeks. She really wanted to see Cassie and make everything alright again between them. She wanted to be there in her best friend's hour of need.

At that moment, she realised that the person she really wanted to speak to was Gareth.

She left him a voice message.

CHAPTER THIRTY-FOUR

SIXTEEN YEARS EARLIER

The next morning Rose and Stella walked round to Cassie's house.

Carolyn came to the door in her dressing gown, her face tearstained and her frizzy permed hair sticking out at various angles. It was common knowledge she liked a drink or three but Rose couldn't recall ever having seen her look as rough.

Stella bustled inside and pulled Carolyn into her arms. Rose expected her to start sobbing uncontrollably, but she didn't. She stood, stock still and frozen with her arms down by her sides, her eyes staring and wide.

It was almost more disturbing than watching her break down.

'I'll make us a cuppa,' Rose said, walking past the two older women towards the kitchen.

'No!' Carolyn shrieked, pulling away from Stella's embrace. 'They've said we can't go in there just yet.'

Rose stopped dead at the doorway at the stretched yellow tape and looked around. It looked as if someone had emptied out half the contents of the cupboards and scattered them all around the counter tops.

It must have happened here. Her eyes were drawn to dark stains on the carpet tiles near the back door.

Sickened, Rose turned and walked back into the living room. Carolyn had begun to talk.

'I nearly didn't go, you know, to our Noreen's. She'd been a bit off colour but I convinced her a drink would do her good.' She covered her face with splayed nicotine-stained fingers.

'Carolyn, you can't blame yourself for this, love,' Stella said gently, stroking the wiry, stiff strands of dyed red hair at the back of her head. 'The only person to blame here is that… that *monster* who attacked Cassie.'

'Don't!' Carolyn wailed. 'I can't bear to think about it. Nobody's seen our Jed; he's taken himself off somewhere. The police are aware but seem to think he's an adult and he'll come back when he's ready but he can't live with it. I'm worried he'll do himself in, Stella.'

Rose walked over to the sagging patterned velour settee and sat at the other side of her mother. Jed had been in a terrible state when she'd seen him rushing off up the road last night; she hoped Carolyn was wrong about his state of mind.

Carolyn looked up suddenly, her tone regretful, accusing. 'You always used to stay over here on Fridays, Rose. Why were you not here this week?'

Rose realised in an instant that Cassie must not have told her mum they'd fallen out.

'I was out with college friends,' Rose replied easily, pushing away the truth of being over at Gareth's flat.

Stella nodded. 'She was home for eleven, weren't you, love?'

'The hospital are keeping her in for a couple of days,' Carolyn said, and Rose began to breathe normally again when she realised there would be no further grilling.

'Can we visit?' Rose asked. 'I'd really like to see her.'

'They've had to do all sorts of horrible tests,' Carolyn said as if Rose hadn't spoken. 'She's got concussion and she lost a lot of blood. They say she grabbed a knife, probably to defend herself, but she cut all her hands up.'

Rose thought again about the rusty-looking dark stains she'd spotted on the kitchen carpet tiles.

'That's terrible,' Stella said. 'The poor love.'

'Can we go, Mum? To see Cassie today.'

'Of course,' Stella replied. 'If that's OK with you, Carolyn?'

Carolyn nodded slowly, reverting to her strange, trancelike state. 'I'm going in at eleven this morning. You can come with me if you like. I'm sure she'll want you there with her, Rose.'

Carolyn appeared at the end of the hospital corridor and shuffled slowly towards Rose and her mother.

Her mouth drooped with fatigue, her expression one of feeling beaten.

'Rose, I'm so sorry. Cassie won't see you.' Carolyn held out her hands and shook her head, perplexed. 'She wouldn't say why but she's adamant.'

Rose looked at her mother.

'She seems really confused.' Carolyn twisted her hands and looked at Stella, her tone pleading. 'She's not herself.'

'It's completely understandable,' Stella said briskly. 'Now, you're not to worry yourself, Carolyn. Perhaps when Cassie's home and feeling a little more stable, Rose and I can pop over?'

'Course.' Carolyn looked at Rose. 'I'm really sorry, love.'

Rose sighed. 'I just want her to know I came, that I was here for her. Give her my love, will you?'

'Of course I will. Thanks for coming, Rose.'

When Carolyn disappeared back down the corridor and into Cassie's room, Stella reached for her daughter's hand.

'Don't take it personally, Rose. Poor Cassie will be traumatised; it's natural. None of us would be able to act rationally after what's happened. There are all sorts of things to deal with after such horror; shame, fear—'

'I know, Mum,' Rose agreed in a small voice.

The two women walked to the bus stop together but got separate buses. Stella had an appointment at the optician's in Hucknall and Rose fibbed that she had some free periods at college so was heading home.

As she settled into her seat, Rose took out her phone and switched the ringer on again.

There were six missed calls and a text – all from Gareth.

CHAPTER THIRTY-FIVE

SIXTEEN YEARS EARLIER

Gareth met her off the bus and she collapsed into his arms, oblivious to who might be watching.

'Hey, what's wrong?' He pushed her gently back to get some space between them and looked into her eyes. 'What's wrong with my girl?'

From the midst of snotty tears and sniffles, Rose blubbed out the awful truth of what had happened.

'What? Oh my God, how terrible... poor Cassie!'

She gnawed at her fingernails 'She's been *raped*. Some evil bastard has...'

'I heard you, Rose,' he said quickly. 'The poor girl, I'm... devastated for her... for *you*, as her friend. I don't want you out on your own after dark.'

Rose shook her head slowly. Gareth was saying all the right things but it just sounded – *hollow*. With Gareth's threat about Cassie wishing she'd never been born echoing in her ears, it was difficult to reconcile his reaction now.

'What's wrong?' He stared at her.

'I – I just can't believe what's happened,' Rose stammered.

'It's an awful business alright but you've told me yourself that Cassie is careless with her personal safety.'

'What?' She felt a heat rising inside her. 'What are you trying to say? Regardless of Cassie's lifestyle, she doesn't deserve to be lying in a hospital bed and—'

'Of course she doesn't,' Gareth said tightly. 'I didn't say that.'

'She's my best friend and I—'

'Best friend? Are we talking about the same girl here?' Gareth gave a short, bitter laugh. 'Sorry, I thought Cassie was the person who's been ignoring you all week and issuing threats against us both.'

Rose swallowed hard.

'We've been friends all our lives,' Rose said levelly. 'The stuff she threatened, it was just a blip.'

'A blip? Is that what you call her threatening to tell your dad about us?'

'I'm sure she didn't mean it, she'd have just said it in temper.'

'Wake up, Rose. Your *friend* might not quite be the angel you think she is.'

'Stop! I don't want to listen to this crap anymore.' Rose shrugged off his embrace and stepped back. 'I can't handle you being like this, Gareth. I can't understand why you'd say such awful things, it's as if—'

She hesitated.

'Go on, Rose.' He moved closer to her. 'You were in full flow there; I was getting a nice little glimpse of where your loyalties lie. It's as if *what*?'

Rose sensed things were getting out of hand but she found she couldn't stop. The words tumbled out of her mouth before she could bite them back.

'You don't even seem surprised that Cassie's been attacked. I can't stop thinking about you saying you'd make sure she'll wish she'd never been born. Why would you even say something like that?'

Gareth snatched her hand and squeezed – really squeezed until she whimpered.

'Do you think it was me, Rose? Do you think I went around to your friend's house and raped her last night?'

'No! Don't say that.'

'Because she'd have liked it, you know. I didn't want to have to tell you this, but when you were upstairs at her house washing your face, she came on to me.'

'What?' Rose staggered back from him. She could hear approaching traffic and crows cawing in the wood nearby and then all the different noises began to swim together in her ears.

'She tried to kiss me, Rose. Asked me, wouldn't I like a real woman like *her* instead of a little girl like *you*.'

'You're lying,' Rose whispered. 'Cassie would never do that. She just wouldn't.'

'It's interesting, Rose,' he said through gritted teeth, 'how when Cassie says something she doesn't mean it. But all I have to do is make a throwaway comment and you can't get over it.'

'My point was that you said she'll soon wish she'd never been born and then Cassie was attacked.' Rose sighed and looked at her hands. 'I don't think you had anything to do with it, Gareth.'

'Doesn't sound that way to me.' He held her gaze. 'I'm sorry if I squeezed your hand so hard, Rose. You'll no doubt get your revenge though.'

'What do you mean… revenge?'

'If you tell the police what I said, they'll pull me in. I'll become their prime suspect.' He looked at the floor. 'I can't blame you if that's what you want to do.'

It was a sobering thought. Rose hadn't thought about the police.

Gareth stepped closer and wrapped his arms around her.

'Don't you see, Rosie? They'll be looking for someone to blame and I'll be the perfect scapegoat. An outsider who was in Cassie's house the night before the attack. You can just hear the villagers gossiping about it, I'd be the highlight of their sad little lives.' He sniffed. 'Maybe I should just go to the police myself, tell them what I said. It'll save you the bother.'

'What?'

'I'll tell them about my off-the-cuff comment, so you don't have to betray me,' Gareth said quietly. 'But I know what places like this are like. The villagers will have their own kangaroo court and I'll instantly be found guilty. I'll have to leave my job, leave the area.'

'Don't say that.' Rose shook her head. 'That's not going to happen.'

'Isn't it? People around here are the forgiving sort, are they, Rose?'

Rose suddenly remembered that a couple of years ago there had been a dishevelled-looking young man hanging around, a wanderer who'd been in the village for about a week. People said he was squatting in a derelict shed in the churchyard.

Rose would see him around the streets, sitting or lying at the edge of the pavement, pale and wiry, holding out his hand for coins.

A couple of the villagers took him food and blankets and Jim Greaves even treated him to a basket of chicken and chips at the Station Hotel.

Then people's garden sheds started being broken into overnight and items stolen. Someone said they'd seen the beggar riding a bicycle just like the one that had been taken from the O'Reilly's house on Byron Street.

The well-wishers swiftly dissipated. A group of local men visited the beggar in his makeshift home, questioned him. They alerted the police, who took him down the station. Rose never saw him again after that.

'I'm not going to say anything to the police,' Rose whispered. 'I know you've done nothing wrong and it was just a silly comment.'

'You must do what you think is right, Rose,' Gareth said, turning away. 'If you feel bound to support Cassie at my expense, then go ahead. I can't expect your loyalty above someone you've known all your life.'

'Gareth—' she reached for him, pulled him gently towards her '—my loyalty is to you. I want to be with *you*. I – I love you.' He liked her to tell him so but the words still felt strange when she said them, as if something inside kicked against it.

He tangled his fingers in her hair and kissed her forehead.

'Then keep away from Cassie,' he murmured. 'She's jealous of what we have. Can't you see that, Rose? We only need each other now.'

CHAPTER THIRTY-SIX

ROSE

PRESENT DAY

I tapped ex-DCI Mike North's postcode into Google Maps and set off in the car to Colwick, a suburb in the east of Nottingham and about a thirty-minute drive away from the village.

I don't drive too often these days and although I'm always a bit nervous at first, once I get going, I can usually relax and enjoy the ride.

I think it's something to do with the barrier of metal a vehicle affords. You look out from a car but pedestrians rarely look *in*. I feel more protected than when I'm on foot.

I'd rather not walk to and from work across the village but it's a valuable part of keeping me from becoming a recluse. I just wish it would get easier.

Stumbling on Mike's contact details at work came as a complete surprise and served to convince me it was a 'sign' that I should carry through my intention to speak to him without delay.

Miss Carter, on a visit to the library, mentioned she'd been at a WI meeting close to Nottingham and that there had been a talk by none other than a retired lawyer called Tessa North.

'She gave a very eloquent talk about women having a career in law and she was especially interested in hearing I lived in Newstead Village,' Miss Carter told me, a little self-righteously.

'Oh, and why was that?' I said, trying to look interested but wishing I could just get on with losing myself in validating a pile of new customers' library cards.

'Her husband is an ex-detective and he had a big case here. His name is Mike North.' She seemed to suddenly realise who she was talking to and her error in bringing up Billy's case. The colour drained from her cheeks. 'Oh! I'm so sorry, dear. I didn't think. I didn't mean to—'

'It's fine,' I said, sitting up in my chair. 'Did she say where they were living now? I don't suppose you got her email address?'

'I can do better than that, dear,' she said, looking pleased with herself again. She delved into her purse and held a business card aloft. 'She gave us all one of these.'

I'd called the mobile number later and left my number and a voicemail explaining who I was. It had been a nice surprise when Mike returned my call himself and readily agreed to see me. Even more so because he'd suggested we meet at his home.

'I don't get out much these days,' he said. 'It'll be nice to see a new face around here.'

I am predictably tense driving over there. I don't put the radio on. Instead, I try to think of how I might get advice from Mike without – at this stage – implicating Ronnie.

They say once a copper, always a copper and Mike North may well feel obliged to pass on any details I give him to the contacts he still has on the force.

If my neighbour is innocent, which despite everything, I'm still ninety-nine per cent certain he is, I have to protect him. At least for the time being.

I turn into Riverside Crescent and drive along the length of the exclusive apartments to the second visitor car park at the end, as per Mike's instructions.

The apartments are situated on the banks of the River Trent and although there is no sign of the river from this, the car park side, the balconies all overlook the water.

I grab my handbag and walk up to the imposing building. There is a lot of steel and glass here and the windows glint in the weak sunlight. I approach block seven and punch in Mike's apartment number, then ring the bell button on the keypad.

'Hello,' a woman's voice says when I tell her my name. 'Come on up, we're on the first floor.'

I ignore the plush lift and take the stairs to the first floor. When I emerge from the landing, one of the doors to the three apartments opens.

I walk towards the smiling woman with short blonde hair.

'You must be Rose,' she says and shakes my hand. 'I'm Tessa. Mike's been so looking forward to seeing you today.'

Tessa looks to be in her early fifties, tanned and attractive, casually dressed wearing cropped white jeans, bare feet and a baggy white T-shirt.

'I'll take you through to Mike,' she says as we enter the hallway. 'And I'll get you a cool drink. Home-made lemonade or water?'

'A lemonade would be lovely, thanks,' I beam, looking down to slip off my flat pumps.

'Oh, leave those on,' she insists, waving me through. 'Mike's waiting for you out on the balcony.'

I nod and walk past her where the hallway opens out into a large lounge flooded with light. Floor-to-ceiling glass windows and sliding French doors are open, fully exploiting a very impressive view of the river.

'Hi Rose,' Mike calls from his wicker chair outside. 'Come on out.'

He doesn't get up so I walk across the lounge and step out on to the immaculate glass-screened, tiled balcony.

'Wow,' I gawp. 'I wouldn't want to get out much either if I had this to wake up to.'

He laughs and reaches out his hand very slowly. And that's when I notice he is shaking. Not a shiver, more of a violent tremor.

I shake his hand and he withdraws his arm stiffly.

'Parkinson's disease,' he says matter-of-factly. 'It's a bloody nuisance, as you can see.'

'I'm really sorry to hear it, Mike,' I say, feeling bad for putting him out with my intrusion into his peace. 'I'd no idea, I'd never have—'

'Don't apologise, Rose.' He shakes his head. 'I'm glad to see you again after all these years. You were just a young girl when tragedy struck your family.'

There's a beat of silence as we both remember.

'I was devastated to hear about your parents. Losing both of them like that after what happened to Billy, well… I don't know how you got through it.'

'Thanks, Mike. They both thought a lot of you, as you know.'

He smiles and I study his lined face. It's sixteen years since I saw him last and my memory is sketchy from that time but he looks much older than I expected; a lot older than his wife. I'm almost certain it's as a result of the Parkinson's he's been forced to live with.

We turn as Tess comes out with a tray bearing two long glasses containing iced lemonade.

'Lovely,' I say, accepting one gratefully, wafting my face with my hand. It didn't seem quite as hot as this down in the car park.

'It's a sun trap here,' Tessa says, setting Mike's drink on the table next to him with an extra-long straw. 'All the balconies are south-facing and even on a fairly cool day it seems warmer out here because we're protected from the wind.'

I sip my lemonade and consider that Mike seems to have done very well for himself on a detective's salary and now his pension.

'It's thanks to Tessa's career we've got this place.' Mike looks out over the river, seeming to read my mind. 'She was partner in a law firm. Gave it all up to look after me, lucky girl.'

'Watch it, Rose.' Tessa winks at me before stepping back inside and pulling the glass door to. 'He'll have you feeling sorry for him before you know it. That's how he caught me out.'

Mike laughs and blows her a kiss. This couple have undoubtedly got a difficult path ahead of them with Mike's illness but it's clear they really love each other. It's nice to see.

I shade my eyes and look ahead, all the way down to the bend in the river. I've been here just a few minutes and already I've spotted moorhens, coots and a magnificent cormorant flying low and fast above the water.

Mike has found his own little piece of heaven in the middle of all the vile crap he's had to deal with in his thirty-odd years with the Nottinghamshire Police.

What happened to Billy is part of a past he'd rather forget and that I'm here to ask him to remember.

CHAPTER THIRTY-SEVEN

ROSE

PRESENT DAY

I try not to stare as Mike leans forward with difficulty, a shaking hand attempting to guide the straw towards his mouth.

'Can I help?' I ask him awkwardly.

'Thanks but no. I actually get satisfaction from still being able to do the smallest things.' He rolls his eyes. 'Pathetic, really. But I never know when things are going to get worse, you see.'

I shake my head. 'I think you're doing amazing. Did you become ill after you retired from the force?'

'No, no.' He settles awkwardly back into his chair, and watches as a rower glides gracefully by. 'It was before. Something happened to me on Billy's case.'

I sit up a little straighter. 'What do you mean?'

'Something changed in here,' he said and tapped at his chest. 'I lost heart for the job.'

'I can understand that.'

'Billy's case, as I've always called it, well, it took something away.' He glanced behind him, I presumed to check Tessa wasn't around. 'I've dealt with some pretty bad stuff over the years, murders, rapes, violent drug deals gone wrong… you name it and, after thirty-three years on the force, I can guarantee I've seen it.'

I sit, quietly listening. Not wanting to interrupt but desperate to say what I've come to talk about before I lose my nerve.

'But something about that lad, your brother, it tore me up inside. I'd come home after a fourteen-hour day and work for another four or five hours sat at the kitchen table.' He shook his head slowly as he remembered the horror of it. Still staring out at the water, he continued. 'I missed family birthdays, my eldest daughter's graduation and me and Tessa, well, we came close to splitting up.'

Having seen how good they were together today that one really surprised me. I felt bad. Mike had gone through all this to get justice for Billy. For us.

'It was all-consuming.' He looks at me. 'I'm not trying to say I suffered like you and your parents did, Rose; of course that's not the case. But you're probably the only person left now who can understand anywhere near how it felt.'

I nod. I don't feel the need to say anything.

'Anyway—' he shakes his head like he's trying to dispel the memories '—once the case was over and Farnham went down, thank God, I found I'd got no oomph left for any more cases, you know? I started dropping stuff like cutlery and having trouble writing with a pen. Stiff joints… you get the picture.'

'It was the Parkinson's?'

Mike shrugged. 'True to form I ignored it for as long as I could, found ways of disguising the tremors. Then one day, Tessa noticed and that was it, she was like a dog with a bone. Within a month I'd been diagnosed and I accepted ill-health retirement.'

'I'm so sorry to hear all this, Mike,' I say, feeling a genuine sadness. 'My parents always said how lucky they were to have you running the case. How you cared about what happened to Billy. I don't think any of us quite recognised quite how much you gave of yourself.'

'Well—' he sighs, seeming to gather himself '—enough of my self-indulgent moaning. It's so good to see you, Rose – see that you're thriving despite what happened to your family.'

I suddenly feel awfully conscious of my skinny thighs displayed on the chair and the bony shoulders that are hard to hide in the top I've chosen to wear.

I think about my crappy, sad life. It doesn't feel like I'm thriving at all.

'You said on the phone that you wanted my advice?' He's prodding me as to the reason I came here and I can feel the resistance in myself. I don't want to overstay my welcome, so now's the time to say what I came to say.

I take a breath. 'It's difficult, Mike. I've spent the last sixteen years trying not to think about what happened to Billy, trying to wipe the memory of Gareth Farnham from my mind.'

'I can totally understand that,' he says, nodding. 'Take your time, Rose.'

'The thing is, I'm going to ask you a big favour. I mean, a *really* big favour.'

'Anything I can do to help, I will.' He holds his shaking hands out in front of him. 'You know that.'

'I'd like to talk theoretically about a certain scenario, if that's OK.'

Mike smiles. 'Ahh, I see, the old *what if* scenario. You don't want to talk hard facts right now? That's fine by me, Rose. Go ahead.'

Do I still want to do this? I ask myself.

Ronnie's tired face flashes into my mind. He's been so ill and still is, lying in bed next door, all alone in his autumn years.

I take in a long breath. I have to do this for myself and for Billy.

I really have no choice.

CHAPTER THIRTY-EIGHT

ROSE

PRESENT DAY

I look at Mike and the words begin to flow.

'What if, many years after a terrible crime, something came to light that cast doubt on everything you thought you knew about who committed it?'

Mike grips the arm of his chair and looks at me. 'What's happened? Is there new evidence?'

I look away and Mike checks himself.

'Sorry, Rose, I forgot. We're just speaking theoretically, right?'

I give him a quick nod. I wish I could lift my arms in the air to let the air circulate a bit. My heart has started to thump but I ignore it. I can't stop now.

'OK. If something came to light, it would depend very much as to what that *something* was,' Mike mused. 'If it was crystal-clear-cut new evidence, then whoever found it ought to go to the police. Simple.'

'But would they listen? And would they be happy not to take any action until the person felt ready?'

Mike looks at me incredulously. 'It's not a game, Rose. If an innocent man has done sixteen years of time behind bars – or however long our theoretical villain has been incarcerated – for a crime he didn't commit after all, then that needs sorting. He'd have to be cleared and the murder case reopened.'

Gareth Farnham is far from innocent. The thought of my actions helping him start a new life after what he did sickens me to my stomach. He'd be freed and, until someone else was convicted, Billy's death would go unpunished.

I look at Mike and I could swear he's thinking the same thing.

'It's black and white.' He shrugs. 'If there was important new evidence then it should be disclosed to the police. The person who reports it loses control the minute they take down the statement, there'll be no bartering about whether or not to progress it.'

'But what if there was nobody working there any more who was on the case?'

'Irrelevant.' Mike shrugs. 'They'd have to reopen it if the new evidence showed there had been an unsafe conviction.'

I take a tissue out of my bag and mop my forehead and chin.

'Do you want to go inside where it's cool, Rose? I can call Tessa to help me in.'

'No, I'm fine,' I say quickly. I just need to get this over with, so I press on. 'If there seemed to be new evidence and someone else was implicated, someone who'd been free all this time, what would likely happen?'

Mike sighed. 'It's really hard to second-guess these things without knowing the full picture. All I'll say is this: it's got to be something big and failsafe for the force to reopen a case once it's been satisfactorily concluded. Particularly if it was a high-profile murder case involving a child. Then the whole country would sit up and listen.'

I feel a stab of panic.

'The person who found the new piece of evidence would have to go to the police and make a full disclosure,' he continued, 'and give a full statement. Then they'd decide what, if anything, they want to do about it.'

'But what if the evidence wasn't what it seemed and an innocent person got dragged through interrogation and—' I press the heel of my hand to my forehead. It's all such a dreadful mess. I feel more confused than ever. 'Couldn't I just have a quiet word with someone first, before I go ahead and report anything?' I catch myself. 'Theoretically speaking, of course.'

'Doesn't work like that, I'm afraid.' Mike pressed his lips together. 'That old style of policing is long gone. An officer could get disciplined or even fired if he or she was found to be meddling unofficially in a closed case. They'd need permission from the highest level to start dabbling again. Nowadays, they just haven't got the resources to be re-opening cases that are done and dusted, the force is under such tremendous pressure.'

'So, if a person was to go and tell them everything, would they free Gareth Farnham and reopen the case?'

'It's really not that simple,' Mike says. 'These things don't happen overnight, Rose, the police can't just go around freeing convicts and reopening murder cases on somebody's say-so.'

I nod, realising I must sound like a simpleton to Mike. I'm aware I might be over-simplifying the whole thing and I'm also aware it comes from a place of wanting Farnham to be guilty and praying there is a perfectly simple reason for a key piece of evidence being squirrelled away all this time in Ronnie's house.

Mike looks up to the sky and thinks for a moment. 'If there was agreement among the powers that be, they'd probably follow up the new evidence lead and then decide whether or not it was worth taking it forward to an unsafe conviction.'

'But what if the *new* person implicated was innocent after all? What if it wasn't what it looked like? They'd be so traumatised.'

'That's precisely why the police can't just go at it full pelt to start with.' Mike looks at me. 'Ultimately, justice must be done, whether folks get upset at being questioned or not. This "talking theoretically" business is all a bit frustrating, isn't it? Why don't you just tell me what's happened and maybe then I can properly advise you?'

'I can't, I just can't.' My voice cracks and I clutch my handbag close to me. My heart is full-on jackhammer now, and I feel sick. 'Can I ask you one more thing, Mike?'

'Anything.'

'When you arrested Gareth Farnham, were you one hundred per cent certain you had the right man?'

'I'm sorry, Rose.' He sighs. 'I said anything, and I do want to do as much as I can to help, but you know I can't legally discuss past cases I worked on. I just can't do that.'

There are two alternating images flashing on repeat in my head.

Gareth Farnham's hateful face and Ronnie's sad, kindly face. I'm so tempted to just blurt out everything to Mike.

Just tell him, the voice in my head urges. *Just tell him and share the pressure before it cracks you up.*

I stand up. 'I'm sorry, Mike, I shouldn't have asked. I don't know, I'm just a mess at the moment. Ignore me, I have to go now, I'm due in work at one.'

'Don't apologise, Rose. After what you went through – I mean you personally – it must be so traumatic to even mention that bastard's name. The terrible things he did—'

I shake my head. 'Don't, Mike, please.'

Mike calls for Tessa and she appears on the balcony almost instantly.

'I'll see you to the door,' she says.

I thank Mike for seeing me and he tells me he's there any time I want to offload.

But just as Tessa and I are about to step into the hallway to the front door, Mike calls out again. 'Rose!'

I turn round to find he is standing at the balcony door, facing me. He's obviously in great pain, his knees buckling slightly and his expression grim. Tessa runs back across the room to help him.

'Gareth Farnham was a despicable man for what he did to you and to Cassie,' Mike says a little breathlessly. 'I've never lost any sleep that he's serving time; he deserves it. But I admit to you now, there was always something not quite right with the case, something I couldn't put my finger on. I think that's the reason it got to me so much.' Tessa reaches him and he leans heavily on her with relief. 'I'm so sorry, Rose. The answer to your question is *no*. I was never one hundred per cent certain we had the right man and despite my intense dislike of Gareth Farnham, if pushed right now, I'd have to say the same thing.'

CHAPTER THIRTY-NINE

SIXTEEN YEARS EARLIER

'I want you to come over to the flat this weekend,' Gareth said. 'For the whole day.'

'I'd really like that,' Rose said. She felt so terribly grown-up these days.

'I thought I'd make you lunch on Saturday and then we can have a lazy afternoon together. What do you think?'

'Oh, I'd love to but I've promised to take Billy to football practice on Saturday afternoon,' Rose said. 'Maybe I could come over in the morning, instead?'

'I have some paperwork to get through in the morning,' Gareth said brusquely. 'It won't hurt for once not taking Billy, will it? Your mum or dad could take him.'

'But I haven't taken him for ages and he'll be really disappointed now, if I don't go.' Gareth's face dropped, so Rose tried to explain her position further. 'It's just that we've always had that time together and this week he's going to be in goal for the first time. It's a big deal for him.'

Gareth's nostrils flared but he said nothing.

'Can I be honest, Gareth? Since I started college and the library and met you, I feel like I've neglected Billy,' she said, wanting him to understand. 'I really need to start making a bit more time for him… perhaps the three of us could do something.'

'Oh, I get it – it's all my fault.' Gareth slid his hand from her knee.

'That's not what I'm saying!'

'What about time for *me*… for us?'

'It's just that I feel a responsibility for him,' Rose tried to reason. 'He's a lonely little thing, I—'

'He's not *your* kid… is he?' Gareth remarked. 'You're not one of those creepy inbred families like on the *Jerry Springer* show, are you? Where the kid thinks his mum is his sister, kind of thing?'

'No!' Rose gave a little grin but she felt a stab of annoyance. 'He's definitely my little brother.'

'Well then, he's not your responsibility at all. Let your parents take him to the football. You make life too easy for them.'

Rose sighed. Gareth was missing the point. She *wanted* to take Billy to his match.

'I was looking forward to spending some quality time together,' he said, his voice softening slightly. 'But if you've got to put your family first then so be it. I've only myself to blame, I suppose, for not getting to know other people here in the village. Perhaps I've been too devoted to you, Rosie.' He kissed her cheek gently. 'I'll find something else to do. No doubt there'll be other people around who wouldn't mind spending some time with me.'

Rose felt a jolt of alarm as the attractive faces of other girls in the village clicked through her mind's eye like a slideshow. Most of them were older than her. They had jobs in places like Mansfield and Nottingham, kept themselves groomed and well dressed.

She wanted to see Gareth at the weekend but she would also like to honour her commitment and take Billy to football.

If Gareth would only be a bit more flexible, she could do both but it was clear that wasn't going to happen.

'I'll ask Mum if she can take Billy,' she said reluctantly.

'Good girl.' Gareth smiled.

*

'You can come with us if you like, Billy,' Rose said brightly.

Her parents were at the regeneration site and Gareth had called at the house on the pretence of Rose sharing her knowledge of the Nottingham & Beeston Canal.

'It's OK, Rose,' Billy said. 'I'm going to see if anyone from school is down on the field.'

'But you love watching the narrowboats,' she persisted.

'I don't want to,' Billy scowled and looked at Gareth.

'It's alright if Billy comes with us, isn't it, Gareth?'

Gareth shrugged. 'He's just said he doesn't want to.'

Rose became aware of a strange electricity in the air. She could feel it, crackling between Billy and Gareth.

'What is it with you two?' She looked frantically at one, then the other. 'Something's happened.'

'Stop making up your silly stories, Rose,' Gareth said smoothly, staring at Billy. 'Nothing has happened. Billy can entertain himself. He's eight years old now, not three.'

She looked at her brother and felt her heartstrings tighten. For whatever reason, Billy wasn't an overly popular boy at school. He had one or two friends but they lived on the edge of Hucknall, miles away from the village.

He'd always been a bit of an outsider and now Gareth was making him feel uncomfortable within his own family. She'd given in and agreed not to take Billy to football training but now Gareth was expecting her to exclude him again.

'Billy, I'd really like you to come, I—'

Gareth grabbed her forearm. 'Leave it, Rose. We're going to the canal on our own and that's final.'

'Oww!' She pulled her arm away and rubbed it, scowling.

'Don't you hurt my sister,' Billy said between gritted teeth. He stepped forward, his small hand clenched into fists.

Gareth threw his head back and let out an exaggerated laugh. 'Why, what are *you* going to do, you skinny little runt?' He pushed Billy hard and the boy stumbled back, banging his arm on the corner of the sideboard. Tears spilled down his cheeks.

Rose rushed to his side.

'How could you?' She spat the words at Gareth, her eyes burning. 'I think you'd better leave.'

Before she could even register what was happening, Gareth stormed over to where she was crouched down rubbing Billy's arm. He seized her by the hair.

She screamed as he dragged her to her feet. Billy began to wail, his expression pure terror.

'We're going to the canal whether you like it or not, Rose. Get in the car right now.' His voice was calm and level, amplifying her fear.

'Gareth, please! No! I can't just leave Billy, there's nobody home to look after him.'

'Get in there.' He pushed her hard towards the kitchen. She crunched her shoulder on the door frame and cried out in pain. 'You!' Gareth turned round to a cowering Billy and raised his forefinger, moving it smoothly across his own mouth. 'Keep it zipped, brat, or I'll hurt your sister.'

In the kitchen, Gareth towered above Rose, his features dark and malicious.

'This is what you're going to do.' His voice kept the same monotonous tone. 'When I've finished with you, you'll go back in there and convince your brother to keep his stupid mouth shut. Otherwise, your dad is going to lose his position on the project and I'll be giving his upcoming job to someone else.'

Rose squeezed her eyes shut, forcing clusters of tears to tumble down her cheeks.

When she opened her eyes and looked up at him, she wondered how such a caring, loving person could have turned into this… this *monster*.

He was threatening her with her dad's newfound purpose. Ray thought the world of Gareth. It was only now she realised he had carefully wormed his way into their lives. In his own way, he now controlled her father just like he controlled her and Billy… and there was nothing she could do about it.

Cassie had been right all along.

'I'll tell him to keep quiet,' she whispered, rubbing her eyes with the back of a hand.

'Good girl. Very sensible.'

She opened the kitchen door and walked back into the living room, where Billy stood in the middle of the room looking dazed.

Rose knew if she told her father what was happening, he'd sort Gareth out in a heartbeat. Job or no job. There was no doubt in her mind he'd sacrifice his promised new future without a second thought if he knew Gareth Farnham was abusing both her and her brother.

But Rose couldn't do that to her dad. *She* was the one who'd got Gareth Farnham involved in their lives. It was up to her to protect her father and brother and to find a way out of this mess.

She'd stupidly excluded nearly everyone who cared about her from her life. She'd genuinely believed that Gareth only wanted her to be with him because he loved her so much but now she finally saw the truth that Cassie had tried so hard to tell her about.

Gareth was threatened by and jealous of everyone Rose cared about. Including her eight-year-old brother.

She decided she'd stay quiet and try to keep Gareth away from Billy… until a solution presented itself.

CHAPTER FORTY

SIXTEEN YEARS EARLIER

She'd waited for him outside the project office at lunchtime.

It was a bright day, not cold, and Rose looked around the enormous site. She tried to see past the mounds of clogged earth, the patches of dead grass and to visualise the clever landscaping and planned fishing lake documented on the site plans her father had spread all over the table at home. It wasn't easy.

There was much work to be done – at least another eighteen months, Gareth had said. Then it would be a case of managing the whole thing, running the workforce and engaging the wider community to play a full part in using the new facilities.

Gareth had plans to stay in the village long-term and Rose realised she couldn't just run away from the situation. She had Billy to think about. He was eight years old and she'd asked him to lie for her, had asked him to protect a man who had treated them both like dirt.

It now occurred to Rose that for a time she'd been carried away by what had appeared to be love's sweet dream. She'd soaked in every compliment, every well-thought-out instruction Gareth had given her.

She'd done it all without a second thought because she'd believed he really did want the best for her.

That perspective had been shattered by how he'd treated her and, more importantly, how he'd treated Billy.

It was as if someone had shone a bright, searching light into a dark, sinister corner… she wouldn't be able to unsee those things again. The old platitudes she told herself to excuse Gareth's controlling manner; they all rang empty in her head now.

She had been a fool, pure and simple.

Rose turned and peered through the window of the project office. The meeting was breaking up now, people standing, shaking hands.

Her father looked up and raised his hand to her in greeting. His face shone. He was part of something again for the first time in a long time.

A few seconds later, the gravel behind her scuffed as Ray stepped outside in his heavy metal-toed boots and overalls.

'Rose! Are you here for me or Gareth?'

'I'm here to see Gareth, Dad.' She gave him a weak smile. 'He needs my help with something.'

Her father turned and smiled. 'Speak of the devil, here's the man himself.'

'Hello, Rose.' Gareth faltered a little, his eyes skating between the two of them. 'Everything OK?'

'I came to speak to you about that stuff you needed me to look at.' Her voice sounded a little terse, even to her, but her father didn't appear to notice.

'Ahh, yes, of course. Ray, any chance you could show the contractor the area for the first dig while I get Rose's esteemed opinion on something?'

'Consider it done,' Ray said, standing a little taller. 'Bye, love.'

'Bye, Dad,' she said faintly, watching as he strode purposefully away.

She wanted to run after him, grasp his arm, blurt out everything that had been happening over the last few weeks.

Instead, she turned to Gareth.

'I need to speak with you,' she said. 'Right now.'

His office was situated in a cramped Portakabin on site. Gareth extended his arm and directed Rose to sit in one of the two office chairs opposite his desk. She felt like one of his visitors.

His desk was neat, a pristine blotter taking pride of place. No doodles or notes, the pad of paper sat perfectly white and untouched. The stapler, hole punch and tub of pens and pencils were lined up perfectly next to the compact cordless phone. The effect was marred only by a couple of badly folded plans strewn on the right-hand side.

Gareth sat down and leaned back in his seat, pressing his fingertips together as if he were about to suggest a proposal to her.

But he said nothing.

Rose took a breath.

'I – I've done a lot of thinking and I think it's best if we… well, if we stop seeing each other.' She hadn't meant to blurt it out so quickly but now, at least, it was done.

She'd expected furious words, accusations, cruel jibes, but none of these things materialised. Gareth watched her but remained silent.

'The thing is—' she dragged air into her lungs but still felt horribly out of breath ' —I can't put what happened the other day out of my mind, how you treated me and Billy and… and there have been other things too but I don't want to go into all that now.'

'I completely understand, Rose,' he said, smoothly.

'You do?'

'Absolutely. I've behaved reprehensibly.' He sighed and looked out of the small, misted window. 'Truthfully, I've had some stress on here at work that I've tried to cope with alone but I can't condone my behaviour. All I can say is I am truly, truly sorry.'

Rose opened her mouth and closed it again. She'd run through a lot of possibilities in her mind but this humble response hadn't been one of them.

'I'm an idiot. I've lost the girl I love through my own arrogance and I've upset little Billy, who I'm really very fond of.'

Gareth had always previously spoken about Billy as if he were a nuisance… was that something else Rose had misread?

'It sounds as if you've thought very carefully about your decision, so I have to respect that,' Gareth said softly. 'But I beg you, can we still be friends, Rose? I can't bear to think we might see each other in the street and not say hello. I couldn't stand that.'

'Of course,' she said quickly, hours of steadily building tension suddenly lifting from her tight muscles.

'I'm so sorry,' he said again, and she thought how wretched he looked, sat there, so remorseful.

'Apology accepted.' Rose smiled. 'I'm glad we can still be friends. Maybe I can help Dad out now and again here at the site.'

'I'd love that.' He nodded, pushing back his chair. 'Take care, Rose. I really hope we can speak again soon.'

And with that, Rose found herself courteously but unexpectedly dismissed.

As she walked home, she felt curiously dazed, somewhat spooked, even.

The breeze billowed under her long, loose hair and it occurred to her what had felt so strange, so out of place.

Gareth had seemed like an entirely different person altogether.

CHAPTER FORTY-ONE

SIXTEEN YEARS EARLIER

Rose heard from her mother that Cassie was out of hospital.

'Give it a day or two, love,' Stella had said when Rose had talked about popping round there. 'I know this is out of character for Cassie but the trauma she's been through… you have to realise that—'

'But I want to help her through it.' Rose had turned her back on Stella. 'I want her to know I'm there for her.'

Whenever she thought about the attack on Cassie, her heart filled with a powerful need to put things right between them. Rose didn't know what she could really do about what had happened but this was the perfect chance to show Cassie none of it mattered any more. She thought that being there for her friend might be enough.

'Another day or so and I'll come with you,' Stella had said. 'How's that?'

Rose had shrugged and walked out of the kitchen; it seemed she didn't have a choice in the matter.

She had intended to send word to Mr Barrow that she wouldn't be around that week to fulfil her volunteer duties but in the event that Cassie wasn't yet ready to see her, Rose thought she might as well go in.

It seemed preferable, she thought, to sitting around moping about Gareth or Cassie and unable to do anything about the situation with either of them.

'Ah, Rose, there you are,' Mr Barrow said briskly, looking up momentarily from his paperwork. 'I've been having a bit of a clear out this morning so I've left you a bit of a pile over there. I hope you don't mind.'

He nodded to the small, square table behind him and gave her a guilty smile. It was piled with tatty-looking hardbacks.

'They're all overdue for a bit of repair work.' He stood up and peered down at her through the narrow oblong spectacles that never moved from the end of his long nose. 'Hope you don't mind?'

'It's fine.' Rose sighed. Actually she didn't mind; it would be nice to become absorbed in something menial but ultimately satisfying, for the afternoon.

She was vaguely aware of Mr Barrow rabbiting on about his allotment. She nodded here and there in what felt like the right places and that seemed to pacify him.

She began to sort the books into piles that she had silently named: spines, pages and cover. Mr Barrow had already placed the archival quality repair tape, the PVA glue and the cellophane wrap on the side.

There was something rewarding about repairing well-used books, of preserving the words within them, so more people could read and enjoy.

As she began to relax into her work, cocooned in the discreet hum of hushed library conversations around her, Rose's biggest worries wriggled their way out of the tight little compartment at the back of her head.

Who had attacked Cassie?

Rose couldn't make sense of why Cassie was so completely shunning her. Yes, they'd properly fallen out for the first time ever but still… all the years of friendship before that surely counted for something?

Had she done the right thing finishing things with Gareth?

He'd been so accommodating, so apologetic. He'd behaved terribly towards both her and poor Billy but to her surprise, he'd fully acknowledged that. Despite everything, Rose already missed him. He'd felt like the only good thing in her life for so long. He hadn't asked for one but was she a fool not to give him another chance?

Rose didn't know if she could keep her father from finding out at least some of what had been happening. It was wrong to ask an eight year old to keep secrets from his own parents, to defend someone who had hurt him. But what else could she have done under the circumstances?

She was trying to protect everybody, and she was trying to protect her dad's job. Her head felt dizzy with it all.

'Miss Rose Tinsley?'

Her head jerked up from her work at the mention of her name. Mr Barrow turned and smiled, beckoning her over to the main desk. A delivery man stood, his arms full of an enormous bouquet of blood-red roses.

'Your lucky day, love.' He grinned, presenting the flowers using both arms, like he might pass her a baby.

'Heavens, Rose—' the librarian raised an eyebrow '—celebrating, are you?'

'No, I'm not,' she murmured, fishing a small envelope out from between the blooms. 'I've no idea who sent them, Mr Barrow.'

Mr Barrow's attention was already back on his computer screen. Rose glanced round and a couple of customers nodded and smiled in appreciation of her delivery but she stepped back to the table, turning her back to the room.

Picking up scissors, she used one blade to slit open the envelope. She pulled out the compact white card, its border a printed tangle of red and pink petals.

She swallowed hard and silently read the neat handwritten print over and over.

Mine forever G. x

At four o'clock prompt, Rose said goodbye to Mr Barrow and left via the back entrance.

Ten minutes before she was due to leave, she realised she'd been repairing the same broken book for over two hours. Mr Barrow blinked at the virtually untouched pile of repairs but he didn't comment.

Her mind had been everywhere but on the task in hand.

What was Gareth hoping to achieve by sending her flowers? He'd seemed perfectly reasonable yesterday, accepting her decision and asking if they could still be friends.

When she'd read his message, those two proprietary words, she'd felt a cold trickle of sweat forge its way down the length of her spine.

Rose supposed that any gift of flowers was meant to make one feel special and valued but something about this had felt so… odd… so… inappropriate.

She'd seen Mr Barrow glancing at her out of the corner of his eye, concerned at her expression. She'd thrown the card in the bin and dumped the flowers in the kitchenette in the back.

Just about to turn the corner at the top of the road now, she stopped in her tracks as someone shouted, 'Rose!' She turned to see Jim Greaves, the library caretaker, striding towards her, his arms full of the discarded bouquet. 'You forgot your lovely flowers, pet!'

She inwardly cursed Jim's blatant interfering. This was all she needed.

'Glad I caught you, pet.' He pushed the flowers towards her, beaming. 'How's your Billy, the little tike?'

'He's fine, thanks, Jim,' she said weakly.

'Tell him to pop round when he has a minute, his Auntie Janice would love to see him, find out what mischief he's been up to.'

'I'll tell him,' she said, then, glancing at the bouquet, she shook her head. 'Thanks, Jim, but I don't want them.'

'Eh?'

'The flowers. Why don't you take them home to Janice?' She smiled and touched his shoulder. 'See you next week.'

As she turned the corner she glanced back to see Jim still standing there, watching her with interest.

CHAPTER FORTY-TWO

SIXTEEN YEARS EARLIER

'Did you sort Gareth out then, love?' Her father's booming voice carried over the television when Rose looked in the living room to say hello.

She coughed to save her having to reply and her mother looked up from her magazine.

'Yesterday, I mean,' Ray continued. 'When you came over to the site?'

'Oh, yes,' Rose said, busying herself by burrowing into her bag. 'It's all sorted now.'

'Gareth's got a bit of a soft spot for our Rose, you know.' He winked at Stella. 'Always asking how she is, where she's been and who she's hanging out with.'

'Dad!'

'I'm just saying. He's a lovely lad, is Gareth. Wouldn't mind him as a son-in-law, even.'

Rose's cheeks flushed.

'Now, Ray, he's far too old for her.' Stella rolled her eyes at her daughter. 'She needs a nice lad who's around her own age. Right, Rose?'

'I'm going up to my room,' she murmured, backing out of the doorway. 'I've got some preparation to do for college tomorrow.'

Upstairs, she passed Billy, playing with his cars on the landing.

'Come to my room, Billy.' She ruffled his hair as she walked by.

'Why?'

'I want to talk to you for a minute, that's all.'

Billy followed her and sat on the end of her bed. He looked pale and tired. Rose wondered if he was having trouble sleeping.

'So, how're things with you, little man?'

'OK, I suppose.' Billy shrugged, picking at his grubby nails.

Rose sighed. 'Billy, I'm really sorry about the other day, letting Gareth get away with being so horrible to us. And I'm sorry I asked you not to say anything to Mum and Dad, it wasn't fair of me.'

'S'alright,' he mumbled.

'It's really *not* alright,' Rose said, sitting next to him and sliding her arm around his bony shoulders. 'Nobody's got the right to treat us like that, Billy. Nobody. That's why I've told Gareth I never want to see him again.'

'But I didn't think he was your proper boyfriend, anyway.' Billy scowled up at her. 'You said you were just helping him out with stuff, like Dad does on site.'

Rose winced, pushed the lie away.

'None of that matters now,' she said. 'The main thing is, he won't be getting in the way of us doing stuff together anymore.'

'What shall I do about coming downstairs?'

'What do you mean?'

'Gareth told me I'm not allowed downstairs if he comes round to the house when Mum and Dad are out.'

'He said that?' She pressed her hand to her mouth. 'Why didn't you tell me?'

'Because he said if I told you then Dad wouldn't be able to help out with Gareth's project any more. But now you don't like him anymore I suppose I can tell you.'

Rose gulped in air and swallowed down what felt like a hairball in her throat.

What on earth had she done to all of their lives by getting involved with Gareth Farnham?

The next day after college, Rose boarded the bus for home, rapidly blinking her increasingly watery eyes.

She missed Cassie so much. Their falling out had never existed, so far as Rose was concerned. She only remembered all the laughs, all the good times they'd had together on the course.

People had tried asking Rose exactly what had happened to Cassie.

Rumours were rife at college and nobody was quite sure what had happened. The local newspaper had reported a young woman had been attacked but no further details had been given. So Rose became a popular target at lunchtime for enquiries as to Cassie's wellbeing and concerned but searching questions about the attack.

She had a stock reaction. 'Cassie has asked me to thank everyone for their concern but police have asked her not to disclose details of the incident yet.'

She felt quite proud of that response, which she'd thought of herself. It made Cassie still sound very much her best friend.

As she passed on her friend's 'message' several times over lunch, Rose had felt certain things would be back on track between them soon, particularly when she confessed to Cassie that she'd been right about Gareth Farnham all along.

And then Vicky Sparkes had approached her just as everyone poured out of the building. Vicky was part of the small group that Cassie had begun to hang around with after they'd had their disagreement.

'Hey, Rose,' Vicky called. Rose turned to face her. She felt hypnotised by a small, white ball of gum flicking over and under the other girl's tongue. 'I've got a message from Cassie. Stay away from the house.'

Three other girls, part of Vicky's group, sauntered up and gathered around her. Their belligerent attitude drew interested glances from passers-by.

'Cassie doesn't want to see you again. Get it?' Vicky flicked back her highlighted hair and grinned. Everyone stared at Rose.

'I don't need you to deliver messages from Cassie,' Rose said curtly. 'I can speak to her myself.'

'She's making out she knows all about what happened to Cassie,' she turned to tell the others, twirling a piece of hair around her finger. 'But Cassie won't have you near her, will she, Rose?'

'Whatever,' Rose huffed, walking away.

Vicky shouted something else but Rose couldn't hear what it was. The rushing noise in her ears was too loud.

CHAPTER FORTY-THREE

SIXTEEN YEARS EARLIER

Rose knocked at Cassie's door and Jed answered.

Her mother had told her he'd returned home but Carolyn was still worried about him. Carolyn had told Stella he seemed to blame himself for Cassie's attack.

'She's in bed,' he said, staring blankly just above her head.

'I want a quick word with her,' Rose pleaded, taking a step forward. 'Please, Jed, just five minutes will do.'

Jed adjusted his stance so he filled more of the doorway.

'She's in bed and she left instructions not to be disturbed,' he said robotically.

She stared at him but there was no reaction.

'Why is she doing this?' Rose's calm countenance slipped. 'I've been her best friend for God knows how many years and she's treating me like a stranger.'

He stood stock still, his face impassive.

'Come on, Jed—' she softened her voice a little '—she's traumatised, it'll do her no good to stay upstairs on her own. You must be worried about her and I can help, you know I can.'

'Sorry, Rose, you can't come in.' He stepped back quickly, closing the door in front of her face.

She banged on the door in frustration and then turned away, tears of injustice spilling down her face. She understood that Cassie didn't want to see anyone, but this was *her*, for goodness sake.

Their friendship had taken a few knocks recently, mainly because of her relationship with Gareth, and Rose understood more now about what Cassie had been trying to tell her.

That's why she just wanted a few minutes alone with her. To tell her she knew now that she'd been *right*.

Just a few weeks ago, Cassie would have been asking for Rose as she lay suffering, not turning her away like this.

They needed each other now more than ever. Cassie was the only person Rose could really confide in.

Her dad would throttle Gareth if he knew how he'd treated her and Billy, even if in the process he lost the only chance of a secure future he'd had.

As she walked along Cassie's street, still smarting from Jed's abrupt rejection of her, a silver car drove very slowly across the bottom of the road. Rose thought nothing of it, until a couple of minutes later, when it drove past again.

She was too far away to be able to see the driver but she felt a little unnerved. The road was very quiet. There was no traffic and she hadn't seen another person walking yet.

She walked on for a minute or two. The car had gone now and she shook her head, had a little chuckle at her imagination.

It had probably just been someone who was lost or looking for a particular road. The village could appear to be a warren of winding back streets that all looked the same, if you weren't familiar with it.

She reached the bottom of the road and stepped out when all of a sudden, out of nowhere, the car sped towards her. She jumped back from the road onto the pavement and cried out as she slipped and fell, twisting her ankle.

She tried to get up but it was too painful. She'd have to shuffle back to the wall and use it as a prop to stand.

Through the pain of her ankle she heard the growl of an engine. She looked up to see the car, on the opposite side now; the driver's side window was down.

'Hello, Rose,' Gareth said, getting out of the car.

She tried to scramble to her feet but she could feel she'd sprained her left ankle. In seconds, Gareth was towering above her.

'I can help you into the car or I can drag you, Rosie,' he said pleasantly. 'It makes no odds to me.'

Rose looked up at him, fearful he could lash out at her at any moment. She had to get to her feet.

'Gareth, we talked about this. We're not together any more, I don't—'

'I just want to talk to you. That's all. Stop making such a big deal about it.'

She'd managed to lean most of her weight on her good leg. Leaning heavily against the brick wall next to her, she inched her way to standing.

'I can't talk right now, I have to get back home.'

He moved fast. One hand pincered her upper arm, the other grabbed a handful of hair. Rose yelped at the pain in her head and ankle as he half-dragged, half-lifted her across the street.

'Stop it,' she shrieked. 'Please, just leave me alone!'

Gareth released her hair and instead clamped his hand over her mouth. She kept screeching but the sound had been reduced to a mere muffled groaning.

Her eyes scanned the surrounding area wildly but there were no pedestrians or other cars around. Rose prayed that someone was watching, that someone could see *something* of her struggle from one of the terraced houses that lined the street. The villagers were a nosy lot as a rule and she had never felt more hopeful because of that.

Nobody knew where she was. Her parents didn't even know she'd been seeing Gareth or visiting his flat. Her father was blissfully unaware of anything that had been happening, that his future with the project was all but finished.

And Billy… poor little Billy, who'd sworn to Rose he wouldn't breathe a word of how Gareth had treated them. It had seemed the right thing to do at the time, to convince him to keep his mouth shut, but now she hoped and prayed he'd spill the beans when she didn't turn up at home.

Foolishly, she'd fallen for Gareth's assertion that they would just be friends. She thought she'd kept him onside.

Gareth bundled her roughly into the passenger seat and slammed the door. When he stalked around to the driver's side, she tried to open the door while the car was moving but he'd got some kind of a child lock in place because the handle rattled loose and useless in her fingers.

When the driver's door opened, Rose tried to lunge across. Gareth pushed her viciously back into her seat and hit her with the flat of his hand on the side of her head.

'Next time it'll be my fist, so shut the fuck up.'

Cowering, she glanced at him out of the corners of her eyes. Both his hands clutched the steering wheel as he hunched forward, eyes wide and staring at the road.

She didn't know who this person was any more.

When the car slowed outside his flat, Gareth turned to look at her.

'We can do this the easy or the hard way,' he said calmly. 'I just want to talk to you and then you can go home. I'm leaving the village soon, and if you act sensibly, your dad will still keep his job. I just want a chat, that's all.'

She'd planned to scream as loud as she could as soon as he opened the car door but what he said took the air from her lungs.

If she talked to him, it could still all be alright. Everything could turn out OK for her dad, and Gareth would soon be gone from their lives.

So she allowed him to help her climb the stairs to the upstairs flat. He seemed quieter now. Laughably, he actually seemed concerned about her again.

Inside, he settled her on the sofa.

'Back in a mo.' He smiled before heading for the kitchenette.

Rose unseeingly stared ahead. There was a dull ache, deep in her core, as the enormity of what she'd done hit her head on.

She had made such a grave error in trusting this man. She'd helped keep their liaison a secret, coerced Billy into keeping quiet, shut out her family and friends… all the people who cared about her had been lied to, hoodwinked.

And the worst part was that it had all been done with her knowledge. She'd been a willing party in Gareth Farnham's deceit.

A glass of orange cordial appeared in front of her face.

'I suppose your throat feels a bit raw after all that fuss you made out in the street,' he said.

Gareth was deluded. Dangerous. She needed to stay calm so he thought everything normal and get this chat over with as soon as possible. Then she needed to get herself safely home.

She had allowed this situation to go on for far too long; job or no job, it was time to speak to her father.

She took a deep draft from the glass. The cool, sweet liquid felt such a relief on the rawness of her throat. For a brief moment, the stupid part of her wondered if everything could be alright again, although she knew the answer, of course.

It wasn't long at all before she started feeling strange. He said something to her and that's when she realised there were two Gareths in front of her. As he laughed, his voice sounded slow and distorted.

She dropped the glass, held out her hands to him. Inside her head, the words formed perfectly, but the sound that came out of her mouth was just one, long, wailing cry.

CHAPTER FORTY-FOUR

SIXTEEN YEARS EARLIER

Rose woke up and, for a minute or two, she didn't know where she was.

The walls were plain white with no pictures. A pulled blind with a leaf print clung to the window. And only the occasional hum of a passing car on the road outside.

Then it hit her. She was in Gareth's bed.

She tried to turn her head but the thumping pain that struck her when she moved, even just a millimetre, was too much. She felt bruised and tender. Everywhere.

She sensed she was alone in the room and this was proven when the door opened and Gareth walked in with a tray.

'I made you tea and toast,' he said brightly. 'Sit up, princess.'

This isn't right, the voice in her head said. She knew this man was Gareth Farnham, her ex-boyfriend… but she couldn't remember how she got here. In this room.

And why was she in his bed?

She searched her memories but it felt as if someone had used an eraser inside her mind and scrubbed everything away.

She opened her mouth to speak but her tongue lay swelled and listless, refusing to form any words.

Gareth helped her sit up in bed and she cried out with the pain in her head.

'Take two paracetamols,' he said, matter-of-factly, shaking the foil pack in front of her.

She looked down and gasped. She was completely naked. She reached for the sheet and pulled it over herself.

Gareth laughed. 'Bit late for that, I've seen it all. And more. Got the evidence, too.'

He walked out of the room and she closed her eyes against the rampaging headache.

A flash of memory… *speaking to Jed at Cassie's door.*

She opened her eyes and heard a screech of brakes… *Gareth's car across the road.*

Rose reached for the mug from the tray and took a sip of tea and the next memory bite slid smoothly into her mind's eye… fighting and struggling to get away from Gareth's firm grasp… being forced into the car… and then…

CHAPTER FORTY-FIVE

ROSE

PRESENT DAY

I run out of Mike North's apartment block. And I mean *run*.

A woman and her small son enter the block and seeing me, stand aside, their mouths falling open with alarm. I crash down the stairs and stumble out into the fresh air.

Mike's dreaded words echo in my head: *I was never one hundred per cent certain we had the right man.*

There are so many feelings swirling about in my mind I can't identify them. All I know is that together they make me feel like running away and hiding in a small, dark place.

But my years of therapy are kicking in. Gaynor would never have let me get away with simply saying *I don't know* how I felt. She taught me to stand back and observe myself, to unpick each tangled rope of emotion, however painful.

So, when I get into the car, I sit for a moment and I do just that.

Anger.

It's taken me completely by surprise that I feel so angry at Mike. But if he had doubts at the time of the investigation, then why didn't he flag it up? He had a responsibility to us, to Billy… to himself… to uncover the truth and ensure justice was done.

Did he share his doubts with Mum and Dad? I'll never know.

I feel incredibly angry at myself for asking him the question in the first place. Can any detective ever be one hundred per cent certain that they've apprehended the true villain? I should never have broached the subject with Mike.

Fear.

I feel terror that the one thing I thought was certain beyond any doubt – the one thing the *entire village* was certain of – is now in the balance. Did Gareth Farnham kill Billy?

I visited Mike today in the hope he'd be able to help me with a dilemma and instead of resolving it, he's managed to double it.

If I listen to Mike then it will force my hand. I will feel, more than ever before, that I have to take action without delay.

The stress of an accusation might just finish Ronnie off... and he might be innocent.

He is frail and unwell and even if an interview is dressed up nicely by a sensitive police officer, the unadorned truth is that Ronnie will know what I suspect him of underneath.

The whole village will know that I have betrayed Ronnie. I'll have to leave this place, start again somewhere else, alone. Amongst strangers.

The fear stretches into unbridled fury when I think that just by going to the police, I might inadvertently start the process to free Gareth Farnham.

Maybe I sound like a really awful person but I don't want him free, roaming the streets. Even if he leaves me alone, he's a predator. Men like him don't change; he'd have his sights set on some other young, naïve girl within days.

He has ruined a lot of people's lives and whatever the do-gooders might say, the one thing I'm certain of is that the man deserves to stay behind bars for the rest of his life.

And yet, here I am, back full circle in my thoughts and it always comes down to this:

What if Ronnie did *kill Billy?*

What if – all the time he watched my family in agony and appeared to be a massive support – he was laughing behind our backs?

Old man or not… why should he be free to live his life now?

I start the car and a few minutes later I'm pulling out onto the Colwick Loop Road.

A deep, long honking noise makes me yelp out loud and I wrestle the steering wheel over to the left. I've wandered over to the middle of the bypass and an approaching lorry, coming the other way, has let me know in no uncertain terms.

'Sorry,' I mouth, as the enormous vehicle rumbles past me.

I lower the window slightly to get some air in.

This problem is going to end up killing me one way or another; either through stress or under the wheels of a HGV.

I reach into my handbag and take a swig from the bottle of water I brought with me. I wish Mike could have explained more about his feelings towards the investigation back then.

Was his doubt just a passing thing or had it been more than that?

He'd said that was why the case had really got to him and he'd explained about the extra time he'd put in, working at home each night.

What had he been doing during those extra hours? Looking for some missing clue or scouring interviews to spot a wrong word… or had it been something more than that?

I can hardly complain about Mike being evasive. I was the one who'd set the tone of our chat, with my 'speaking theoretically' so-called brainwave.

There's a single thing that shines like a beacon of truth in all the confusion. The one thing that can't be ignored no matter how many options I give myself: *Billy's blanket.*

It's just a matter of asking the right questions of the right people. Someone stuffed that blanket in a box in the Turners' spare room. Who, when and why… that's all I need to know.

CHAPTER FORTY-SIX

ROSE

PRESENT DAY

Half an hour later I arrive home. There's a car I haven't seen before outside Ronnie's house.

I decide I'll go home and change before I call round to see how he is on my way out to work. Taking care of Ronnie feels like being in the middle of a tug of war. Am I helping Billy's killer? Or am I caring for an elderly neighbour who is a genuine, wonderful person?

I try really hard to block such thoughts. It's the only way I can function.

I lock the door behind me, check everything looks as I left it downstairs and then climb up to my bedroom.

I peel off my jeans and top and realise my back is wet through. I feel so uncomfortable I decide to have another quick shower. Ten minutes later I feel fresher and get dressed in my black work trousers and white blouse.

I'm walking downstairs when I hear a low rumble and realise it's emanating from my own stomach. I haven't eaten since yesterday but the moment I think about food, my mind shuts off, revolted.

I remember being in this place once before. Back then, in the midst of the horror, controlling food somehow made me feel more in control of my life. I know now that this thinking isn't logical and it would make little sense to any sensible person but, nevertheless, I know myself enough to acknowledge this was *my* reality.

I have to eat; I know that. Just not now.

The home help lady is round at Ronnie's house.

'Hello,' she says brightly with an Eastern European accent as I tap on the kitchen door and walk in. 'I am Claudia, I will be coming here each day for one hour morning, one hour afternoon, to help Mr Turner while he recovers.'

'Hello, Claudia.' We shake hands. 'I'm Rose, Ronnie's neighbour.'

'Ah yes, he tells me about you, Rose. He says you are his angel! He is happy because his son is coming to visit.'

'Eric?' I'm surprised.

'Yes, Eric from Australia.' She beams.

I chew the inside of my cheek. 'How is Ronnie?'

'He is good. Would you like to take his drink up and I will bring his sandwich in one minute.'

Ronnie is sitting up in bed.

'Rose!' He smiles. 'Our Eric's going to be here in a few days. I gave him your phone number at the library to confirm the details, I hope that's OK.'

'That's fine, Ronnie.' I set his drink down on the bedside table and try my best to push all other thoughts away. He looks old and frail with his pyjamas on, stuck in bed. 'How are you feeling?'

'You know me, Rose—' he smiles weakly '—I'll be fighting fit in no time.'

'But for now you must rest, Ronnie,' Claudia scolds him playfully as she steps into the room. 'No fighting yet.'

'Tell Claudia what I was like when I was younger.' He winks. 'Strong as an ox, wasn't I, Rose?'

I freeze. I see Billy, chasing his kite into the woodland in the abbey. Ronnie, as he used to be, appearing from nowhere, grabbing my brother in a vicious headlock, dragging him into the bushes and—

'Rose?'

I unclench my fists and begin to breathe.

'Are you feeling a little unwell, Rose?' Claudia is concerned.

'I'm fine. I'm sorry, I have to go.' I turn to Ronnie, my eyes burning. 'I'll come round later, Ronnie, make you some tea and we can have a chat.'

He looks away from Claudia and stares at me.

'Is that OK with you?' I ask him.

'Yes,' he says, the hint of a smile on his lips. 'That's OK, Rose.'

CHAPTER FORTY-SEVEN

SIXTEEN YEARS EARLIER

Gareth had taken her phone away and there was no clock in here but Rose estimated she'd been awake a couple of hours.

The light in the room told her it was still early morning. Her memory, although not fully functioning, was patching things together now. The awfulness of what she remembered almost made her wish it had stayed blank.

The bedroom door opened. He was dressed for work and came in to sit beside her on the bed.

'You told me that we were finished. You said you didn't want to see me again, Rose. Can you imagine how that made me feel?' His voice was calm and smooth and that made her feel even more afraid. 'Tell me you didn't mean it.'

'I—' She reached for the right words. She'd learned to listen to Gareth's tone to determine how she should respond, but that had also got her into this mess. 'I think it's best if we just stay friends.'

'Are you fucking serious?' He stood up, towering next to her, his fists clenched.

'Don't hurt me anymore,' she cried out. 'You used to love me!'

He crouched down next to her. 'And I still love you, Rosie. But I'm sick of all the other people in your life trying to ruin our time together.'

'Who do you mean? Nobody even knows about us... apart from our Billy, that is.'

'He drives me crazy, hanging round us.'

'He's eight years old!' Rose said. 'He's just a kid and I love him more than—'

His features twisted and she bit back, realising what she'd said.

'More than what, Rose? More than me?'

'It's just an expression, saying that you love someone more than anything.' She sighed. She felt so tired and in pain and sick of saying the wrong thing.

'But you've never said you love *me* more than anything.' Gareth's front teeth dug into his bottom lip. 'You've only ever said that about him.'

'He's my brother!' she retorted.

'And I'm supposed to be your soulmate,' he growled.

Rose stayed quiet. He was impossible to reason with.

He stood up. 'You can't get away from me, Rose; you belong to me. If you try I'll ruin you and your family's life.'

He meant fire her father from his volunteer position, Rose supposed. But he was ruining her life right now. She'd never felt so unhappy and he'd hurt and threatened Billy. She wouldn't stand for that.

'I'm not your pet, Gareth. You don't own me,' she said, sounding braver than she felt. 'If people hear how you've treated me and Billy, there'll be real trouble.'

'Which is why I took the liberty of putting a little insurance policy in place.' He smirked and took a small camera out of his pocket. 'When I get these little beauties developed, nobody is going to believe anything dirty girl Rose says any more.'

She shivered as he laughed.

'I'm locking you in,' he said matter-of-factly. 'I'll be back at lunchtime, and, if you were wondering, the windows have locks and there's no phone here.' He waved the camera at her. 'Don't do anything stupid or these photos will be plastered on every lamppost in the village.'

'Why are you doing this?' she whispered.

'Because you're being difficult,' he said, walking to the door. 'And until you come to your senses, life won't be pleasant.'

He closed the door and she heard a bolt slide to, on the other side. A lock on the outside of the bedroom door?

It was as if he'd planned all along to keep her here.

CHAPTER FORTY-EIGHT

ROSE

PRESENT DAY

I look up from the computer screen to see Jim standing there, staring at me.

'Are you feeling OK, pet?' he asked. 'Only I've asked you twice now about what time you'll need me until today.'

'Sorry, Jim.' I click out of the online publishing catalogue I've been pretending to view. 'Just after closing time is fine, I need to get home today.'

For once, I actually can't wait to get home and lock the door behind me. Putting on this act is exhausting, and I just want to pull the blinds and curl up on the sofa.

Jim breathes a sigh of relief. 'That's great, Rose, thanks. Janice has a hospital appointment this afternoon, you see, and it'll be a bit tight to get her there unless I get off on time.'

'No problem.' I smile, feeling bad that he's had to ask.

'How's Ronnie?'

I look at him blankly.

'Ronnie,' Jim says again. 'Is he improving any?'

I swallow. I don't want to tell him Ronnie is home; the whole village will be round there visiting and I need to speak with him in peace later.

'He's feeling a bit better. They were busy on the ward this morning, they don't tell you much.'

'Aye.' He nods. 'Run off their feet, those poor nurses. They'll be looking after Ronnie, though. Best place for him until he's feeling fit again.'

'Yes,' I say.

Ronnie's face floats into my mind's eye: his well-worn features, his eyes crinkling when he laughs; his yellow teeth, narrowing towards the gum, the way his skin stretches over his mottled lips, and his sneering fury and banging on the kitchen window when he spots one of the local cats in his yard.

I stand up, suddenly eager to get away from Jim and Miss Brewster, who I've just spotted walking towards the counter.

'I'll be back in a sec,' I stammer, nearly knocking over my chair. 'I just need to—'

I storm past Jim to the staff bathroom and catch him sharing a concerned look with Miss Brewster. Inside the larger cubicle, I lock the door and lean against the cracked sink, staring into the mirror at my own pasty face and wild eyes.

How am I ever going to face Ronnie later? Just the thought of spending time with him again makes my flesh crawl.

Then I go the opposite way; when the feeling subsides, I start questioning myself.

There has simply got to be a logical reason for the blanket being there. I mean, if Ronnie had anything to do with what happened, why on earth would he keep such an important piece of evidence?

He could have burned it, dropped it into a public waste bin… anything.

It just doesn't make sense.

*

I'm tinkering with the book inventory database to kill time, when someone coughs. When I look up; a man and woman, both in dark suits, stand at the desk.

'Sorry!' I push my papers away. 'I was in another world altogether, there. Can I help you?'

The woman holds up the plastic laminated card at the end of her lanyard. 'Cynthia Colton and Greg Allsop from Notts County Council? We rather thought you'd be expecting us.'

Oh God. Oh God. *Oh God!*

The council's visit to inspect the library as part of the closure consultations. It has completely and utterly disappeared from my mind. I can't remember the last time I checked the library diary. It used to be my first and last job of the day.

'Goodness, is it that time already?' I tried desperately to settle my expression and back pedal. 'I'd remembered you were coming, of course, but time has just completely run away with me this morning, I'm afraid.'

They glance at each other.

From the corner of my eye I can see the children's reading corner hasn't been tidied yet after our toddler story time session just after lunch. I'm also behind with returns and piles of unshelved books are stacked around the edge of the curved reception desk like a small barrier. It's far from perfect.

'Can I get you a drink? Something hot, perhaps, or maybe a cool water?' I babble.

'We're fine, thanks, we haven't got that long.' Cynthia gives me a tight smile. 'As we said in our letter, it would be good to take a look around your facilities.'

'Of course.' I can sense I'm smiling too widely. 'I'll just give our caretaker, Mr Greaves, a nudge so he can give you a bit of a tour.'

I page Jim, trying not to look at Cynthia's reptilian eyes darting around the mess that is my desk right now. Any luck and I can signal to Jim to show them around the back office area and small yard first, while I whizz round and spruce things up a bit.

'You called, ma'am?' Jim appears in his usual informal manner, grinning in the doorway.

I cough. 'Err, yes. Cynthia and Greg have arrived for the inspection I told you about,' I say pointedly, widening my eyes at him to encourage him to play along. 'You were going to show them around, just a little tour of our facilities, if you remember?'

For a moment Jim looks perplexed and then he gets it. 'Ahh, yes. I remember now. Would you like to come through?'

I almost faint with relief when they trot out of the main library into the back. Jim grins and winks at me and follows them.

CHAPTER FORTY-NINE

ROSE

PRESENT DAY

With the worst possible timing, Mrs Brewster and Miss Carter come in at that very moment, chattering and laughing together.

'Afternoon, Rose,' Mrs Brewster calls as she begins to unload what seems like dozens of hardback returns onto my desk from the depths of her wheeled shopping trolley.

Ordinarily, I'd smile and engage in a bit of friendly chatter with our customers but not today. As fast as I'm trying to tidy the desk, Mrs Brewster is undoing it. I sigh and give up, walking over to the children's reading corner instead.

'You look flustered, Rose,' Mrs Brewster says. 'What's wrong?'

I look round furtively before saying in a low voice: 'The council officials are here to do an inspection.'

'Is this to do with closing down our library?' Miss Carter's nostrils flare.

'I'm afraid so,' I reply, nodding. 'As part of the consultation they have to do an inspection. So they can say how useless we are, I expect. Anyway, I forgot all about it and—'

Suddenly I can't remember what I want to say.

'Are you feeling alright, dear?' Miss Carter and Mrs Brewster glance at each other. 'You seem a little… disorientated.'

My mouth is dry and I'm sweating so much my top is sticking to my back and arms. I don't reply.

I hear Jim's booming voice.

'What do you expect us to do if we get rid of the buckets, like? We'd be swimming in water back there.'

'That's rather the point, Mr Greaves,' Greg replies in a monotonous tone. 'For health and safety reasons you shouldn't be occupying a flooding space at all.'

'It's only a few roof leaks, man,' Jim replies dismissively. 'When I was a lad, our house used to be full of buckets to catch the leaks and I managed to survive it.'

I try and take some deep breaths to keep relaxed but it's not working. I feel grateful it's not so cold that we need the heating on. If they knew the boiler failed nearly every other day, they'd certainly have something to say about that.

'I'll leave these two… *officers* with you then, shall I, Rose?' Jim growls when they all reach my desk.

'Thank you, Jim,' I say brightly. I turn to smile at Cynthia and Greg but they stare back, po-faced. They're obviously not too impressed with our back office.

'So, this is the main library area.' I lead them over to the far-side wall. 'We keep a good, wide range of fiction and non-fiction titles. And we try to keep the education section stocked with useful books relevant to the national curriculum. Miss Jennings, a local teacher, helps us to choose—'

'How many end-users do you have using the facilities at present?' Cynthia consults her keyboard. 'It looks as though your figures have declined steeply in recent years.'

'Customers, you mean? Readers?'

'We refer to them as end-users,' Cynthia says blankly.

'If the library closes, then what happens to all our jobs?' I blurt out. 'Is that it, we're just finished?'

'It might be you're selected to work elsewhere if there's a vacancy, perhaps a school, or—'

'I can't!' Moisture prickles on my forehead and I lean against a shelving unit until the dizziness passes.

'Are you alright, Miss Tinsley?'

'Yes.' I stand upright again. 'It's just that relocation isn't really suitable for me, you see. On… health grounds.'

'That's jumping the gun a little.' Cynthia sniffs. 'Nothing has been decided about the library's future as yet.'

We're coming back full circle in the library space now.

'And here we have our children's corner,' I say, managing to gather myself a little. 'It's very well used. The local primary school bring classes here once or twice a week during term-time and we also have mother and toddler story sessions on two lunchtimes each week.'

Cynthia's eyes widen. 'Looks as if it could do with a bit of a tidy!'

'Yes, it's a bit of a mess but a session just finished before you arrived,' I explain. 'There's only me working today but it will get done before we close.'

'I think it's safe to say the whole place needs re-carpeting,' Greg observes.

'We're doing our best, you know?' I hear myself say steadily. 'We're doing our best under difficult circumstances.'

I'm actually afraid that Mrs Brewster's eyes are going to pop out of their sockets at any moment but it's too late by then. I've gone and said it.

'We're well aware of that, Miss Tinsley—'

'I'm sorry, will you excuse me?' I push by them, heading for the back office. 'I'm sorry, I just… I just need a moment.'

CHAPTER FIFTY

ROSE

PRESENT DAY

How I've managed to get though the afternoon in this daze and propel myself out of the door, I honestly don't know, but I find myself walking home after work.

Earlier this afternoon, when the council officials left the library, I promptly burst into tears.

Jim, Mrs Brewster and Miss Carter all rushed to console me but I brushed their concerns away. I didn't feel at all worthy of their sympathy.

'It's not your fault, pet,' Jim kept saying. 'You seem very uptight; perhaps things are getting on top of you a bit.'

I said nothing and buried my face in the tissue Miss Carter proffered but, in my head, I berated myself. I'd known about the visit for over a week but, because my head was elsewhere, I'd done zero planning for it. In fact, worse still, I'd totally forgotten it was happening and I felt sure, judging by their faces, they gathered that.

I'm making mistakes, forgetting important stuff and blurting things out inappropriately without thinking about the consequences.

Ordinary, everyday things just seem too hard to think about on top of everything else. Even my safety checks are half-hearted today.

My stomach has been growling all morning, so loudly that one or two people have joked about it. Jim offered to pop out and get me a sandwich but I can't stand the thought of eating anything. It would have to be the right kind of food. Nothing else will do.

But it's not long before I stop feeling so nonchalant about my surroundings. My heart begins its fretful pumping and my mouth is dry as sawdust. I hasten my pace, just wanting to be home.

As I turn the corner, I see the familiar and reassuring sign of the local Co-op up ahead and, before I realise I'm making a conscious decision, my feet divert me there.

Inside, I whip round the aisles in record time, loading my wire basket with items. I don't go to the checkout; I stand instead in the short queue for the self-service where a new young man, who mercifully is not a master of polite conversation, stands sentry, ready to help any confused shoppers.

Just fifteen minutes later, I'm walking into the house with my two shopping bags.

I lock the door behind me, dump my shopping on the floor and close the front room curtains. Carrying the stuff through to the kitchen, I pull down the blind and double-check all the deadbolts are still in place on the door.

I pour a large glass of fizzy pop, sit at the kitchen table and begin the process that I know without doubt will bring me relief.

First, I eat the three chocolate eclairs. The choux pastry is so light I barely need to chew at all before the chocolatey cream slides down my throat.

As I fiddle with the packaging of the large lemon drizzle cake, I cram a couple of chocolate Hob Nob biscuits in my mouth and, finally, I start to feel the tension in my neck and shoulders begin to dissolve.

I don't bother with a plate; I cut a large slice of cake and deposit a dollop of extra-thick double cream on the end. My mouth is almost too full to chew but I manage just fine, relishing the moist, clogging sweetness that is everything.

I close my eyes, and all the worry – all the awful thoughts that plague me – disappear. All that matters is that wonderfully full sensation in my mouth that negates everything else around me.

Within minutes I have wolfed down half the tub of double cream and two-thirds of the cake. I start on the large tub of cookie dough-flavoured ice cream. It freezes my mouth and throat and numbs the pain, burying it under the weight of the calories.

When the tub is empty, I stagger into the living room and lie down on the settee. I close my eyes and try to ignore the roiling of my stomach, focusing on the warm, reassuring feeling that covers me now like a warm blanket.

I start to drift in that strange place betwixt sleep and wakefulness, and after a while I force myself to sit up. It's time.

I walk upstairs, unbuttoning my work blouse as I climb, discarding it on the top step. Outside the bathroom door I slip off my trousers and step into the room in just my underwear.

I lift up the loo seat and bend forwards, pressing my index and second fingers together and inserting them smoothly into my mouth. I press down on to my tongue and increase the pressure as my fingertips reach the back of my throat.

And voila! Up it comes in all its glory: the lemony, creamy, chocolatey goo that has wrapped itself around all my worries and taken them down the pan with it.

I feel so relieved I still have the knack.

After washing my face and hands and swilling out my burning mouth, I change into leggings and a loose T-shirt in my bedroom.

I flush the loo again, wipe around the rim and squirt some bleach in there before replacing the lid. I open the window a touch and sit on the top step while the air circulates for a few moments.

I don't leave windows at home open and unaccompanied, ever. It's one of my safety rules.

When I've closed it, I go back downstairs and clean up the mess in the kitchen. I sweep up the strewn lemony crumbs with the edge of my hand into a small pile on the worktop before depositing them into a pedal bin liner. In goes all the ripped packaging and the almost empty tub of cream.

I feel sick as I mop up the litter of creamy smears on the counter. My acid-burned throat is smarting so I take a sip of water but that only seems to make it worse.

I touch my lips gently and remember back to when the bulimia was at its worst. I had blisters on my lips and sores in the corner of my mouth. My throat was permanently sore and my skin broke out in spots.

But all I could see was that my ugly, fat body had got a little bit more acceptable and my mind had ceased its almost constant torture. It only lasted a short time before I felt the need to purge again.

I don't want to revisit that place. I silently promise myself I won't do this again.

I can't delay what needs to be done any longer. I put what I need in my handbag, pick up my keys, Ronnie's key and head for the back door.

It's time to talk to Ronnie.

CHAPTER FIFTY-ONE

ROSE

PRESENT DAY

It's only five-thirty in the afternoon but it feels like the end of a very long day.

I feel like a bit of a zombie, like my mind has drifted on to autopilot to get ordinary tasks done but nothing more. My conversation with Mike North this morning, the visit from the council officials, stuffing my face with food when I got home… it all seems fuzzy in my mind's eye. As if it happened a long time ago.

More's the pity it didn't because then I might have dealt with my problems better and move past them. I lock the back door and stand still in the garden for a few moments. The air is warm outside but the sky is grey and overcast. It's not the sort of evening for sitting out.

I look back at the house. The mortgage is paid on the property now; it belongs to me but I still couldn't manage without a job. If the library closes there is nothing else going around here, I'd definitely need to look for work out of the area.

What that might do to my anxiety levels, I can't afford to think about.

I turn my back on the house. I had the chance today to impress the council officers at work and I blew it. Yet worse than that was the feeling of panic, of lack of control in my own life. It brings back the worst sorts of memories, makes me fear I'm slipping again.

I push thoughts of the library closure away for now. There is something more pressing that needs to be dealt with as a matter of urgency.

I open the adjoining gate and walk through, leaving it open ready for when I return, after speaking to Ronnie. I tap on the back door and try the handle but, as I'd expected, it's locked. Claudia, the home help, must've locked up before she left.

I open it with my key and then lock it behind me once inside. At the bottom of the stairs I slip off my shoes.

'It's only Rose,' I call as I begin to climb the steps.

I hesitate on the landing, transfixed once more by the spare room door. I'm still finding it almost impossible to grasp that, for all these years, Billy's blanket has been concealed in there. Nobody, including me, ever thought to look there.

I hear a rattling cough, which brings me back to the present moment, and I turn the other way so I can try and forget the room is there.

When I knock on Ronnie's bedroom door, there is a hoarse reply. 'Come in.'

Ronnie's bedroom is gloomy and there's a sour smell in here. Claudia has only opened the curtains halfway, probably because during her visit earlier, the light outside was much brighter.

Ronnie is in bed, padded upright with several pillows.

I can see how much weight he's lost since he's been in hospital. His face looks gaunt and pale.

'Hello, Ronnie,' I say, forcing a little smile. 'First things first, do you need help getting to the loo?'

He shakes his head. 'Claudia only left about an hour ago.'

'OK,' I say, and sit on the end of his bed. 'How are you feeling?'

'I'm tired,' he says, subdued. 'I feel really tired, Rose.'

He does look tired to be fair but I can't help wondering if he's paving the way to evade speaking to me. I told him earlier, in no uncertain terms, that I wanted a chat…

He says he's not hungry but that he'll have a cup of tea.

Downstairs, I put the kettle on and then stand looking out of the small window on to the bleak concrete yard, wondering how I'm going to broach the subject of finding Billy's blanket.

Ronnie has been really poorly – still is – so it's quite possible his memory is patchy. It might be a good idea to get him generally thinking about the past first, with no pressure attached.

I take up his tea and two digestive biscuits.

He leaves the biscuits on the plate and sips the tea, watching me over the top of his mug.

'You don't look that well yourself, Rose.' He frowns and his voice crackles like screwed-up paper.

'I'm OK,' I say.

'Your cheeks look a bit flushed like they used to be before. When you were ill.'

I ignore the comment.

'Have you taken your tablets?'

'Yes,' he says, nodding.

'When I came through the gate just now, I started thinking about some of the parties we'd have in the garden,' I say lightly. 'When you and Dad would crank the barbecue up. Remember that?'

He takes another sip of his tea and makes a small grunt at the back of his throat.

'Happy days. Where did all those years go, eh, Ronnie?'

'I don't know.' He sighs. 'But I wish I had them back. I'd do things differently then.'

My ears prick up.

'Like what? What would you do differently?'

I hope I sound casual but inside my heart starts banging. Sometimes, when people get old and ill, they decide, on impulse, to unburden themselves. Maybe this is one such moment.

'I wouldn't work as many hours for one thing.' He clears his throat. 'The money came in handy, it gave us a good life, but I wish I'd have spent more time with little Eric and with Sheila.'

'You did your best,' I tell him. 'I bet most of the men round here feel the same. You all worked so hard down the mine.'

'Aye. Didn't know the government would shaft us then though, did we? Thought we'd all keep our jobs for life.'

I nod.

'And… I—' he hesitates and the air around us seems to crackle with electricity '—I regret what happened with Billy,' he says, his voice dropping to a whisper.

CHAPTER FIFTY-TWO

ROSE

PRESENT DAY

'What do you mean by that, Ronnie?' My throat's tightened and the word comes out strangulated. 'What do you regret?'

'I know it's painful for you to even hear his name, Rose. But something's tortured me ever since that night.'

I hold my breath and stare at my old neighbour. He seems to move closer and then further away and he's speaking but his words sound vague as if they're bleeding into each other.

He's going to tell me about the blanket. He's going to confess everything.

'Rose?' Ronnie raises his voice and everything sounds clear again.

'Sorry—' my eyes focus again '—what did you just say?'

'I said, I blame myself that we didn't find him on the search,' Ronnie said, turning his face to the window and the fading light. 'I guided the volunteers towards the lakes and the abbey, and away from the residential area of the grounds. Away from the bushes where he… where it happened. I deeply regret that.'

I stare at him. I'd never considered that Ronnie had had the power back then, as organiser of the village search, to divert the volunteers away from Billy's body. If he'd had anything to do with Billy's death, it would have been the perfect foil. These days the police would have taken control of every last detail but back then things were different.

'Are you alright, Rose?'

I tear my eyes away from him. He'd seemed to remember the past perfectly well just now, despite his insistence yesterday that he couldn't recall anything at all.

'I suppose you did what you could,' I mumble, trying to keep him engaged. 'Back then, I mean.'

A dread settles over me as I realise I'll never get a better time than this to talk about the spare room discovery. This is my one chance, probably my *last* chance, to get information out of Ronnie, because soon I've got to decide what to do about the crucial new evidence.

Without speaking, I reach for my handbag and close my fingers over the clear plastic bag within it. I pull it out and place it on the bedspread between Ronnie and me.

The red blanket, although faded, sits on Ronnie's pale bedding like a puddle of spilt blood.

His eyes settle on it and he puts down his mug on his bedside table.

'Do you remember this, Ronnie?' I ask him gently. 'It's Billy's blanket.'

'I – I'm not sure,' Ronnie replies, his fingers worrying at the edge of the quilt. 'Since I fell, my memory is patchy, Rose. It keeps coming and going.'

'Billy used to take it everywhere with him. He had it on the day he was taken. I saw it in his rucksack as he left the house. The police tried to find it for weeks afterwards.'

Ronnie can't seem to tear his eyes away from the blanket.

I keep my voice firm and level. 'When you were in hospital I found this blanket in a box. In your spare room, Ronnie.'

He shakes his head.

'Yes. I did find it in there and I need to know how it got there.' I look at his baffled expression. 'You understand what I'm saying, don't you, Ronnie? The police searched everywhere for this blanket and then I find it sixteen years later in *your* house. I can't ignore that fact; I'd be failing Billy.'

'But… how… I don't know why it's there, Rose. I mean, if Billy had it on the day he went missing, then how can it be *here*?'

He's either acting very stupid because he's playing it smart or he's genuinely confused. I can't figure out which it is.

'That's exactly my dilemma, Ronnie.' I hesitate and then, realising that the seriousness of the situation overrides the risk of upsetting him, I continue. 'Only the person who harmed Billy could have his blanket, do you see? It's the only possibility.'

Ronnie frowns and nods. He narrows his eyes and looks upwards. 'But that still doesn't explain how it got in here,' he muses.

I've spelled it out as clearly as I can without outright accusing him of having something to do with my brother's murder and that hasn't worked.

I take a breath.

'The thing is, Ronnie, when I go to the police, they're going to want to know—'

'The police?' He's already pale but any remaining colour drains from his face.

'Yes. The blanket is a crucial piece of evidence. I can't just pretend this hasn't happened.'

'No, but—' he raises a shaking hand to his mouth ' —they might think I've had something to do with Billy's death… What will my Eric say?' His eyes well up and he brings his hand to his forehead. His breathing is sporadic.

I stand up and rush to him.

'Breathe, Ronnie. Breathe.' I press the glass of water Claudia has left on the side to his lips and he takes a tiny sip. 'It's OK.

Don't get stressed out, I just had to ask. You understand that, don't you, Ronnie?'

'Yes,' he says in a small voice.

'Let's leave it there for now; you can't get this stressed when you're trying to recover.' I hear myself say the words and part of me screams in frustration. But a bigger part just cannot reconcile this frail old man with hurting my brother. 'There's just one thing I have to ask you again, Ronnie. You specifically told me not to come upstairs when they took you into hospital. Even if you can't remember saying it, can you think why that might be? That you wouldn't want me to come up here?'

He shuffles against his pillow and closes his eyes. When he opens them briefly, his mouth trembles.

'It's the stuff in the ottoman.' His voice shakes as he reaches for my hand and I let him touch me. 'I'm so ashamed, Rose. It's been a burden over the years. I've wanted to tell someone for so long but—'

I jump up and dash to the bottom of the bed, flinging open the top of the heavy carved wooden lid of the ottoman.

'Rose, please—'

I hear the hum of his words but I can't make any sense of them. I did search in here but…

I pull out the sheets, cast them aside. Nothing…I keep going. Blankets, pillowcases. I look up at him in frustration.

'Inside a folded sheet, there's an envelope—'

I pick up the neatly folded bedding again, shake out the sheets one by one and then – the faint crackle of paper and my fingers close around a large envelope. I lift it out and sit with it in my lap.

Ronnie is still speaking, rattling on and on about family and loss and… I zone his voice out and, with quivering fingers, I remove the top from the box.

It's just paperwork. I swallow down the lump that's rapidly rising in my throat and take a breath. I unfold the first document; a birth certificate with a name I don't recognise.

'He was born George but Sheila was hell-bent on changing that, you see.'

The next three folded papers are death certificates. The scrawled writing of the registrar swims before my eyes.

'Our first little Eric only lasted a week but the second, he was a stronger chap and we were blessed with him until he was five months old.' I look at Ronnie, aghast. I don't fully understand what he's telling me but it's too late to stop him now.

He is smiling, looking towards the light, and I realise he isn't here anymore. In his head he has time-travelled to the past. I say nothing and suddenly his head jerks back to me.

I unfold the next yellowed sheet and hold it to the light. A horror clouds Ronnie's face when he sees the adoption certificate.

'He doesn't know, Rose! Eric doesn't know he's adopted.' Fat tears roll down his pinched, wrinkled face. 'I know it was wrong, not to tell him, but… it would've broken Sheila's heart. She had to believe it was true, you see. That he was really *ours*.'

'Ronnie, I—'

'She would never talk about it. I tried once or twice but it made her ill. Eric has a right to know but... I've been so weak, so ashamed of the secret. I've just left everything as Sheila wanted it so I could try and forget, but these past few years it's loomed much larger in my mind.'

I think about the untouched memories and items in Ronnie's house. Cupboards and boxes full of stuff that he can't bear to part with, or so I thought.

Turns out he's been afraid to face the secrets of the past.

I let him ramble on as, with a certain shame, I refold the highly personal papers in front of me. Not all of what Ronnie says makes sense – but he explains how Sheila feigned pregnancy and they adopted a three-month-old boy called George Holland, an orphan who became Eric Turner, their son.

'After Sheila died I became terrified that it would somehow get out that Eric was adopted and that he'd hear about it through village gossip. He might never speak to me again and I couldn't bear that, I…' Ronnie swallows hard and turns his wizened hands over and studies them. 'I thought about destroying the paperwork, of course, but that wouldn't make the truth disappear, would it, Rose?'

I shake my head slowly and think how hiding Billy's blanket didn't make the awful truth of what happened to him disappear.

'I couldn't bring myself to do it. I already felt such an ogre for lying to Eric all these years, I suppose I just accepted that when I'm gone, he would find the truth.'

'That's why you told me not to go upstairs?'

Ronnie nodded. 'Stupid, I know. I never go out because I'm guarding Eric's secret, you see. When they carried me off to hospital I thought that was it, I was a-goner. I wanted Eric to find the truth when he cleared the house.'

Ronnie closes his eyes and I adjust the pillows behind him a little so he can rest his head back comfortably.

He appears to be falling asleep but then his eyes flick open.

'I'm so sorry you found Billy's blanket here, Rose. I swear, I don't know how it got there.' His long, cool fingers grip my own, vicelike. 'You have to believe me, Rose. I didn't know.'

I press my lips together, as close to a reassuring smile as I can manage, and I extract my fingers from his.

As Ronnie dozes, I put Billy's blanket back in my handbag and leave the room a little shell-shocked but with a new sense of resolve.

Ronnie has unburdened himself with a secret he's kept for the best part of fifty years. He must be very good at keeping secrets. Is he protecting himself or someone else by denying the knowledge of Billy's blanket or is he telling me the truth?

What's clear is that there is only one path of action available to me now.

I have to speak to someone who could answer all my questions and get to the truth far quicker than the police ever could.

Despite my promise to Dad, I know now that I have no choice but to contact Gareth Farnham.

CHAPTER FIFTY-THREE

SIXTEEN YEARS EARLIER

Things moved fast after that, although Rose wasn't aware of much of it.

The fever took her mid-morning and she slept through everything in a soupy daze, permeated only by light and the occasional noise.

She opened her eyes briefly when her father entered Gareth Farnham's bedroom and took his daughter into his arms.

'She wanted to be here, with me,' Gareth Farnham shouted at his back as Ray carried his daughter out to the car. 'She's an adult, you can't tell her what to do.'

Back at the house, Dr Nadin came round and checked her over. With Ray's permission, he took a blood test.

'I think she may have been drugged,' he said before leaving.

Stella had never seen Ray so angry.

'Calm down,' she said. 'You have to calm down, Ray.'

'There are witnesses to him forcing Rose into his car, Stella,' he yelled, his eyes shining. 'Look at her. Look what he did to her.'

An ex-miner on Cassie's street had seen everything but had been caring for his grandson and hadn't walked round to tell Ray until the next morning.

'I thought it was just a lover's tiff,' he shrugged when Ray asked why he hadn't called the police.

Ray called to see Carolyn then, to ask if she'd seen Rose, and Jed had told him about his daughter's relationship with Gareth Farnham.

'She's ditched Cassie, and when you think she's out with her college mates, she's round at his flat,' Jed told him almost with relief. 'It's been going on for ages behind your back, Ray.'

Ray's legs had almost given way. Carolyn made him strong black coffee.

'I'm sorry,' he kept saying. 'I know you've got your own problems.'

When his strength returned, Ray drove over to the regeneration site. Farnham was talking to council officials over by the proposed fishing lake.

Ray covered the rough ground in moments and seized Gareth's lapels, almost lifting him off his feet.

'What the devil—' The officials scattered.

'He abducted my daughter, took her against her will and… and… he's been having sex with my daughter!' Ray screamed as the other volunteers tried to pull him off Gareth. 'She's barely eighteen and he's almost thirty. I trusted you, Farnham. You bastard!'

Ray Tinsley's arm braced and then he let his fist fly, feeling the satisfying crunch of Farnham's nose as he made contact.

Rose woke up in her own bed. Her mother sat at her side, weeping.

'I'm sorry, Mum,' she whispered.

'Don't think about that now,' Stella whimpered. 'You need to get yourself well. There'll be plenty of time to talk through what happened.'

Her father nodded and Rose could see his pride was wounded.

'Dad, I – I shouldn't have lied. Your job, I—'

'We're looking to the future now, Rose,' Ray said, inspecting his already-bruising knuckles. 'Farnham has been suspended and they've put a temporary manager in who has asked me to carry on working with the project.'

Rose breathed. In, out, in out.

Her dad was going to be fine.

'Nobody's seen Farnham for days,' Stella told her gently, at the weekend. 'We think he's left the village but – if you'd just press charges for—'

'Mum, please. I just want to forget what's happened and make a fresh start.'

'Leave it, love, for now.' Ray placed his hand on Stella's arm. 'Rose is an adult now. She has to decide for herself.'

She couldn't share with them why. She couldn't tell them about the photographs Gareth had taken.

If he shared them around the village as he'd threatened, if her friends and family saw them… she'd never dare show her face again.

Her face brightened when Billy walked in the room.

'Is it windy out?' she asked him.

He nodded, his face beaming. He knew what Rose was getting at. 'Windy enough for the kite!' he chuckled.

'Come on then,' Rose said, standing up. 'Let's not waste it: kite flying at the abbey it is.'

'Yesss!' Billy punched the air in glee and they all laughed at him.

She'd neglected her brother for far too long, Rose thought, as she pushed her feet into her trainers. She intended to put that right along with a lot of other things. Gareth Farnham had left the village, there was no reason for her to be afraid any longer.

Her mum had spoken to the college a couple of days ago and they'd agreed she could get back on to the course next week if she felt well enough. Her parents, whom she'd thought so restricting, were helping her start again. She realised now that all they'd ever tried to do was keep her safe and love her.

The last couple of weeks with Gareth were a nightmare she'd been lucky enough to escape from, thanks to the people around her.

Cassie still wouldn't see her but that was a bridge she felt sure she'd cross in time.

Rose and Billy walked across the village to Newstead Abbey, chatting all the way.

Weak rays of sunlight broke through the scattered clouds and even the wind felt quite warm. Rose had only needed to wear a cardigan and hardy Billy was ruddy-cheeked, wearing just a T-shirt, despite Stella's fretting.

The abbey grounds were dotted with people but not nearly as busy as it was in high summer.

Rose had bought the kite for Billy's birthday in March but they hadn't really seen many windy days like this one. Lots of rain and storms, but kite weather was rare. That's why she knew they had to seize the day and it was the perfect chance for her to spend some time with her brother. To start to make up for her bringing trauma into his life with her terrible choice of boyfriend.

The sun felt warm on her face, Billy was full of life and wonder, and Rose felt good. She felt hopeful for the future and grateful for what she had.

Billy had disappeared into the rhododendron bushes to rescue his kite and hadn't yet emerged.

Rose sat on the grass with her legs stretched long and watched from afar. She turned her face towards the sun and tried to keep her thoughts positive.

A coach party poured from the car park and headed down towards the abbey, obviously here for the tour of the house and Lord Byron's ancestral home.

Rose lay flat and closed her eyes.

She felt exhausted all the time just lately but her mum had said it was completely normal after what she'd been through. It had only been a matter of days, after all. Sitting here amongst nature, she felt more relaxed than she'd done for weeks and weeks.

She just wanted everything to feel normal again and that included her friendship with Cassie.

She could understand Cassie had felt betrayed, felt Rose had chosen her new relationship with Gareth above their lifelong friendship, but, once she had the chance to explain everything, Rose felt sure they could get back on an even keel.

The police had so far drawn a blank in terms of finding Cassie's attacker and Stella said the village grapevine reported screaming arguments from their household with Carolyn being worse for wear with drink day and night.

The faces, voices, events of the past week swirled and merged in her head. She felt warmth on her face and the delicious coolness of the grass beneath her bare arms. She let her mind drift… relaxed into the blur of shapes and colours drifting behind her closed lids…

The bang of a car exhaust from the parking area caused Rose to shoot up to standing within seconds. Had she fallen asleep? Perhaps just for a few minutes but that was all. The coach party must have all funnelled into the house now as they were nowhere to be seen.

'Billy!'

Rose glanced at her watch. He'd been gone over ten minutes now, she thought with alarm. Then she realised the little scamp was probably hiding from her. It wouldn't be the first time.

She used her hand as a visor against the sun and scanned the long, bush-lined road leading to the multi-million pound residential properties located within the abbey grounds.

Rose bit her lip. The kite had crashed down over there somewhere and Billy had insisted on going to fetch it alone.

'I'm not a baby, Rose,' he'd complained when she'd begun to walk with him.

But now, from where she stood, it seemed quite a way away… further than she'd originally thought. She grabbed her cast-off cardigan and began striding towards the area Billy had disappeared into.

'Billy!' she called. 'Time to go home now.'

She looked around her as she walked. There were still a few people around but the visitors seemed to have thinned out all of a sudden.

'Billy?'

No response, and the further she walked up the road, the quieter it became.

'Billy! Stop messing about. Come out here, right now!'

What if he'd tripped over a branch or a root and hit his head on a rock or something? Her mother would throttle her.

Rose remembered that very thing had happened when she'd been on a school trip to Cromford Mill in Derbyshire. The boy had tripped on the stony ground and bashed the side of his head. He'd needed stitches and the trip had to be cut short.

Rose neared the area she'd last seen Billy before he'd disappeared into the bushes. Another month and the rhododendrons would be in full bloom, but for now it was a sea of thick, shiny, green foliage.

'Billy, come out. Please… you're scaring me now.'

It was true. Her heart was banging against her chest wall like a tin drum and her mouth and throat were dry with fear.

For five full, long minutes she walked up and down the long road, stepping into the bushes wherever there was a gap, searching everywhere for her brother.

But Billy was nowhere to be found.

CHAPTER FIFTY-FOUR

SIXTEEN YEARS EARLIER

Virtually the whole village carried on searching well into that first night.

Rose thought how the field looked fairy-like in the dark, the horror masked by a sea of torch light that looked like lanterns from where she and her family stood at the window.

DCI North had been forced to physically restrain Ray from leaving the house to join the search party.

'I need you to stay here, Ray,' he'd said firmly but kindly. 'Your family need you here. Leave the search to everyone else, we have more than enough people.'

Rose and her mother held each other and watched the strong, dependable man they loved crumple into his chair, bow his head and quietly begin to sob.

DCI Mike North held up his hand as they moved to comfort Ray.

'My advice is to let the emotion come,' he said softly.

When she'd run back home from the abbey, breathless and faint with fear, her mother had been in the kitchen, holding an enormous bouquet. 'They're for you.' She smiled as Rose flung open the door. Then her face changed as she registered Rose's hysteria.

The detective was very interested in Gareth Farnham. He spoke to Rose in the kitchen, with the door closed.

'Tell me everything,' he said, pencil poised above his notebook. 'From the very beginning.'

So she did.

'I've been such a fool,' she whispered at the end. 'Everything that's happened… it's all my fault. I brought Gareth Farnham into our safe, ordinary lives.'

'You're wrong, Rose; you're a victim,' DCI North tried to reassure her. 'You've been controlled. Groomed.'

'But I chose to stay with him!' she cried out.

DCI North pressed his lips together and looked at her. 'Listen to yourself because it's right there in your very words. The control. Farnham was good at it, Rose. You didn't even know it was happening. You thought you had a choice but, in reality, you never did. Think back, even to the small things; somehow you would've ended up doing everything *he* wanted…'

Rose began to object again and then stopped.

The ice cream flavour she ate, the film choices; no matter what her initial preference was or how he'd ask for her opinion, they always ended up with Gareth's recommendation.

Later, of course, there were no initial choices. Gareth would tell her what would be happening and she'd simply accept it.

If she didn't, there would be hell to pay; it just wasn't worth the fight.

'How could I have been so stupid,' she whispered, knotting her fingers together. 'How could I not have seen it?'

'Don't beat yourself up, Rose,' DCI North said grimly. 'That's the nature of control. It's pervasive; it creeps up on you. Believe me, you are not alone.'

Yet even as the detective uttered his supportive words, deep inside, Rose still felt as if she was to blame for Gareth's behaviour.

She felt responsible for this awful, awful mess.

All through the early hours the Tinsley family sat silently, wrapped in blankets, staring unseeingly into space.

As dawn came, a thick wall of silence fell over the house and the street. Then, a noise… a scuffling sound out in the yard. Could it be Billy, found his way home?

She dashed to the window and looked down on to the dark, still garden. Her heart sank back down.

'Where did you go, Billy?' Rose whispered, a solitary tear rolling down her swollen face.

But nobody answered.

A few hours later, at around seven-thirty, Rose decided to walk over the road to the playing field. She had to get out of the house and away from the oppressive air. She knew she was trying to run away from herself, from her thoughts. Impossible but still… It was raining and dreary and everyone else had had the sense to stay inside, the village search party due to reconvene at 9 a.m.

Rose yelped and jumped away when a familiar voice spoke behind her, chilling her to the bone.

'Rose, please listen to me. Just give me a couple of minutes to explain.'

Rose turned away so he couldn't see her shaking. 'Go away, or I'll start screaming, I'll ring the police.'

Her breath left her and she gulped in more air. Rapid, shallow inhalations that couldn't begin to fill her lungs.

'You know I'd never do this.' Gareth touched her arm from behind and she jumped away. 'You know I'd never hurt Billy.'

'I don't know that!' She whipped round to face him again, heat spiralling up from her solar plexus. 'You said he was a nuisance. You got so angry with him and hurt him before we split up.'

'That doesn't mean I'd hurt him, Rose!'

'You said Cassie would wish she hadn't been born and the next day she was attacked. *Raped.*' Her eyes darted around the field, across the road, searching for other villagers but there was no-one.

'Is that really what you think of me? After how I've loved you, shown you such respect?'

She shook her head and stared at him incredulously. 'You are *deluded*! The things you did to me – the photographs you took and threatened me with…'

'Oh Rose! I never took any photographs. I was just bluffing. You have to believe me.'

But Rose's days of believing anything Gareth Farnham said were over.

She saw, as if for the first time, the lines of discontent between his brows, his worn, grey complexion… but something in his eyes pinned her feet to the floor and she realised he completely believed his own words.

He really believed that he'd been respectful to her, even after drugging her and keeping her a prisoner!

At that moment, she felt more afraid than ever and began to walk briskly back towards the street.

'Rose, I need you to do something for me. Please. The bouquet I bought for you and left at the door – I've looked everywhere for the receipt. I know the florist gave me one because she handwrote it in front of me but it isn't in my wallet. I've turned the flat upside down and the car. I think I must've stuffed it in the bag wrapped around the bottom. I paid cash but it will show I was well out of the area at the time Billy went missing.'

He wanted her to help him escape arrest, that's what this was about. He wanted her to help him get away with whatever he'd done with Billy in the same way he'd cleverly convinced her before not to tell the police the comment he made about Cassie wishing she wasn't born the night before she was attacked.

'I'm not listening to your lies any more. If you really want to help me then tell me what you've done with my brother.'

'Rose, please!' He grasped her arm and she immediately shook him off.

Silently, the power had shifted between them. Rose thought for a moment about the things Gareth had said and done to her. She thought about the way he'd controlled her, which she'd been unable to grasp until now… until DCI North had made her understand.

It was as if a veil had been lifted and now everything made sense: each cunning step he'd taken, isolating her from friends and family, domineering her in every way, even when they'd been in bed together.

And the lies… so many lies.

'Stay away from me, you bastard,' she hissed.

His mouth fell open as she turned and walked away.

She expected him to call her name, to run after her, plead with her – even threaten her to help him escape whatever he'd done to Billy. Anything.

But he didn't.

He never said a word and Rose did not look back.

When Rose got back to the house, her parents were talking to the police in the living room.

She stood in the kitchen and looked at the long wooden cupboard in the corner. It was in here that Stella stored all the plastic carrier bags from her trips to the supermarket and from her other purchases.

It was there Rose would've stuffed the bag that had been wrapped around the bottom of Gareth's dripping bouquet of Stargazer lilies that had been waiting for her when she returned from the abbey.

She'd initially thought they were from well-wishers until she'd read the small card in Gareth's handwriting.

She'd immediately dumped them in the bin outside.

She'd felt so bad for the flowers; they were dazzling… such incongruous beauty amidst the horror of Billy's disappearance.

She did not open the cupboard door to search for the receipt.

She stood and considered why Gareth's words were still rattling around in her head.

She'd always considered herself to be a fair person. A *pushover*, Cassie would say. But Rose had always tried to see the good in people; it was just in her make-up.

Unfortunately, she had tried to see the good in Gareth Farnham for far too long.

It had resulted in her being controlled; some might say brainwashed. Maybe it had resulted in her best friend being brutally attacked… would she ever know the truth?

Rose shook her head and looked again at the cupboard.

Periodically, the bags built up and Stella had a good clear out. Perhaps she already had done so and Rose was too late.

Regardless, although she didn't want to believe another word Gareth Farnham said, if she didn't thoroughly check now she would always wonder. Rose's hand hovered above the handle.

Did she want to know? What difference did it make, really?

CHAPTER FIFTY-FIVE

SIXTEEN YEARS EARLIER

Two days after Billy went missing, the village had their major suspect.

Farnham had something to do with Billy's disappearance; everyone was saying so. And if she was honest, in her heart, Rose knew it, too. Just as she knew on some level it was no coincidence that Cassie had been attacked after his barbed comments.

The thought of him doing that… of what happened to Cassie… it made her want to throw up. But she couldn't think about that at the moment; only Billy filled her head.

Finding him was all that mattered and she knew Gareth would not tell her anything that could help because all he cared about was himself. He was still trying to enlist her to help prove his innocence when he was clearly as guilty as hell.

He was currently the major suspect in the investigation. Nottinghamshire Police kept taking him in, questioning him and then letting him go.

Villagers had reported seeing Gareth with Billy, shaking him, pulling him by the arm in the street when the family thought the child was playing down the field with his schoolmates.

Rose had spotted the odd bruise on Billy and asked him about it, worried he was being bullied. She'd just not realised a grown man was doing it.

The last straw for her had been when Gareth had been aggressive with Billy in front of her and she had told the police this. She had also told them about Gareth's comment about making Cassie's life a misery.

She point-blank refused to cover for him any more.

It was as if Rose had swallowed a phial of truth serum and she could now see Gareth for what he was: sly, conniving, *dangerous*.

She couldn't trust herself when it came to Gareth Farnham. But she could trust others, and everyone she cared about and whose opinion she valued thought the same thing.

Gareth knew where Billy was.

She grasped the handle and pulled open the cupboard door. Crouching down, she pulled all the tangled plastic bags out on to the kitchen floor and began sorting through.

She couldn't remember the colour or logo on the bag that had contained the flowers. She stuffed all the obvious supermarket ones in a bag and pushed them back into the cupboard. That left about a dozen others.

Her eyes were drawn to a pink bag with silver writing. She reached for it with a slightly shaking hand.

The writing read: Simpkin the Florist. She shook out the creases and opened up the top.

There was a small, handwritten white receipt chit inside. She hesitated and listened to the continuing hum of voices in the other room. Once she was satisfied nobody would be walking in anytime soon, she turned her attention back to the bag.

With shaking hands Rose smoothed out the receipt on the floor in front of her.

She ironed it out repeatedly with the edge of her hand, delaying the moment she would need to look at it.

She scanned down to the bottom of the receipt. It was unusually detailed. The smooth, looped handwriting recorded they were purchased at 3.26 p.m. on the afternoon Billy went missing.

Rose sat back on her haunches and the receipt slipped from her hands, fluttering in the slight breeze from the open window.

At this exact time, she and Billy were still flying the kite at the Abbey.

Gareth had apparently been in Derby – at the florist's. It would have taken him at least forty minutes to get back to Newstead. Theoretically, he could've taken Billy but the timeline would be tight. Very, very tight.

Of course, that was only if he was telling the truth.

She wasn't sure when it had started but Rose became gradually aware that there were hushed voices in pockets all around the house but never in her earshot.

Any sense of time had long ago slipped through her fingers in this new hell. It was either night or day and that was the extent of her awareness. The knowledge that Billy was still missing was all that filled her head.

She could hear them now, low, worried voices in the kitchen. She crept halfway down the stairs to listen but still couldn't decipher any words amongst the low, concerned hum.

A WPC, Collette, Rose seemed to recall her name was, appeared at the bottom of the stairs.

'Hi Rose—' her voice sounded too bright '—nothing happening down here. Why don't you just relax in your room a while?'

Was she serious? *Relax*?

'Nobody else is relaxing.' Rose frowned, stomping down the last few steps. 'What are they talking about in there?'

The police officer's eyes darted to the closed kitchen door.

'I'll ask your mum to pop up to see you shortly, if you like.'

'It's OK, I'm down here now.'

Rose pushed open the kitchen door and the low voices immediately stopped. Her parents, DCI North and a couple of the other villagers, all looked at her, their eyes wide.

'Have you found him?' Rose cried out, her eyes darting to her mother's pale face. 'Have you found Billy?'

'No, Rose. We haven't found Billy yet,' DCI North said.

'What, then?' She rushed up to her father, grasped his upper arm and shook it. 'Tell me, Dad… what's happened?'

The room was silent. The air crackled around them as if it were filled with static. Ray Tinsley's whole body tensed, and then he sighed and his shoulders sagged.

'I'm so sorry, Rose—' he pulled her close to him '—it's Cassie.'

CHAPTER FIFTY-SIX

SIXTEEN YEARS EARLIER

Afterwards, the only thing she clearly remembered was the primal wailing noise that had filled the room.

It had begun as a low growl and spiralled into a shrill scream.

Her mother's hands had flown up to her ears and her father had stepped away from her, his mouth open and hopeless.

Rose had crumpled to the floor.

It was only when she'd begun to sob that the screaming had stopped.

When Rose woke, the room was bright with beams of sunlight bouncing off the white walls.

There would be no happy reunion, no holding her friend and remembering the good times together.

Cassie was dead.

'She just couldn't cope after the attack, she overdosed on her sedatives,' her mother had explained. 'It's so, so sad but you must focus on getting stronger, Rose. We have to pull together.'

Why did Rose feel that somehow Cassie dying was *her* fault?

Why hadn't she been more persistent, camping out on the doorstep of Cassie's house until she agreed to see her, barging past Jed to get upstairs?

Now Cassie's entire family was in crisis and the one last thing she could do for her friend – look after her mother and brother – was impossible because she was *here*.

Rose's fingers clawed at the starched, white bed sheet, the guilt growing thick and fast in her mind, as if it sensed the upper hand.

Why hadn't she gone with Billy to find his kite?

'Hello, Rose.' A middle-aged nurse with dark hair pulled back from her round, smiling face appeared next to the bed. 'I'm Avril.'

'Where am I?' Rose whispered.

'You're in Ashfield Community Hospital. You've been here three days now but we're hoping that—'

'Billy,' Rose croaked, more of a statement than a question. Her throat felt parched and sore but she tried again. 'Please, tell me... where's my brother? Where's Billy?'

Nurse Avril reached for her hand, squeezed it. 'I'll get Dr Chang,' she said.

Billy and the kite were up ahead.

As the kite began to plummet, Rose ran towards it. There was still time, if only she could reach them before...

'Run!' she told herself. 'Run!'

And she did, she ran for her life, for Billy's life. But her legs moved ever-slowly, as if she were running through treacle and, every time she looked ahead, Billy seemed a little further away.

When she looked down at her bare feet, they were wrapped in thorns and bleeding.

But she didn't stop running.

She never stopped running.

Voices chipped into her dreams. Sounds that were far away at first and then drew closer.

Rose opened her eyes. Her parents stood at the end of the bed now with a doctor and nurse.

'Rose!' Her mother dashed forward and touched her face.

'Nice and relaxed, Mrs Tinsley,' the doctor said tersely. 'Hello, Rose. I'm Dr Chang, remember?'

Rose squeezed her eyes shut to force the memory to appear.

'You… injected me,' she said accusingly.

Dr Chang smiled. 'A little injection, yes. Just to help calm you, Rose.'

Rose looked at her father, still standing at the bottom of the bed. He looked thinner, weaker. Rose thought he looked… beaten.

'How long have I been here?' The nurse had said three days when she last woke up but then she'd drifted away again . . .

She kept her eyes fixed on her father but it was Dr Chang who answered her. 'You've been here about a week now, I think, Rose.'

'Yes.' Stella nodded, her hand still on Rose's cheek. 'Eight days today. They had to sedate you, Rose, you've had a… you're not well—'

'Where's Billy?' Rose said quietly, still looking at her father.

He turned away and looked out of the window. Rose followed his gaze.

She could see only sky and clouds, no ground. As if they were all in a bubble together, floating in the air, away from reality.

She knew Billy was gone then, even before her mother told her.

'I want to die too,' Rose said softly.

And that's what she'd tried to do, she thought now, as she sat reading by the open kitchen door.

Reading helped. At least part of her brain engaged with the story if the book was a good one. She felt safe holding it in her hands, as if it was some sort of good luck amulet.

For some reason she felt like revisiting all the old Enid Blyton titles of her youth. Dear Mr Barrow had sent over a box full of much-loved books.

Not *The Famous Five* – she was in no mood for adventure – but *The Faraway Tree*, *The Wishing Chair*, *The Naughtiest Girl* series… unlike people, books didn't monitor her reactions, ask her any questions or sigh at each other in disapproval.

Instead, they felt like a balm on her scorched, scarred heart.

The breakdown had lasted the best part of a month.

They'd sedated her during the worst part, when she'd tried to escape from everything, tried to run away dressed only in her hospital gown.

'You're back on the road to recovery,' a smiling Dr Chang had announced to her, the day of her discharge.

It was true she'd stopped screaming, stopped starving herself, stopped trying to escape.

She'd chopped off her hair to shoulder-length herself and dyed it dark brown so she didn't have to look in the mirror at the long red tresses he'd loved and tangled his fingers in.

Now, two months later, she just felt dead inside. She was zombified when awake and saw only Billy and Cassie's faces when she closed her eyes.

She wouldn't, couldn't, go outside.

'He's in prison, Rose,' her mother told her repeatedly. 'He can't hurt you now.'

'He's going to rot in hell in there,' her father added. 'They'll never let him out.'

Rose noticed they'd long stopped saying his actual name. Everyone tiptoed around her, thinking things through before they spoke.

Her parents were colourless, pale imitations of their former selves. They were trying to carry on whilst grieving for Billy and

Rose felt she was adding to their already unbearable burden by giving them something else to worry about.

They were trying so hard to help her get better and, for that, Rose was grateful.

The thing they didn't realise was this: it didn't matter where Gareth Farnham was or that he couldn't physically get to her.

Because his voice was always right here. Inside her head.

CHAPTER FIFTY-SEVEN

ROSE

PRESENT DAY

It would be a lie if I denied I constantly think about the past. I think about all of it but in particular, it's always that first, fateful meeting that changed my life and everyone else's around me that really bites.

I think about it all the time. I recreate what I might have said or done that would've shut Gareth Farnham down the first time he offered to carry my art stuff home from the bus stop.

I think about the people I might have confided in when I first saw the signs that his façade was slipping.

But then, truthfully, how was I to know at barely eighteen years old that such people existed? How could I have possibly second-guessed how it would all turn out when, at the beginning at least, everything seemed so… so perfect?

These questions are amongst the first things on my mind when I wake and they're often the last thing that flits across my consciousness before I fall to sleep each night.

I realised a long time ago that what happened is never going to go away. Ever.

'It will get easier,' my therapist told me continually. 'It will.'

But you see, it doesn't get better.

It's more that you somehow begin to acclimatise to blaming yourself. The strength of feeling, the shame… it *never* goes away but you do kind of get used to having it around. You begin to accept you will never feel happy or at peace.

But this… what I'm feeling now… it's simply impossible to live with.

The not knowing… the awful possibilities that present themselves, each one worse than the last.

The compartments in my head that I constructed all those years ago and used to bury the pain? Well, since the day I ventured into Ronnie's spare room, they are all emptied out. Every single one of them.

My mind is one hot mess of freshly released unbearable memories and I seriously don't know how long I can stand it.

Billy hadn't tripped and hit his head while searching for his kite; he was abducted.

We searched for him for two days before his body was found amongst the rhododendron bushes in the abbey grounds. The post mortem revealed he'd been suffocated.

A manhunt ensued. The village filled with well-wishers, volunteers and the national press.

There was only ever really one suspect. Gareth Farnham was arrested, questioned and eventually convicted of Billy's murder.

He denied killing my brother, as he always has done since. But by then I'd found out he was a skilled liar, a manipulator who said exactly what needed to be said in order to get what he wanted.

In court his defence had presented a psychiatrist, a Dr Simeon Chambers, who'd tried to convince the jury that Gareth was a sociopath who couldn't help controlling the people around him. This, she'd said, although regretful, was not the same thing as murdering a child. That hurting Billy was not in his make-up.

I'd seen his lies and aggression first-hand and I'd gotten into the dock and told them so.

In his summing up, the judge had said, in his learned opinion, 'Farnham is more of a scheming narcissist than a sociopath. He fully understands his actions.'

I'd wanted to rush over and kiss that judge for refusing to let Farnham evade justice but I hadn't, of course. I'd sat with my fingers knotted together to stop my hands shaking. I'd stared straight ahead and hadn't looked at Gareth, even when he was speaking.

When he hadn't been giving evidence, I'd been able to feel his eyes burning into me, willing me to look up so he could inject his silent poison into me. Warn me to keep my mouth shut, plead with me to help him… he could do all this without uttering a word to me, such was the extent of the control he had over me.

But I had not done it; I wouldn't look at him.

The final time our eyes had briefly met, he'd been a man convicted to life imprisonment being led down to the cells.

I'd sworn I'd never speak to him, look at him, and I'd promised myself to do my best never to think about him again.

Of course, that was before I made the discovery in Ronnie's spare room.

CHAPTER FIFTY-EIGHT

ROSE

PRESENT DAY

Decision time is here.

I could try to forget about finding Billy's blanket. I voice it silently in my head but of course I know the thought of doing so is just fantasy.

It's completely impossible to forget something so shocking, so profound.

Even if I managed to push it to the back of my psyche – which I've hardly succeeded in doing with other traumas – it would poison everything. I'd live out the rest of my days wondering and hating myself for taking the easy way out.

I could talk to Ronnie for a third time but I honestly think there is nothing to be gained by this. After our last conversation, his memory does appear to be sketchy and he is still ill. I look at him one minute and see my kindly, supportive neighbour, and the next minute I'm imagining Ronnie younger, stronger and capable of doing harm.

I've spoken to Mike North, the committed detective who led the case, and even he wasn't able to give me any cast-iron answers. It all seemed a bit too wishy-washy; speak to the police but, in the end, they might do nothing anyway, because declaring an unsafe conviction and re-opening a closed investigation is an enormous undertaking.

I could still go to the police but I feel it is the absolute last option on offer. If Ronnie is traumatised by police interviews and found to be completely innocent then I don't think I could ever live with myself.

I could end up destroying the only true, supportive friendship I've had since Billy died. I'd be vilified by everyone who loves Ronnie, and I'd really have no choice but to move from the village.

No. The next step is horribly clear. I must do something I vowed to myself I would never do, something that goes against a promise I made to Dad on his deathbed.

I must make contact with Gareth Farnham.

I shudder and knot my fingers together so hard it hurts. But still, I really feel it is the only logical step for me to take now.

Closing my eyes, I think back to the first letters he wrote me from prison. I read only two before Mum destroyed all his subsequent mail. But the first two were virtually identical.

He followed the same pattern in both the letters. In the middle of his tirade of accusations that I had abandoned him, betrayed him, he would switch to declarations of love for me.

He begged me to visit him, to talk things through. He said he had things he needed to tell me about that day, things he wanted to talk to me about.

'Keep away from him, Rose,' Dad had said one morning, tossing another of Gareth's letters on the fire. 'He's evil and his only aim will be to control and destroy you. For God's sake, don't fall for it again.'

He didn't realise it but Dad made me feel so stupid when he said stuff like that.

I know I deserved it entirely. I mean, what idiot lets someone take over their very thoughts to the extent they stop listening to anyone who ever cared about them and take a virtual stranger's word as gospel?

I once watched a fascinating nature programme about sinister parasites that control their hosts' minds.

Toxoplasmosis is a single-celled creature that infects rats and mice. It actually changes the whole way the rodents think, in that they stop being afraid of the smell of cats and instead are attracted to a pheromone in the cats' urine.

Ultimately, this means they stop hiding under the floorboards and get eaten. The parasite then reproduces in the cat's stomach.

I remember I'd turned the programme off early because it made me feel queasy.

I'd somehow been invaded by Gareth Farnham when I was eighteen years old. I allowed him to get inside my head and it felt like he'd changed my very DNA.

Dad was so right. I need to stay away from Gareth Farnham for the rest of my life. And I absolutely intend to… once I've got what I need from him.

I soon discover that writing the letter is much harder than making the initial decision to do so.

This is the man who is serving a life sentence for killing my beautiful brother, Billy.

This is the man who got inside my head so easily and ruined all our lives.

How do I begin to find the right words to reach out when I'd rather spit in his eye?

The tone of the letter is everything. I can't sound too hopeful. I have to pitch it just right or he'll immediately sense an opportunity for control again. But if I am too offhand he might ignore the letter.

Somehow, I have to try to pique his interest. There has to be something in it for him; that was always the case with Gareth Farnham.

The very act of writing a letter by hand seems so personal. So much is done electronically these days.

Some prisons do allow emailed communications but I don't like the thought of my letter getting lost in cyberspace. When Gareth was sent down, emails were a lot less popular than they are today. He might not be up to speed with the latest technology and I can't take that risk.

A letter, although difficult to compose, is failsafe in that I know it has a good chance of eventually reaching him.

I have a pen and paper. I've already researched how to send a letter to a prisoner and I have the postal address for HMP Wakefield.

Now I just have to write.

Dear Gareth, I begin.

The nib of my pen jerks away from the paper and I snatch it, screw it up. There can be no 'dear.'

I start a fresh page.

Gareth.

After Billy died, you said that…

Still too personal. I don't want to address him in such familiar terms and I don't want to sully Billy's memory by mentioning his name in the letter, either.

I screw up the paper and set it aside. My pen hovers again above a clean sheet.

Confident, direct and formal is undoubtedly the approach to take.

<u>FAO: Gareth Farnham, HMP Wakefield</u>

Many years ago you told me you had details you wished to discuss with me.

If you still wish to do this, I am now in a position to read your letter.

Rose Tinsley

206, Tilford Road, Newstead Village, Nottinghamshire

NG15 0BX

I grimace as I write my address, knowing those eyes of his that started off looking at me with love and ended up despising me, will feast on it.

But this is no time to allow negative emotions to take hold of me. He knows my address already. I'm not telling him anything new and providing a home address is a condition that HMP Wakefield stipulates before allowing mail through to a prisoner.

I re-read the note twice and then, to avoid obsessing, I fold it up and tuck it inside the envelope I have already addressed to the prison. HMP Wakefield is situated, ironically, in a place called Love Lane in Wakefield, West Yorkshire. A strange place for a person who destroyed so much love to end up, I think.

I sit for a moment and look at the letter.

I did it.

I glance at the wall clock and see it is just before 9 p.m. I never go out after dark; it's one of my rules. But I want to post this before I get cold feet.

Filled with bravado after writing the letter, I slip on my shoes and grab my keys.

I can do this. I can see it through for Billy.

CHAPTER FIFTY-NINE

ROSE

PRESENT DAY

Predictably, I barely sleep and I wake up to a drab day. Rivulets of rain channel down my bedroom window like tears.

I feel exhausted and I'm dreading the day at work.

Last night, when I left the house to post the letter, the street was eerily quiet. Apart from a bus trundling by on the top road, lit up and dotted sparely with passengers, there was no traffic and no pedestrians.

I left the house by the front door, double checking to ensure the lock had caught and was secure. When I turned round, gathered my courage to walk up to the top of the road to the post box, a quick movement caught my eye.

My head jerked up immediately, my eyes scanning the street.

There; I spotted something… a change in the gloom, a vague shadow rather than a person. I blinked and then the shadow disappeared and all seemed still. Was it just my overactive imagination?

I looked at the letter in my hand and hesitated. I could always post it in the morning on my way to work. It would still get sent the next day. And yet…

There was something that felt so definite about the action of taking it that made me set one foot in front of the other, even though it felt like I was wading through treacle.

I slid the letter in the narrow opening of the post box that glimmered a dangerous red under the streetlight. After glancing around me and satisfying myself there was nobody nearby, I ran back home. Literally ran.

Key in hand, I opened the front door, slammed and locked and deadbolted it.

Then I stood, with my back leaning against the cool UPVC of the door and I laughed at myself. Would there ever be a time I'd stop this nonsense and just live my life?

There had been nobody watching me and no dastardly shadows disappearing into the field.

Still, I wish I could just stay home today and catch up on my sleep in a room reassuringly bathed in daylight. Sadly, that's not an option. My routine is my lifeline.

I shower, wash and dry my hair and breakfast is a banana that I eat while getting dressed.

A sinking sensation fills me when I remember I'll have to pop round to check on Ronnie before I leave. I get what I need for work and then lock up fully so I can leave for work straight from leaving his.

Two minutes later I'm climbing the stairs next door.

'Only me,' I call.

He's out of bed, sitting on the floor looking dazed. His face is deathly pale and his head is hanging.

'Ronnie!' I rush up to him.

'I'm alright,' he croaks, allowing me to help him up. 'I needed the bathroom and… I coped just fine until I felt dizzy when I got back in the bedroom. Stupid legs gave up on me.'

'Did you faint?'

He shook his head. 'Just stumbled. I'll be fine now, Rose, you get yourself to work.'

There he is again, worrying about others. I desperately need this to be the *real* Ronnie. It has to be or I might never trust a human being again.

I'm so glad I posted the letter last night. The only way to move forward is to get some answers from Gareth Farnham.

I pray he is ready, after sixteen years of thinking about it, to finally face the truth.

At the library, Jim seems a little jumpy around me.

'How are you feeling, pet? You shouldn't worry about those fools visiting yesterday, you know. The decision whether to close the library won't be theirs alone.'

'I know that, Jim, but these so-called consultancy groups work on recommendations. I feel I wasted a really important chance to show them how important the library is to the village.'

'They put my grandad out of work when they closed the steelworks up north, the troubles at the pit killed my brother and then they went and closed it anyway.' Jim's jaw flexed. 'They're not going to do it to our blinking library, Rose.'

I wish I had a fraction of Jim's certainty. His words are determined but they won't save this place. Over the past couple of years, I could name at least five libraries they've closed in Nottinghamshire and I'm sure it wasn't through lack of local protest. The balance sheet is king and they went ahead and did it anyway.

'I'll put my thinking cap on,' Jim said, with a smile. 'People around here often under-estimate me, Rose, but they shouldn't. You know what they say… still waters run deep.'

CHAPTER SIXTY

ROSE

PRESENT DAY

'You must be mistaken, Rose,' Miss Carter says in a frosty tone. 'Check again, please.'

She's just appeared at the desk to return three books, all of which are overdue by a day. There is just a very small fine to pay but she's having none of it.

I sigh and move the scanner across the first one again.

'There, see?' I twist the monitor round to show her. 'They were due back on the twenty-third, Miss Carter.'

Her mouth knits into a tight line and she stands a little straighter. 'And what date is it today, may I ask?

'It's the…' I glance at the bottom right corner of my monitor, 'Oh!'

'Quite.' Miss Carter's face lights up with the satisfaction of being proven correct. 'It is the twenty-third, Rose.'

'I'm so sorry, I don't know how I—' I feel my face burning as I blather. 'I thought it was the twenty-fourth. I'm an idiot. So sorry, Miss Carter.'

'Don't mention it, Rose,' she says piously. 'We all make mistakes.'

Trust me to pick the righteous Miss Carter to make mine with.

'Sorry,' I mutter again, setting the books aside, hoping she'll soon wander off to the women's fiction shelves.

My mind returns to the thoughts that are crowding my head.

The post box I left the letter at last night has an early collection this morning: 9.30 a.m.

If the prison is efficient, Gareth Farnham could have the letter in his hands tomorrow. Is that possible, I wonder? I know the officers have to check the content of any communications but I only wrote a few lines, it's hardly Tolstoy's *War and Peace* they've got to wade through.

'Rose!'

I look up quickly at the sharp tone to find Miss Carter is still standing there, now bending forward so her face is in front of mine.

'S-sorry!' I stammer. 'I was just—'

'You were in cloud cuckoo land is where you were.' Miss Carter frowns. 'I asked, how is Mr Turner?'

I stare at her.

'Your neighbour?'

'Oh! Yes, he's very well, thank you. Home now and recovering nicely. His son's going to be visiting soon from Australia.'

'Eric? Well, I never. Let's hope it's not just to stake his claim on Ronnie's assets; he's never been much of a son and I think Ronnie can count on one hand the number of times he's seen him in the last twelve years. But no doubt Ronnie will be pleased.' She sighs. 'I'll have a word with Mrs Brewster and we'll try to pop over and say hello to him later.'

'He's getting more mobile but spends much of the day in bed still,' I say quickly.

'That's fine, we won't stay long.' She smiles tightly and finally moves away from the desk and heads off towards the fiction shelves.

An hour has barely passed when a tanned man dressed in jeans and a sports jacket enters the library and approaches the desk.

'Hello, Rose,' he says with a strange mixed accent, his eyes darting around the shelves of books behind me.

'Eric! I wasn't expecting you, Ronnie said you'd ring the library.'

I push away the forbidden thoughts, the secret that I shouldn't be party to.

'Trust Dad to get mixed up.' He rolls his eyes. 'I'm here now, and I wondered if you have the spare key for Dad's, save him getting out of bed to let me in.'

'Yes, course. One sec.' I root in my handbag and pull out the key, handing it to Eric. 'How are you?'

'Good. Fine thanks, you?' He has an unfortunate habit of not meeting my eyes when I speak to him. I remember noticing it about him when he still lived next door, too.

Maybe Eric always felt different but never knew why. Maybe his parents felt like strangers to him at times and he blamed himself. A secret he knew nothing about, yet the truth behind it was real and he felt it.

'I'm well thanks,' I say, although I feel rubbish.

There are a few moments of silence. We'd never really had anything to say to each other. He was three years older than me but to say we'd been neighbours, we never made an effort to get along.

Eric had been a mummy's boy. 'Always hanging on his mother's apron strings,' Mum used to complain. She said she could never have a good gossip with Sheila without Eric earwigging.

I remember he'd been a bit of a loner but Ronnie and Sheila treated him like a little prince. Some good that did them; he upped sticks with not much warning and hardly anyone saw him since.

Somehow, I can understand his decision more now.

'Best be off and see the silly old bugger then,' he says, smiling. 'See you around.'

*

The days trundle on. Work, home, sleep – all peppered with checking the doors, checking the road outside, the yard at the back.

Checking on Ronnie two or three times a day.

The truth is, despite my best efforts, I can't really think of much else apart from this: has Gareth Farnham read my letter?

He might not even have it yet. It's so frustrating. I think about ringing the prison but I doubt they'll tell me anything.

Yet again he is controlling me, only this time he probably doesn't know it.

Five days after I sent the letter and after another unremarkable day at work, I fight the urge to call at the Co-op for comfort foods and walk briskly home in the drizzle.

I usually use the back door to enter and leave the house but today, because of the rain, I unlock the front door and step inside, into the miniscule hallway.

I shiver and peel off my anorak, turning to hang it on the coat hook by the door. I feel something under my foot and look down to see I've inadvertently stood on the mail.

Snapping on the light, I ignore the unsteady feeling in my legs and bend down to gather up what's there. A pizza home delivery flyer, a generic house insurance communication marked simply 'Property Owner' and a white envelope with my name and address printed neatly on the front.

I allow the other mail to fall from my hands and I turn the envelope over in my hands. There is nothing on it that suggests it's come from prison but, somehow, it looks different. It has a bar code sticker on and a couple of handwritten illegible marks as if it's been through some kind of vetting process.

I won't know until I open it.

I lock and bolt the door, kick my shoes where I'm standing and drop my handbag. Then I sit down in the chair and, finding a small unsealed piece of the flap, I inch my index finger along and pull out the single piece of folded paper in there.

I open it and smooth it out on my knee. My shoulders slump as I realise it isn't a letter from Gareth Farnham but then I read the first printed line and my hands start to tremble.

Forcing myself to read the short paragraph that is there, I clamp my elbows into my sides and swallow hard as I stare at the bold heading on the sheet.

VISITING ORDER
Prisoner 364599 Gareth Benjamin Farnham
has granted you permission to visit.
Please select 3 possible dates and times for your visit below.
You will receive a confirmation email within three
working days.

I brush the paper from my knee and shuffle my feet away from it.

My chest feels tight and sore as I grapple with the implications. Why couldn't he just have written to me? I never considered this…

How is it still possible that he can knock me off my feet? I feel like the prisoner here.

I leave the discarded paper on the floor, stand up and walk upstairs for a lie down. A single thought is throbbing repeatedly in my head.

I can't see him.

I just can't.

CHAPTER SIXTY-ONE

ROSE

PRESENT DAY

A week later, I join the M1 and drive all the way up from Junction 27 to Junction 40.

It sounds straightforward but I talk to myself all the way to calm my pumping heart and cool my burning face. It's not just a reaction to the fact I haven't driven on the motorway in years but also what waits for me at the end of the journey.

I don't even want to think about the stress and strain I've put myself through since I received the visiting order in the post. I'd lay upstairs staring unseeingly at the ceiling for hours. When I came back downstairs I checked Ronnie was OK and then I sat down and wrote another letter to Gareth Farnham. It was identical to the first one, except I added:

It is not possible for me to visit the prison. Please communicate by letter.

Three days later I'd received another visiting order in the post.

I felt furious enough to ignore him and desperate enough to make the journey to speak to him. After several sleepless nights and a day off sick from work, desperation won through in the end.

At Woodall services, between junctions 29 and 30, I park up, and, despite the drizzle, lower the windows to get some air into my ten-year-old Ford Fiesta. I've parked by a bank of stringy-looking trees but I know there's a blackbird in there somewhere. I can hear it singing, a throaty warble so clear it feels like it's sitting on my shoulder.

I wish my head felt clearer. Am I doing the right thing? I draw in a long breath through my bared teeth and then release it.

I'm honestly not sure there *is* a right thing to do.

I lean my elbow on the rim of the open window and allow my forearm to drape outside, a thin breeze trickling through my fingers.

If I hadn't been with Billy that day at the abbey, it might have been possible for me to come up with a logical reason for Ronnie having his blanket and ultimately push it from my mind.

It wouldn't have stayed pushed away though, how could it?

Besides, I *was* there that day; I *do* know that Billy had his blanket with him at the Abbey.

Everybody loves Ronnie, and if I'd ever been in any doubt, then the outpouring of affection and concern after his short illness proved the point.

He'd helped so many people over the years, I'd look like the wicked witch of the west if I dared to suggest otherwise.

I'm shaken out of my thoughts by a family – parents and two small children – piling into the car parked next to me. The boy and girl are chattering excitedly and, although the parents look weary, there's a comfortable and relaxed manner between the two of them that I find myself envying.

One adult either side of the car, they get the kids strapped into the back seats and the father grins and shakes his head at the parcel shelf, stacked to the brim with clothes, toys and carrier bags.

Mum and Dad always made sure we had a family holiday once a year. Usually it was a week at the coast; quite often Whitby or

Morecambe. But the year we stayed in a small cottage in St Ives sticks in my mind.

The glorious light, the azure sea and sky, the sound of seagulls when we woke in the morning and when we returned from each scorching day at the beach.

Every day, we'd start with a hearty cooked breakfast, one of Dad's specials usually reserved for a Sunday morning at home. Mum would pack up a picnic each day that we'd eat against the backdrop of the waves and the sun beating down on our shoulders.

On top of all this were ice creams and cream teas and, most days, fish and chips eaten out of trays at the harbour.

We'd gotten friendly with the family next door. There had been a girl, Bethany, who was just a year younger than me. We'd often pop to the corner shop together, our respective families needing bread or milk or some other essential item we'd run out of.

The shop owner, whose name I can't recall, had taken a shine to us, and given us tips about the best places for teenagers, and we'd occasionally help bring in the sandwich board outside, a job that needed doing before the shop closed at 6 p.m.

Then one day, just before we were due to go home, the police had called at our cottage. The shop owner had informed them he'd suspected that Bethany and I had stolen a cloth bag containing cheques and around a hundred pounds in cash from under the counter.

It'd been awful. Our mums had been crying, the dads looking at each other suspiciously, as though they'd suspected the other one's daughter. The next day we'd heard a local boy had been apprehended for the theft; he'd done the same thing in shops dotted along the coast.

I've never forgotten that feeling though, of being accused, of being desperate to prove your innocence but finding it impossible to do so and actually realising that the angrier you get, the more guilty you look.

I wondered for years after that if Mum and Dad would've doubted me, if we hadn't heard the police had found the culprit.

I don't want to be responsible for making Ronnie feel like that if he's an innocent man. I think too much of him.

I pop inside the services to use the loo and a grab a latte on the way out. I have to sit and drink the coffee before I set off because my old car doesn't have the luxury of a coffee holder. I keep meaning to get one of those plastic ring contraptions that clips on to the air vent but it's rare I use the car these days.

It's an expense I often wonder about having but it gives me comfort to know it's there, outside the house. In case I need to get away fast.

And it's been very useful to have on hand today. Because after churning the possibilities over yet again in my mind, I feel renewed vigour to get to Wakefield to see Gareth Farnham.

I need to stay strong, stay focused and find the truth. After all, he's the one in prison.

I'm not a naïve, young college girl any more… what can he do to hurt me now?

CHAPTER SIXTY-TWO

HMP WAKEFIELD

PRESENT DAY

Rose was forced to drive around the prison car park twice before she eventually found a space.

Under different circumstances, she could've almost tricked herself into believing she was parking up, about to go shopping… until she got out of the car and looked across to her right. A stark biscuit-coloured building with a flat, dark-green roof and long, high wall crouched there, as if daring her to approach.

She locked the car and, slinging her handbag over her shoulder, she made her way over to the pedestrian path and walked towards the prison. Rose was aware she was walking too slow, dragging her feet and choosing to walk the long way around, instead of cutting through the parked cars.

But she gave herself a break. As long as she got there, it didn't really matter how long it took. After all, she'd waited sixteen years.

The grey sky offered no contrast to the gloomy colours that surrounded her. Heavy, rain-filled clouds hung over the trees at the back of the prison, threatening to pour at any moment.

As she approached the building, electronic doors whooshed open and an older couple emerged. The man slid his arm around the woman's shoulders as tears rolled unchecked down her cheeks.

She tried not to stare but it was hard to ignore. As she approached the reception area, her heartbeat sped up a notch.

'Rose Tinsley,' she said at the desk. 'I'm here to visit Gareth Farnham.'

The middle-aged woman behind the desk checked her paperwork and asked her to sign the visitors' book and then directed her to the visitor's centre.

'Straight down the corridor and turn right at the bottom. There'll be a few security checks and then you'll be able to begin your visit.' She smiled as if she'd assumed it was something Rose had been looking forward to.

The level of noise that assailed her ears as she entered the visiting area took her by surprise.

Rose stood for a moment or two, frozen in the doorway, her eyes scanning the crowded space. Men, women, children, clustered together in small groups, dotted around the room like buzzing insects.

She hadn't really known what to expect but had naively visualised a quiet, calm area where there would be a prison guard standing quite close to the table where she would meet with Gareth Farnham.

There *were* several officers, dotted here and there around the periphery of the room but – she couldn't help thinking – not close enough to stop a prisoner punching someone in the face, or worse, if they were compelled to do so.

Rose swallowed hard and looked around her at the sea of heads.

The room was organised simply in rows of low, white tables, each served by four hard, black, plastic chairs.

The tables were set surprisingly close together, wobbling and rocking as small children dashed between them, clutching toys to take to their oblivious parents who all seemed either in deep conversation or staring at each other accusingly, with seemingly little to say.

'Excuse me,' someone said in an annoyed tone behind her.

'Sorry.' She hurriedly stepped out of the doorway she was currently blocking and into the main room. Still, she found she couldn't quite bring herself to walk towards the visiting tables.

'You OK there?' a stocky female officer with cropped brown hair and a friendly smile asked her. 'First time here?'

Rose nodded, grateful someone was taking the time to check on her. 'Yes, I've come to see—' she scanned the room again to see if he had appeared before looking back at the officer '—Gareth Farnham.'

'Right.' She felt sure the officer's eyes seemed to widen slightly as she stared closer at her and then turned to view the room. 'Doesn't look like he's out yet but you can wait for him at that free table over in the corner. He doesn't have many visitors.'

There were only a handful of tables not occupied and so Rose moved over to the one the officer had indicated.

She realised she'd been holding her breath and now, as she moved towards the vacant seat, she made an effort to release the tension that cramped at her chest.

She pulled out a chair, wincing as it scraped the tiled floor, although everyone else appeared oblivious to the grating noise, amid their conversational din.

Rose placed her handbag on the chair next to her and looked up, gratified to see a uniformed officer standing with his back to the wall and quite close to where she sat.

Consciously making an effort to do her 'calm' breathing – that was, in through the nose for three counts and out through the mouth for six – she laced her hands in front of her on the table and stared at them.

She didn't want to look around her at the prisoners and their families. They talked, laughed and, as she'd walked across the room, she'd even seen some crying, totally oblivious to their surroundings. Most of them appeared to be perfectly comfortable in a situation that had obviously become normal to them.

Rose found herself surprised at the stark, bare quality of the prison. Like most people, she'd read the newspaper stories about the lax and luxurious life that criminals enjoyed in Britain's cushy penal institutions but, now she'd seen it for herself, she wasn't so sure.

There was an air of abandonment here, a hopelessness that permeated the place.

Rose could imagine, if one had to spend day and night here for some time, it might soon become difficult to imagine a prosperous future. Even more baffling would be how to make a new start back in the outside world, when the time came.

She became aware of a shape… a shadow looming over her.

The chair opposite was pulled back and, suddenly, there she was… looking up into Gareth Farnham's eyes.

CHAPTER SIXTY-THREE

HMP WAKEFIELD

PRESENT DAY

Sixteen years ago, those same eyes had pleaded with her to help him prove his innocence. Rose had declined because she truly believed, like everyone else, that he had taken Billy.

And she still *did* believe that.

Her instinct was to look away from him but, instead, she found herself holding his stare. There they were; those lying eyes that looked so dependable.

But Rose was no longer that naïve, impressionable girl. She now knew the essence of this man was rotten. She knew what he was capable of.

She could detect nothing in his eyes today; no anger, love, regret… they looked darker than she remembered them, more vacant.

His lips were pressed together in a tight, straight line and his mouth curved down at the edges, reminding her of a Great White.

'Hello, Rose,' he said smoothly, sitting down. She was reminded of how his strong, deep voice used to turn her knees to jelly. Today, it sounded thinner, more reedy.

He laced his fingers together and mirrored her own position.

Rose parted her lips slightly but couldn't speak to him. She just couldn't do it. It had taken all her resolve not to push back the chair and fly out of the place but she forced her attention back to him.

He had put on a lot of weight. The flesh on his face and hands bulged, pale and bloated, his chin and forehead spotty. He opened his mouth to speak and she caught sight of yellow, neglected teeth.

'Oh, Rose. What have you done to your beautiful hair?' he murmured.

Before she realised, her hand drifted up to self-consciously touch her dyed, dark hair, lazily pulled up into a little top knot. Her fingers brushed her exposed damp neck and she shivered.

She snatched her hand away immediately but he noticed, of course, and a faint smirk fluttered over his mouth.

'You know how I loved it long and red.' He leaned forward and stared at her intently. 'Maybe you cut it because you didn't want anyone else to look at you. Is that it, darling?'

She felt the heat in her face, knew she'd be slowly turning crimson in front of him. He would no doubt enjoy the public display of her wretched nerves but she knew herself well enough by now to accept there was little she could do about it.

There were far more important things at stake.

'So, how's my Rosie?'

Rose did not respond.

'Finally, you came. I'd like to think it's because you can't live without me.' He paused, studying her blank expression. 'But now I'm not so sure.'

She slipped a hand inside her bag and pulled out a photograph from the side pocket. She slid it across the table so it faced him.

'Ah,' he said. 'Billy.'

She wanted to punch him when he said her brother's name out loud but, instead, she spoke levelly. 'Yes. I'm here because of Billy.'

Her tongue felt swelled and parched; it lay listlessly on the bottom of her mouth as if it was reluctant to form the words she needed to utter.

She wished she had thought to pick up a plastic cup of filtered water from the machine when she came in but it was too late now. She needed to keep Gareth's attention, keep him communicating.

'I don't want to talk about Billy,' he said evenly. 'I want to talk about us.'

'No. I'm here to talk about my brother.'

She forced air in through her nose but it wasn't enough to reach her lungs and she felt almost breathless.

He shuffled in his chair, and leaned a little closer.

'You know, I can still taste you, Rose. At night, in my cell, I imagine I'm on top of you, behind you… inside you. It's what's kept me going all these years.'

She felt the heat breaking through into her face and ignored it.

'So sweet.' Gareth smiled and slid his hand towards her own. She pulled her fingers back. Tucked both hands under the table. 'Still like a shy little girl, even after all this time.' He tipped his head to one side and studied her for a moment or two as if he was trying to make his mind up about something.

'You've not been with another man since me. I can tell I'm still the only one.'

'Can you just stop?' she snapped.

Gareth threw back his head and laughed. 'Oh dear, hit a nerve, have I? I can read you like a book, Rose. *I know you.* I know everything about you.'

She swallowed hard and looked at Billy's photograph. She'd taken it at the park just a few months before he died. He'd been swinging from the climbing frame like a little monkey, his face alive with dare and glee.

'You've completed half your sentence now.' She felt surprised to hear her voice sounded calm. 'There's no sense in denying what happened any more.'

She watched as his fingers beat a rhythm on the table and she noticed that both thumbnails were long and manicured.

She looked away.

'With good behaviour I might get out early, they say. Did you know there's a possibility? You and I... we could carry on where we left off, Rose.' His tongue flicked out and back in again. 'Would you like that?'

She tasted a metallic tang in her mouth and realised she'd been biting down on her tongue. She relaxed her jaw and blinked steadily at him. Let him think it was a possibility... it was worth it, to get closer to the truth.

'Tell me what you did with Billy's blanket,' she whispered, clenching her hands under the table.

'Why do you suddenly want to know that? It seems a very specific question to ask, Rose.'

'No reason,' she said quickly. 'I've always wanted to know what you did with it.'

He narrowed his eyes. 'You're bluffing, I can see it in your face. What's happened? Has new evidence come to light?'

She felt a brief flutter of panic that everything inside her head, all her thoughts, her worries, were transparent to him.

'It's something I've always wondered,' she said. 'That's why I'm here, to finally ask you. I wanted to just do this by letter but—'

Gareth gave a long, low chuckle, interrupting her.

'Good try, Rose, but not good enough by far. Like I say, I know you. Wild horses couldn't drag you here unless it was something special.'

CHAPTER SIXTY-FOUR

ROSE

PRESENT DAY

When I get back home, I dump my bag at the bottom of the stairs… and freeze.

The hairs on the back of my neck suddenly prickle and I walk slowly into the living room. It feels… different in here. A subtle change in the air, that's all it is.

I scan around the room. Everything seems as I left it. The visiting order still on the arm of the chair, the cup and plate I forgot to take through to the kitchen.

I shake my head. I'm turning into a nervous wreck here.

I kick off my flats and head upstairs to take a long, hot shower.

I close my eyes and bend my head forwards, wincing as the needles of scalding water beat down on my terse neck and shoulder muscles.

As I gulp in the thick, steamy air, I try to imagine the layer of invisible grime that visiting Gareth Farnham has left on my skin, dissolving and disappearing forever down the plughole.

But despite repeatedly soaping and scrubbing myself, I can feel it there. Settled slick as a layer of grease, clogging my pores. Still, when I do finally step out of the shower, thankfully, I do feel a little fresher.

Purging my mind proves to be a little more difficult.

His words have taken hold inside my head, like a tick that grabs on to a hapless cat or dog, burrowing deep into its skin.

With the heel of my hand, I rub steam from the bathroom mirror and study my ruddy face. My damp hair sticks up in clumps, exposing the bad cut I had done at a little back road salon in Hucknall that still had a row of old-fashioned hairdryers against one wall.

There's no doubt about it; my hair is very unflattering. It was always meant to be; part of the healing process was in getting rid of the long, red locks he loved. In the end, all that time ago, I'd felt my hair belonged more to him than me.

Yet, as much as I hate him, Gareth's criticism had hit home. I felt a jolt inside, as I did sixteen years previously, eager to please him and keen to avoid his disapproval.

What the hell is wrong with me?

Why is my first reaction to act like his puppet again?

I felt OK when I first arrived at the prison but then, the more he talked and the more he looked at me in that way, the more I became aware of an awakening of the old me… young Rose, dithering, rising to the surface. And he sensed that.

My plan had been simple enough; get to the point quickly and succinctly. Demand Gareth tell me the truth about Billy.

Surely, I thought, after all this time inside, I could convince him to unburden himself.

But he soon put paid to my plans. Despite my best efforts, within minutes he'd taken control of the situation. Looking back, I don't know how he even did that.

In my mind's eye, I'd imagined a Gareth who'd been beaten into submission by years of incarceration.

I imagined a man, riddled with remorse, who would eagerly seize the chance to finally tell me the truth about Billy. I was very much mistaken.

For the first three months after the judge imprisoned him for Billy's murder, Gareth Farnham wrote to me every single day. Sometimes, it was more than one letter a day; two or three would drop through the letterbox.

I grew to dread that sound, the clatter of the metal flap and the dull plop of folded paper on the entrance mat. After the first couple, my parents had destroyed every letter without opening any of them.

The next three months saw maybe two or three letters a week and the six months after that it dropped to just a couple a month.

On top of this, there were the phone calls. Daily ones for the first ten days or so, dropping to three or four a week for the next few weeks.

Mum and Dad were still alive then, so it wasn't always me who picked up the phone to be greeted by a recorded message.

A disembodied voice would ask if we wanted to accept a call from an inmate at HMP Wakefield.

The first few times, Dad would yell and swear into the phone until Mum explained there wasn't actually anyone listening at the other end at this stage in the call. Soon, we were calling out 'just the prison again' and replacing the receiver.

We couldn't bring ourselves to use his name.

After the first few weeks, we'd just kill the call without announcing who it was. We all knew who was trying to get through on the other end and it sickened us to the pits of our stomachs.

And then, as fast as it started, just before we reached the first year, all contact stopped. No letters, no calls… nothing at all.

'With any luck, somebody in there has done away with him,' Dad kept saying hopefully but, of course, we knew that hadn't happened because DCI North would've let us know immediately.

I turn away from the mirror and begin to dry myself.

How I wish I'd had the foresight to keep those letters he sent. Why did I never think that there might be a time I'd feel strong enough to open them, a time when I might want to scrutinise his loaded words for clues of his guilt?

For all I know, one of those letters might have contained a confession. Too late to find out now and besides, I know why I never gave a second thought to getting rid of his communications.

It was because there wasn't a shred of doubt in my mind.

I was entirely convinced of Gareth Farnham's guilt.

When the police arrested and charged him, nobody in the entire village had a flicker of doubt. When I gave evidence in court against him, I did so with a firm conviction that I was doing the right thing.

The small detail of the receipt placing him somewhere else entirely was, in my mind, a barely concealed attempt to evade justice for my brother's death. I didn't believe a single thing that came out of his mouth in the end.

He was shameless; we all knew that. He'd have throttled his grandmother to save his own skin.

He had strangled my little brother in a fit of pathetic jealousy. I will sit with my own corroding guilt until the day I die.

Billy was killed because of me and my choice to have a relationship with Gareth Farnham.

In the days leading up to his arrest, it was as though someone shone a bright light into the dark corners of my life. I saw everything with a stark and painful clarity.

The way he had schemed and burrowed into my life in record time, how he'd controlled even the slightest details of my appearance. Censored what I read and what I watched on TV.

I asked myself why, if it was so obvious, how could I ever not have seen it?

I still don't have an answer.

A slight breeze shakes me out of my thoughts. I head to my bedroom and stand, wide-eyed on the landing. The window to the spare bedroom is slightly ajar.

I rush in and pull it shut, my hand shaking a little.

I open the windows upstairs periodically to air the rooms but… I never, ever leave them open. It's part of my routine. Check, check, check… it's all I ever do.

Lately I've been so stressed, is it possible I've neglected to properly maintain my security measures? I think about the strange feeling I had downstairs, as if something had changed – yet everything was as I left it.

There's only one answer that fits all.

In getting back in touch with Gareth Farnham, I'm finally losing my mind…

CHAPTER SIXTY-FIVE

ROSE

PRESENT DAY

'How's Rose doing?' Jim asks from behind me when I arrive at work.

'What? Oh, fine; thanks, Jim. Sorry, I've been a bit distracted lately, I think you've had to repeat everything you've said at least once this past week.'

'Don't worry about that, pet. You've been a good neighbour to Ronnie but the old girls tell me he's picking up a bit now. It's probably helped with Eric coming back.'

I grin, thinking what Mrs Brewster and Miss Carter might say if they heard what he just called them. I feel relieved Jim assumed I've just been busy sorting Ronnie out. God only knows what he'd think of me if he knew I'd been to see Gareth Farnham.

In the afternoon, Mrs Brewster stops at the desk. 'Your hair looks nice today, Rose,' she says, tipping her head to one side and studying me. 'You've got a bit of a glow about you.'

'Oh,' I mumble, fiddling with a protective book jacket. 'Thanks.'

'You're not one of *those people*, are you, Rose?' She tucks her chin in and peers down at me over her gold wire-framed glasses until I look up from the desk. 'I mean someone who is more comfortable being criticised than taking a compliment?'

She smiles at me in a kind of reprimanding way if that makes sense, as you might do to a mischievous child.

'No,' I say brightly, shifting in my chair and turning away from her incisive eye. 'Just busy. You know how it is here, always busy.'

The truth is, I don't receive compliments very often and on the very rare occasion I do, I feel my skin crawling in protest. Like it's crawling right now, under Mrs Brewster's gaze.

My first thought is always that the person giving the compliment is lying, saying something nice just to make me feel better. How could they possibly mean it?

A few months after Billy died, I remember my therapist telling me about a concept she called 'self-loathing'.

'It's a way of coping,' Gaynor said in that rather convoluted way therapists have of speaking. 'Fostering low expectations to avoid further disappointments.'

Over a couple of sessions, to use the therapist speak she was so fond of, we 'explored the concept'.

'I want you to think about some of the things you tell yourself on a regular basis, Rose,' Gaynor said. 'The words that play in the background like a tune on a loop. I'm talking about the stuff that's been there so long you barely notice it any more.'

I hummed and hawed a bit, to use more session time up, but Gaynor was having none of it. She sat back in her seat, folded her hands in her lap and waited in silence.

'I suppose I tell myself I'm a bad person quite a lot,' I mumbled.

'And why's that?' she instantly prodded. 'Why do you think you're a bad person?'

'Because of what happened to Billy,' I said, as if it should be obvious.

'*You* didn't hurt Billy.'

'No, but it was because of me that it happened, wasn't it?' I said quickly, wishing we could just move on. 'I brought Gareth

Farnham into all our lives. I stopped spending as much time with Billy, maybe if he'd felt he could talk to me, he could have…'

I swallowed hard against the dryness of my throat but shook my head when she offered me water.

'What else do you tell yourself?'

I shrugged but ended up saying the thing that popped in my head next just to avoid that awful silence again. 'That no one will ever want me again.'

I hated this self-examination. It felt so indulgent, for one thing, when the only thing that mattered was losing my brother.

Me, me, me. Nobody will ever want plain old me.

But that's what Gareth Farnham had told me repeatedly towards the end and I knew it was the truth. The feelings of inferiority had risen up back then, taken hold and never left me to this day.

Very occasionally, before I cut my hair, I'd occasionally see a man send an appreciative glance my way. I'd shrink away as if scalded, allowing my hair to fall across my face until he'd gone away.

Maybe other people couldn't see my negative qualities but for many years now, I've known they are there and I know I'm not remotely good enough for anyone decent to be interested in spending time with me.

But I'd faced my fears. I'd done more than write a letter to Gareth Farnham, I'd spoken to him as an equal.

I hoped he could see how I'd changed. How I'd managed to live my life without him.

He'd be delighted if he knew the truth of my pathetic existence.

CHAPTER SIXTY-SIX

ROSE

PRESENT DAY

I pull down the ladder, tentatively climb it. At the top I click a switch on the floor and the lights snap on. I'm amazed it still works but Dad was a thorough handyman and, knowing him, he'd have fitted a light bulb with a fifteen-year life span or something… if such a thing exists.

I take a breath and heave myself up into the attic, which is somewhat easier said than done. The last time I came up here to help Dad organise the space, I was a strong and healthy young woman, not a bag of half-starved bones.

I sit for a moment and look down at my legs dangling down out of the hatch. It almost represents how I'm feeling inside now; my body in the real world and my mind clouded with dark thoughts and unbearable possibilities that I'm terrified to explore.

Mum had a big clear out and the stuff she wanted to keep but needed out of our living space came up here. After Billy's funeral and after we started to try and pick up the pieces of our lives, Dad put all the stuff – paperwork, notes we'd made, contact names and numbers – in a big packing box and shoved it up here.

Mum had been fastidious in recording any piece of information she thought we might need or refer back to. She'd volunteered as clerk and secretary to the village committee for years when I was younger, so she knew how to keep an organised desk.

It hadn't been touched since; why would it have been? The evidence box, as we'd named it, hadn't been touched since Dad resigned it to the attic. Why would it? The murderer had been arrested, tried and imprisoned for life. As we'd fallen apart, DCI North and his team slotted all the jagged pieces into place until the ugly picture was complete.

It wasn't something we wanted to revisit but it wasn't something we'd wanted to discard, either. It showed we'd done our very best for Billy, covered every angle and explored every piece of information that came our way.

And now… now everything I thought I knew is threatening to fall apart, I'm so glad and grateful we kept it all.

I shuffle back on my bottom on the dusty chipboard Dad laid up here and bring my legs up to join the rest of me. There are numerous boxes up here, far more than I remember. It's ironic that Mum felt she needed to keep all this stuff – she never touched it again after it was relocated.

I stand up and shuffle round the boxes, peeking in. Dozens and dozens of school photographs of both me and Billy. And greetings cards, written with love, that Mum just couldn't bear to throw away. My throat catches when I open a 'Happy Birthday, Mummy' one that's filled with Billy's childish scrawl.

My finger traces over his letters and the faint pencil lines he's used as a ruler to keep his words straight.

'Oh Billy,' I sigh softly. 'I miss you so much.'

My brother would have been twenty-four years old this year. He was tall for his age; Mum always said he'd be a six-footer. It would've been strange to see… my little brother, towering above me. I'll never know what that feels like.

Would he have made it, become a pilot, like he dreamed? Probably not. I don't think he'd have put the necessary schoolwork in but so what? He'd have been brilliant at what he did end up doing and that's all that counts.

I replace the greetings card carefully in the box and close it up again, protecting it against the dust and ravages of time that Billy himself is no longer at the mercy of.

I've been up here all of five minutes and inside I feel weighed down, as if something has sucked all of my energy out. I don't want to look amongst the memories and be reminded of everything I've lost: Mum, Dad, Billy… my entire family.

I pick my way across to the other side of the hatch. The attic is small, like the rest of the house. There are breeze-block walls either side of the space, which cut us off from next door. When I was a teenager I read a serial crime thriller where the killer was crawling along the roof space, peeking in at all his neighbours. It freaked me out so much that I couldn't sleep until Dad dragged me up to the attic laughing his head off and showed me the walls that had been erected.

Most of the packing boxes are white. I can see the one I need: a slightly smaller, ordinary tan cardboard box a few yards in front of me. I'm moving slowly, taking longer to get there than I need to. I give myself a break, pretend I'm just being careful and sure-footed.

The flaps of the box are open, tatters of no-longer-sticky tape hanging off, like useless, curled tendrils. This is strange because I have a distinct memory of Mum taking great pains to lay a sheet of packing paper on top of the contents of the evidence book and tape the flaps down securely. This was a woman who even used masking tapes on the tops of sun creams when she and Dad went for the odd weekend away.

I bend down and fully open the box. It looks like it's been rifled through. Who would have done that? I've no way of knowing if it's been done last week or sixteen years ago. I tell myself it's not significant but there's a small lump as hard as a nut in my throat.

I don't feel strong enough to go through each item in here. One day I will, when the time is right. For now, I keep delving under the layers, looking for Mum's notebook with all her old contact numbers in.

I pull something out thinking it's the notebook but it's a small white prayer book with Billy's name printed in pale gold on the front. Probably sent by a kind villager to comfort Mum and Dad. As I hold it up, something falls from it that had become stuck to the back cover.

It's a letter.

I stare at the handwriting and a shudder travels throughout my body. It's not *just* any letter; it's a letter from Gareth.

I swallow, momentarily frozen. I felt absolutely certain that all the mail he sent had been destroyed.

My hands feel hot and unsteady but I take out the folded sheet within and flatten it out. And I read Gareth Farnham's poisoned words all over again.

My dearest Rose,
I am so sorry for your terrible loss.
One day you will know that I am innocent. That day, you will understand your betrayal of me, your abandonment in my hour of need. I would have never abandoned you, Rose, but I forgive you. I FORGIVE YOU for not listening, not helping me… I NEED TO TALK TO YOU, ROSE.
It's not too late. There are things I need to tell you… things that could prove my innocence so we can be together again.
I am so sorry for what happened to dear Billy but it was not my fault, my darling. The real killer is still out there, living his life unpunished.
Nobody will listen to me. Nobody wants to hear I did nothing wrong. That village condemned me the moment Billy went missing.

But I thought better of you, Rose. I honestly thought you loved me.
I NEED TO TALK TO YOU. Please, Rose. Billy's killer needs to be punished NOW.
Whether we are together or apart, always remember, Rose… you will always be MINE FOREVER.
All my love,
G xxx

I push the letter aside and close my eyes, willing his vile words and lies to leave me. I should never have read it.

I shiver, cross my arms over my body and hold myself as I rock back and forth.

How can he have such power over me after all these years? How could I have gone to see him… given him the opportunity to control me all over again?

After a few moments I shake myself and reach for Mum's notebook. In the back, right where I left it, is a small white envelope containing a small white piece of paper.

As I put the other stuff back inside, I catch sight of a headline on a folded newspaper:

MAN, 28, ARRESTED FOR LOCAL BOY'S MURDER

Gareth's words play in my head: *The real killer is still out there, living his life unpunished.*

I take the envelope, turn away and make my way back downstairs. I leave the box undone and in a mess. How a box of stuff can still control me like this I'm not sure… but I can't face it any longer.

I turn off the light and clamber down the ladder.

I walk to the front door to check for mail and stop dead in my tracks. There is something wedged in the letter box.

I walk over and pull it from the door. It's a brown, used envelope with a window. Inside is a folded white piece of paper.

Still standing by the door I open it up and read the four printed words.

Let sleeping dogs lie.

CHAPTER SIXTY-SEVEN

HMP WAKEFIELD

PRESENT DAY

'Hello, Rose, it's so nice to see you again,' Gareth said, sliding the chair back and sitting down. 'Did you bring the things I asked you for? The Imperial Leather soap and the magazines?'

'Yes,' she lied. 'But I had to leave your parcel at the desk.'

'Thank you, I appreciate that.' He smiled at her. 'So, what have you been up to since I saw you last week?'

He spoke to her in a strange, conversational manner, as if they'd just met up in the local pub for a drink.

Rose bit down her impatience and answered him.

'Just the usual. Work, checking on Ronnie, my neighbour. He's not been well.'

'Oh, I'm sorry to hear that,' he said, not sounding at all concerned. 'He's had a good innings though, hasn't he? Probably on his way out, and you've done such a lot for him, Rose; you never know, he might leave you his house.'

Rose laughed. 'I doubt that. He has a son, Eric, who lives in Australia.'

He looked up, searching his memory. 'Yes, I remember Eric. Creepy bloke he was, a bit of a loner if I recall.'

That was rich, coming from him, Rose thought. How he'd relish learning of Eric's secret.

'He's married now, apparently.' She shrugged, fixing her eyes on him. 'When Ronnie went into hospital for a few days, I cleaned his house, even did the upstairs.'

'Little angel, aren't you?' He winked without hesitation. 'Always helping others and yet you wouldn't help me out when I so desperately needed it, would you, Rose?'

'My priority was my brother,' she said, looking at her hands and thinking about the wording of his letter. 'You can't blame me for that but perhaps we can help each other now.'

His head jerked up. 'In what way?'

'You tell me what you did with Billy's blanket that day and I'll bring you more stuff that you need.'

Gareth laughed. 'There you go again, trying to hoodwink me, Rose. I'm afraid you've taken up some rather sly habits since I had to leave you.'

'What do you mean?'

'Something's happened. Nobody waits sixteen years to ask what happened. Not even you.'

'Just tell me why you did it. You've constantly denied it like a coward… I want to know what happened that day.'

She clamped her mouth shut, annoyed with herself. She'd managed to keep her venom under wraps so far but it was so hard.

'One thing I'm not, little girl, is a coward.' Gareth glared at her and his face darkened in that way she remembered, which made her insides turn to liquid.

But she brushed this thought aside and reminded herself that she was far from Gareth's *little girl* now. She wasn't anyone's little girl, she was a woman. A woman determined to find out the truth at long last.

'Then prove it!'

'Rose, Rose.' He laughed softly. 'Let's not get annoyed with each other; we've waited too long to spend time together.'

'If you still cared about me you'd do this for me,' she said. 'You'd tell me what happened to my brother.'

'I'd do anything for you, Rose, I would.' His face grew serious. 'But I can't help you with this request because I didn't kill Billy.'

She sighed.

'I admit I lied to you at times when we were together, Rosie. All men do, it's just the way we are.' He flipped his palms and shrugged. 'But the day I told you I was innocent of Billy's murder, I was telling the truth. I know it's hard to hear, Rosie, but the truth is this: Billy's killer is still out there.'

The wording of his letter echoed in her head.

'Stop it!' Her voice raised in volume and a nearby officer frowned and looked over. She raised a hand apologetically to him and turned back to Gareth. 'If you continue to lie, I won't come here anymore.'

'I'm not lying,' he hissed, exposing ruined teeth that used to form the winning smile she loved so much.

She took a breath, then spoke the words before she lost her nerve. 'Who did you ask to hand deliver me the message? I haven't gone to the police yet but I will, if I have to.'

'I haven't sent any messages,' he said curtly.

'Nobody knows I'm coming here except you and me. Last night I had a note hand delivered through my door.'

He scowled. 'Nothing to do with me, Rose. What did it say?

'It said, "Let sleeping dogs lie".' She watched his face carefully.

He was doing a good job of looking confused but then she knew only too well what a good actor he was. But that open window… the strange feeling she'd had in the house…

'If I never see you again, Rose, the truth is this – so get it into your thick skull. I. Didn't. Kill. Billy.' He looked around him furtively, dropped his voice lower. 'I asked you to help me because

I was telling the truth. I was out of the area. Now someone has dropped you a note that I've had nothing to do with. The killer is out there. *He* must've sent you the note.'

She stared at him without speaking. Ronnie was back on his feet now. Was it possible that…

'Do you remember the flowers I bought you?' he asked.

'Yes,' she said. 'The Stargazer lilies.'

'That's right. If only you'd listened to me, you might have found a receipt in the bag that—'

'You already told me that back then.'

'I told you because it was true!' He groaned and clamped a hand to his forehead. 'You could have found that receipt and then—'

'A receipt alone wouldn't clear you if you *were* innocent,' Rose stated, interrupting him. She suppressed a smile when a darkness flared in his eyes. He didn't like being interrupted, she remembered, and it felt like a tiny victory. 'You could've got someone else to pick up those flowers while you hurt Billy. A receipt in itself proves nothing.'

'Agreed but it could have provided the basis for them to reopen my case. When the police checked out my alibi, the florist's assistant claimed she couldn't recall me making a purchase and the duplicate receipt book *apparently* couldn't be located… very convenient, don't you think?' Rose watched his face twist with suppressed rage. 'I always got the feeling I'd been shafted by the coppers. That receipt was the one piece of evidence that could have put enough doubt on that lead copper to force him to slow down his persecution of me. But you wouldn't even look for it, you'd already condemned me like everyone else in that shitty little village.'

Had Mike North covered up evidence that could have helped Gareth's case… was it possible? Rose decided she didn't care. As far as she was concerned, he was guilty as sin.

'I did find the receipt,' Rose said simply.

She watched as his mouth fell open but forced her own face to remain impassive.

'What did you do with it?' he whispered urgently. He reached his hand out across the table but didn't touch her. It was as if he'd become frozen in anticipation of her answer.

'I still have it,' she replied.

CHAPTER SIXTY-EIGHT

HMP WAKEFIELD

PRESENT DAY

For the first time since she'd known him, Gareth Farnham was rendered totally speechless.

'I found it when you told me that day, when you tried to get me to help you. But I didn't believe you, didn't believe it wasn't another of your tricks, your lies.'

'Rose, listen to me, sweetheart. If you were willing to give a statement that I bought you the flowers, and with the receipt to back it up even after all this time, that might be enough to start the process to get me an unsafe conviction.' He looks away and smiles in wonder. 'Oh my God, it really could happen.'

He reached across the table and grabbed her hand. She tried to snatch it back but he held on fast.

'Rose, listen to me. I've made mistakes. There are times I didn't treat you well but you have to believe me… whatever I've done is only because I loved you so much.'

He looked at her for a response but she remained silent. His words slid off her like hot butter from a knife. He really wanted her to accept he abducted her, sexually assaulted her… and God knows what else… all because he *loved* her?

She shook her head slowly.

'Just listen to me,' he said hurriedly, as if he knew she was ready to walk away. 'My solicitor contacted the florists about that day, you know. But it was around Mother's Day and they'd seen so many people, they couldn't say for certain they recognised me. No CCTV, no number plate recognition in those days … our hands were tied. That copper – North – he just wanted to send me down. If they'd had the receipt, they would've *had* to investigate my alibi more fully.'

'What if someone else bought those flowers? What if it wasn't you?'

'I bought you the flowers, Rose. To say sorry, to try and win you back. I swear to God that's the truth. I didn't hurt Billy but someone out there did and we'll find them together. When I'm out, I will hunt him down for you, my darling, I give you my word.'

She wished she hadn't mentioned still having the receipt. His face was animated, full of hope, like he could see it, smell the promise of freedom. He was a desperate man.

'I'll ask my solicitor to contact you, Rosie. He'll probably want a statement and the receipt… I love you. You do know that, right?'

Despite Gareth's protests, Rose left the visitor's centre early. She was getting nowhere fast. If anything, she was more confused than ever.

She simply couldn't tell if Gareth was telling the truth but one thought chilled her.

He was either working with someone on the outside to send Rose a threatening note or he really was innocent and someone else was watching her.

Someone else who knew her every move.

CHAPTER SIXTY-NINE

ROSE

PRESENT DAY

I promptly fell asleep on the sofa when I got back home.

I made a cup of tea and sat down and that's the last I remember. The sheer effort it took to face Gareth Farnham had exhausted me.

I woke with a start, my heart hammering in pure alarm at the pounding at the back door.

A familiar figure stood, distorted by the opaque, patterned glass.

'Eric!'

'Sorry to disturb you, Rose,' he gasped, a little breathless. He leaned his portly frame against the edge of the wall. 'We've got a problem round at Dad's… a visitor we simply can't get rid of and he's been *drinking*.'

Since Eric had been back, Ronnie hadn't needed me to help care for him and, although I struggle with the guilt despite the suspicions I still harbour, I just can't bring myself to call round even on a social call. With everything I'm dealing with, seeing Gareth, I honestly think it will take me over the edge.

'Rose?' Eric frowns and peers at my vacant eyes. 'Did you hear me? He's distressed, won't stop drinking.'

'Who?'

'Jed! Haven't you heard a word I just said?'

'Sorry, I—' I look out, over his shoulder as if Jed might be in the garden. 'What do you want *me* to do?'

'I don't know, just talk to him, get rid of him, hopefully. He's trying to cause trouble, insisting Dad talks to him about when we were all young, who said and did what, but Dad can't remember that kind of detail anymore.'

I sigh but don't move.

'He keeps mithering on about his dead sister,' Eric stated. 'Cassie. She was your friend.'

'She was my best friend. I'll get my shoes.'

I've no intention of discussing anything to do with Cassie with Eric. Empathy is clearly not his strong point; never was, as I remember.

He doesn't wait for me, so I grab a cardi and my pumps, lock the door behind me and slip next door.

As I open the connecting gate, I think about the last time I saw Jed. He'd been walking past the Co-op, a sad, grey figure, clutching a beer can for dear life and staggering in his effort to keep upright.

I've said hello the odd time the last few times I've spotted him but he always looks at me as if he doesn't recognise me anymore and then he moves away.

I did call at the house and try and chat properly to him years after our tragedies. I knew Cassie would have wanted us to talk but Jed didn't want it… couldn't handle it. True to form, he closed the door in my face.

Even now, in the street, it's as if, when he looks at me, he sees Cassie and the unbearably painful memories of her vitality and love for life are disturbed in his head.

Ronnie's back door is open and I can hear raised voices within.

'If you don't leave I'll have to call the police,' Eric's raised voice declares as I rush through to the living room. 'Nobody's going to believe a thing you say, anyway. Your brain is pickled.'

I freeze in the doorway.

Jed half sits, half lies across the armchair. He is more dishevelled than I've ever seen him. Torn, frayed jeans and filthy black feet in open sandals. His hair is grey now, greasy and plastered to his scalp.

He pales when he sees me.

'What *you* doing here?' he slurs. 'Cassie's dead. *Dead!* D'ya hear me?'

'I know that, Jed,' I say, keeping my voice level and calm. 'Cassie wouldn't want to see you in this state. If you let me, we can get you some help.'

My words were pathetic. I should've tried to stay in touch with Jed more over the years.

He throws his head back and laughs at that, sparse teeth anchored to his pale gums like rotten pegs.

'Help? You need help, you and that boyfriend of yours.' He's virtually incoherent but I catch the odd word and manage to piece it together. 'Cassie hates him. Hates him. I want to talk about what happened.'

He obviously can't distinguish whether he's in the past or the present. He's in a bad way.

'If you don't leave I'm ringing the police,' Eric snaps. He's pacing up and down the room, his face flushed. 'Nobody is interested in your made-up stories about the past.'

I look at Ronnie and he shakes his head and looks down at the carpet.

'Where's Billy?' Jed suddenly yelps and I gasp and take a step back. 'Where's Billy Tinsley?'

'Enough!' Eric surprises me with his loud booming voice. 'We'll not have Billy's name said in here.'

I open my mouth to protest. What does Eric mean by that? Billy's name isn't something to forget about or to censor.

Before I can say anything, Jed lets out a mighty roar and runs for the door, tipping out onto the street.

'Thank God for that!' Eric fumes, slamming the door closed.

'We can't just leave him there, the state he's in,' I say and open the door, stepping outside.

Jed is already on his feet again and limping up the road, his arms swinging wildly.

'Jed, wait!' I run up to him. 'Let's talk, please.'

'I can't,' he wails, tears pouring down his face. 'Everything is gone, nothing can be made good ever again.'

'Things will never get better for you until you let some of the poison out, Jed,' I say gently. 'I should know.'

He stops walking and looks at me and, for a second, I see the Jed I used to know behind his deep-blue eyes. When he speaks, he does so slowly and sounds clearer and calmer than in Ronnie's house.

'I will talk to you, Rose, but not here, not in front of Eric and Ronnie. Come to the Abbey at ten tonight.'

'What? I can't! Not at ten,' I call to him as he lumbers off up the road. 'Why not now?'

'Ten o'clock at the abbey,' he calls back without looking round.

I shake my head and head back to the house. I'm not going back to Ronnie's, I don't want any more of Eric's insensitive remarks.

For the last sixteen years, I have never gone out at ten o'clock at night on my own. My guts twist at the mere thought of it.

I want to help Jed but he's asked something that's just too hard for me to do.

And why won't he talk in front of Eric and Ronnie?

CHAPTER SEVENTY

ROSE

PRESENT DAY

The stone gargoyles leer down from their lofty platform, their grimacing faces seeming to change as the clouds race by, obscuring and then exposing the pearly light of the moon that shines down on them.

I catch sight of the odd small, black shape flitting around the old tower. Bats. All the ingredients of pure horror right here in front of me. I shiver and hug the tops of my arms. I'm so, so tired of being afraid.

I must be crazy. I still don't know why I had to come here but, somehow, I convinced myself it would be safe, that I'd drive here and park at the abbey. I told myself it was something I could do for Cassie, to gather courage and do it for myself too.

'Jed!' I call, shivering.

What is he playing at? What on earth can be so desperate here that he couldn't speak to me at home?

A faint cry draws my eyes upwards and I see him – high up on the abbey's peak. How has he got up there?

'Rose!' he calls.

I walk closer and spot a ladder propped up against the wall next to the building Jed is standing on. As I get closer still, I see his face: ghostly pale, his eyes burning out of dark, manic sockets.

I'd slipped on my trainers before leaving the house and I'm grateful for that now, as I climb the ladder and sit gingerly on top of the wall. Jed is only about ten yards away as I sit there, my pounding heartbeat in my throat.

'Have you lost your mind?' I shout over to him. 'Come back down, Jed.'

If I was closer I reckon I'd probably be able to smell booze on him. Nobody in their right mind would be messing around at this height, standing up, too.

'I want to talk to you about Cassie, Rose. She always loved it here at the abbey.'

He's definitely still drunk, slurring his words. But what he says about Cassie is true; the abbey was her favourite place to come when we were kids. It occurs to me that sometimes, life gets in the way and we let go of the things we love as we get older, forget what makes us happy.

'You're right, she did love it here but let's talk back on the ground, Jed,' I suggest. 'This is crazy, you'll—'

'No! I'll say what I need to say from up here.'

'OK, fine! Just get on with it... please... ' I look up, watch the rolling, angry clouds in the black sky. Panic seizes me and I begin to clamber to my feet again. 'I can't do this, Jed. I just can't.'

'She told me it was Gareth that raped her, Rose,' he spits out the words like rotten teeth. 'Cassie told me and she swore me to secrecy.'

That stops me in my tracks. The wind catches in my throat and my mind whirs with the awful truth that I now think I knew on some subconscious level but buried.

'But Carolyn told me that Cassie never saw the attacker's face, that he wore a mask.'

I had wondered so many times… had Gareth attacked Cassie? They'd never arrested anyone, the word in the village had been that the attacker was a stranger, someone passing through the village who'd happened upon Cassie home all alone.

But I'd been unable to get that night at Cassie's house out of my mind, when Gareth had looked at her in that awful way. He'd told me to choose between them and I had done. I'd unflinchingly chosen him.

Had I unknowingly condemned Cassie when I told him what she'd said about him controlling me and her threat to tell Dad about us?

I didn't want Jed's words to be true yet the truth seemed to shine from them…

'He did wear a mask.' Jed nods. 'A balaclava. He kept it on while he… attacked her... but Cassie told me that when he left her lying in the kitchen in a pool of her own blood, he peeled it off at the door and smiled at her.'

My hand flies up to my mouth and I frantically swallow down the bile that's rising in my throat. *Why couldn't she find the strength to tell me?*

'He told her that if she breathed a word he'd ruin your entire family. He said if she was a true friend of yours she'd pay the price to keep you safe.' Jed shakes his head. 'She was a bloody soft touch, our Cassie. She acted hard but was soft as butter in the middle.'

It was true. Like her mother, she'd put on a hard-as-nails front that had no substance. Only the people closest to her had realised that.

'Oh, Cassie,' I breathe. The wind plasters wisps of hair to my mouth. I wish it would choke me. Finish everything.

'She said she'd tried to talk sense into you before about how poisonous he was.'

My mind drifts back to the day at college in the common room when Cassie had tried to warn me about Gareth's controlling nature. And what had I done? Run straight to Gareth and told him everything.

Of course Cassie wasn't going to trust me again. She would have totally believed that he'd carry out his threat.

The heartbreaking thing was that, despite our fall out, Cassie had still been hell-bent on protecting me. All the times she'd refused to see me at the house, ignored my calls – it was to protect *me* from the monster that was Gareth Farnham.

'I asked him a hundred times if he attacked Cassie,' I said faintly. 'Every time he lied. And he swears he never killed Billy. The lies – they just never stop.'

Jed emits a curious wail, a sort of howl and yelp rolled into one. He sounds like a wounded animal. I step forward.

'Stay there! Don't come any nearer,' he shouts.

'Jed, this is senseless. Cassie is dead, your mum died an alcoholic. For God's sake, not you as well. I'll help you. I swear, I can get you the help you need.'

'You can never help me, Rose.' The pain is palpable in his voice. 'You can never help me because I'm the one, you see. I'm the one who killed Billy.'

I sway a little, then lean heavily against the stone wall.

'What?' I whisper.

'It was an accident, Rose. I only meant to give you a scare, to take him for a day or two. I planned to put out a rumour that Farnham had something to do with it, so the villagers would blame Gareth. I thought that then it would all come out about him attacking Cassie. I'd been drinking and I think little Billy got scared… I only tried to make him stop shouting for help.'

My fingers claw at my thighs. I can't stop them. I can't speak.

'This big group of people came by on the road and I just put my hand over his mouth to shut him up but… I must've just left it there too long. I didn't know I was covering his nose, that he couldn't breathe… I swear it was an accident. I swear!'

I can feel my strength running out of me like lifeblood.

He must have been there. It must be true. The coach load of visitors that headed towards the house tour; they walked past the area Billy had run after his kite.

Ronnie was innocent. Dear, dependable Ronnie. And Gareth Farnham – for once in his life – *he'd told the truth*. That day, before he'd been arrested, he'd tried to tell me he was out of the area – it was the truth. His alibi was sound.

'Rose, I'm so, so, sorry. I am. I—' Jed is sobbing so hard I can barely hear him '—if I could bring Billy back I would. Oh, dear God, what I would give to—'

'Did you send the note… through my door?' My voice sounds strangely calm. I stand up, wait at the top of the ladder until he gives me my answer.

'I wanted you to stop. I just wanted you to leave it alone. I've always watched you, Rose. I've always wanted to tell you the truth. But I just knew you were up to something because you started going out, changed your routine. I came into the house and found the visiting order from Farnham. I saw Billy's blanket wrapped in plastic on the side… I knew you were on to something but I couldn't tell you the truth because Farnham would go free and he's *guilty*. Guilty as hell for hurting Cassie so bad she wanted to die.'

I squeezed my eyes shut against the poignancy of his words. Thought about how I'd been careless, leaving a window open, feeling like someone had been in the house…

'Jed,' I say urgently. 'There's something I need to ask you. Billy had his red blanket the day he went missing. What happened to the blanket? If you're telling the truth, you'll know.'

'It was caught in the bushes,' Jed whimpers. 'Even looking for his kite he was dragging that bloody blanket around. When I took my hand away and I realised he was dead, I panicked and ran.'

I close my eyes. I can't bear it, can't bear to listen to Billy's last moments when I was just a hundred feet away from saving him.

'Please, Rose, don't cry. I hate myself. I don't want to live.'

'What happened to my brother's blanket?!' I scream at him.

'I panicked when I realised Billy was dead. I covered him up as best I could with leaves and branches and I ran. The blanket was caught in the bushes, I was scared someone would see it so I took it with me.'

'What did you do with it?' I growl at him.

'I knew they'd search everywhere. Mum was round at Ronnie and Sheila's and as I walked past they shouted me in. Wouldn't hear of me not having a drink with them. I made an excuse to use the bathroom and stuffed the blanket into one of the boxes in their spare room. I figured nobody would search Ronnie's house but they might search ours.' He hung his head. 'When Sheila let slip she was having a spring clean, I even offered to help her with the spare room, lifting boxes and making sure that box was never touched.'

'Oh Jed.' My body trembles with my cries. 'What have you done? How could you… to our Billy?'

'I'm sorry, Rose.' The crying, the wailing, has all stopped and his voice sounds strangely calm. 'I'm truly sorry. I can't live with it anymore.'

And he jumps. Jed jumps from the top of the abbey wall.

I sit for a few moments with my eyes closed.

'I love you, Billy,' I say.

Slowly, using the wall for support, I climb down the ladder. It takes me a long time to walk home. When I get back, I lock the door and sit for a while, empty inside but strangely calm.

And then I ring the police.

CHAPTER SEVENTY-ONE

HMP WAKEFIELD

PRESENT DAY

Rose walked into the visiting room and smiled at Gareth as she approached the table.

'Here's my princess.' He beamed. 'Wow, look at you! Is that all for me?'

She'd been to a hairdresser in Mansfield that very morning and had her hair cut, blow-dried and lowlighted with a burnished red. She wore a new, long-line emerald-green top and she'd used mascara and a tiny bit of dark lipstick; in fact, it was the one Cassie had given her all those years ago.

'I made a bit of an effort as today is so special.' She smiled.

'Good girl. Now, have you got the receipt?' He glanced at the clock. 'My solicitor should be here within the hour and he's booked a room in the main block to take your statement.'

'Yes,' she said. 'I have the receipt with me.'

She looked at him with new eyes. This wasn't Billy's killer in front of her. He'd actually been telling her the truth.

'Thank you, Rose,' he said, his eyes glistening. 'For believing in me. I swear I never hurt Billy. I teased him at times but I loved him like a little brother, you know.'

She looked at him.

'What's wrong, princess?'

'I've one last thing to ask you, Gareth, and I need you to tell me the truth. Did you attack Cassie?'

'No!' he said, swallowing hard. 'It wasn't me, Rose. I was devastated when I heard the poor girl had taken her own life, I really was.'

'You didn't rape her and then take off your mask and smile at her? Threaten her with ruining me and my family if she ever told the truth?'

'No!' His face is glowing red. 'No! Whoever has told you that is a liar, Rose. A liar, I tell you.'

'I'll get the receipt,' she said, reaching for her bag.

'You can give it my solicitor,' he said, his shoulders relaxing a little.

'I want you to see it, your ticket to freedom, Gareth.'

'That's sweet, go on then.' He grinned. 'My solicitor said if we handle this the right way, prove a police cover-up, I could be out in weeks, maybe even earlier.'

She pulled the small white envelope from her handbag; the very same one she'd taken from the back of her mother's notebook, squirrelled away in the attic.

'Rose—' he watched her open the envelope, his eyes sparkling with anticipation '—let's put all this awfulness behind us. Make a fresh start. What do you say?'

Rose upended the envelope and a hundred charred, tiny pieces of blackened paper fluttered down on to the desk.

His mouth dropped open and he looked at her in horror.

'*This* was the receipt that I'll deny I ever had. I turned it into ash when I found out you raped and effectively killed my best friend,' she said pleasantly. 'You see, I've already made a fresh start, Gareth, and it doesn't include you.'

His lips made word-like movements but no sound came out.

Rose laughed. 'For what it's worth, I know you didn't kill Billy now but I know you definitely hurt Cassie. It can be our little secret, Gareth. I won't be sharing it with anyone else and helping you to your freedom. You're stuck in here until you're old and grey.'

'You… you bitch! You're making a terrible mistake. Oh God, what have you done?'

He jumped up and launched himself across the table at her but Rose was ready for him. She sprang back so he fell well short of being able to grab her. Nearby women and children began to scream and, within seconds, an officer reached their table.

'That bitch, she's destroyed—'

The officer grabbed him and Rose moved smoothly back as two others closed in on a raging Gareth. He picked up his chair and smashed it down on one officer's head. Rose grimaced as blood began streaming from his eye.

The female officer with the cropped hair rushed across to her. 'Are you OK, love? What the hell happened there?'

'He just flipped,' Rose said, looking bewildered. 'He started rambling on about getting out of here and making a fresh start together. He's serving time for killing my brother! When I told him he was deluded, he went crazy.'

Other officers milled around, clearing the room of visitors. They both walked slowly to the door.

'I'm leaving the job at the end of the month,' the officer told her in a low voice. 'So I'm going to tell you something that I'll thank you to keep to yourself. He's got a large photograph of the two of you on the wall of his cell, told me you were his wife when I asked about it. I recognised you on the first visit.'

Rose looked at her.

'You seem like a nice, level-headed woman. I'd keep away from him, love. He'll have at least another five years added on to his existing life sentence for attacking Officer Renshaw today.'

‘Thanks.’ Rose nodded. ‘I won’t be coming here again. I promised my dad a long time ago I’d never have anything to do with Gareth Farnham again and this time I mean it.’

‘Pleased to hear it. I wish you a happy future.’

‘Thanks, I’m excited.’ Rose smiled. ‘I’ve got a whole new life waiting to start.’

And for the first time ever, she found that she really meant it.

A LETTER FROM K.L. SLATER

I want to say a huge thank you for choosing to read *The Mistake*. If you did enjoy it, and want to keep up-to-date with all my latest releases, just sign up at the following link. Your email address will never be shared and you can unsubscribe at any time.

www.bookouture.com/kl-slater

When I first got the idea for this book, I was interested in what might happen if a mistake that we considered to be safely buried in the past suddenly came to bear on our present. What if we not only put our trust into the wrong person back then but we made a serious error of judgement, such as having important information at our disposal that we decided to ignore?

And, as I began to write *The Mistake*, I also began to explore the nature of controlling relationships and the long-lasting effect such a negative experience can have on a person, even years later.

We tend to assume controlling relationships are of a romantic nature and often something that men particularly do to women but, of course, this definition is far too limiting. Any one person can feasibly control another and that includes adult children controlling their parents, parents controlling their own children, a controlling, manipulative boss or – in a relationship situation – a woman controlling her partner.

Some people may not even realise they are in a controlling or coercive relationship. It's not about physical strength or being weak-willed. They get used to treading on eggshells around someone, putting up with criticisms (even minor ones can hurt and damage, when consistent) and readily blame their own behaviour rather than being able to identify who is really at fault.

Sadly, people may have put up with this sort of behaviour from another person for so long, they've almost forgotten what it's like to relax and be themselves anymore. The first stage is always to identify and acknowledge what is happening.

For anyone who thinks they might need help, advice or clarification, there are some fantastic resources available online at the touch of a button when searching for 'controlling relationships'.

The book is set in Nottinghamshire, the place I was born and have lived in all my life. Local readers should be aware I sometimes take the liberty of changing street names or geographical details to suit the story.

I hope you loved *The Mistake*, and, if you did, I would be very grateful if you could write a review. I'd love to hear what you think, and it makes such a difference helping new readers to discover one of my books for the first time.

I love hearing from my readers – you can get in touch on my Facebook page, through Twitter, Goodreads or my website.

Thanks,
Kim x

www.KLSlaterAuthor.com

ACKNOWLEDGEMENTS

I really am so fortunate to have a wonderful group of competent and talented people around me.

Huge thanks to my editor at Bookouture, Jenny Geras, for her uncompromising vision of the book's cover, which I loved immediately; she has supported and advised me brilliantly, as always, during the writing and editing of *The Mistake*.

Thanks to ALL the Bookouture team for everything they do – which, believe me, is an awful lot – especially to Lauren Finger and to Kim Nash who are both so diligent, and a pleasure to work with.

Thanks to my writing buddy, Angela Marsons, who is always on hand to have a laugh, provide a shoulder to cry on or give astute writing advice. And provide cute doggy pics when required.

Thanks, as always, to my agent, Clare Wallace, who continues to give valuable support and advice. Thanks also to the rest of the hardworking team at Darley Anderson Literary, TV and Film Agency, especially Mary Darby and Emma Winter, who work so hard to get my books out into the big, wide world, and to Kristina Egan and Rosanna Bellingham.

Massive thanks as always go to my husband, Mac, for his love, support and patience, even when my writing schedule borders on crazy! To my family, especially my daughter, Francesca, and to Mama, who are always there to support and encourage me in my writing.

Special thanks must also go to Henry Steadman, who has worked so hard to pull another amazing cover out of the bag.

Thank you to the bloggers and reviewers who have done so much to help make my first three thrillers a success. Thank you to everyone who has taken the time to post a positive review online or has taken part in my blog tour. It is always noticed and much appreciated.

Last but not least, thank you SO much to my wonderful readers. I love receiving all your wonderful comments and messages and I am truly grateful for each and every reader's support.

Printed in Great Britain
by Amazon